Manila takes Manhattan

**Also by
Carla de Guzman**

Carina Press

The Laneways

*Sweet on You
A Match Made in Lipa*

Visit the Author Profile page at Harlequin.com.

Manila takes Manhattan

CARLA DE GUZMAN

Recycling programs
for this product may
not exist in your area.

ISBN-13: 978-1-335-04160-9

Manila Takes Manhattan

Copyright © 2024 by Carla Marie Angela K. de Guzman

Harlequin Enterprises ULC
22 Adelaide St. West, 41st Floor
Toronto, Ontario M5H 4E3, Canada
www.Harlequin.com

Printed in U.S.A.

To fandom friends and enablers everywhere—you run the world

Author's Note

This book is set in April–May 2022, when the
Philippines was on the cusp of something akin to hope.
I do not need to explain to Filipino readers why this time mattered,
and why this was the conflict that needed to be written.
If I do, then perhaps this is not the book for you.

Please also note that there is no glossary. This is intentional.

Carla de Guzman

One

Now Playing: "A Case of You"—Joni Mitchell / "Nakauwi Na"—Ang Bandang Shirley / "American Boy"—Estelle

In the future, when asked about their love story—because everyone was *dying* to know—Mon Mendoza would have two answers. One, the easy, composed, mature answer. That boy met girl, boy and girl fell in love. Simple. Effective. Only sort of true.

Two, the more accurate truth, was that boy saw girl in a hallway, girl saw boy's pancit canton, they had sex, then they fell in love.

He was telling this badly.

The night they met was Mon's first night in the US. In New York, in particular, because if you were going to visit America for the very first time in your thirty-two-year-old life, you might as well start in New York. And this was big, because Mon—producer, occasional singer and rapper, semiprofessional overthinker—was here to work on music for a *movie*. An honest to goodness, will actually maybe be shown in theaters or on streaming platforms movie. Because someone on this side of the world had listened to his music and thought he would be perfect for the job. Thought it was worth paying for a flight, hotel, visa and a *significant* talent fee to get him to New York.

Wild, no? It was a big break to end all big breaks.

He was still a little jumpy with nerves when he arrived— he'd managed to explain to an immigration officer why he had a special work visa, how he could afford this trip, and there was always that nerve-wracking moment of wondering what if this guy just decided Mon should get on a plane back to Manila ASAP? But it was fine; he'd made it to the taxi bay, luggage intact. Only to forget the address to the serviced apartment he was supposed to stay in, which was just classic Mon.

But he managed to sort that out, because he was an adult, damn it.

"Hello, sir, how are you?" the woman at the front desk asked, a touch of curiosity in her voice as Mon approached with his massive luggage, his backpack and his wallet fully open because he'd gotten confused at the payment situation for the taxi. He hoped this was the right place. "Can I help you?"

"Ha? Um, well—"

"What name?" she asked without waiting for Mon's answer, glancing at his slightly beat-up luggage like she fully expected a chicken to rip its way out from inside. Which felt racist. But it was all in Mon's head, so he was *fine*.

"Mon Mendoza?" he said, his own name strange to him when it came out in an American accent. Men"dou-za."

"Hmm. I don't have a Mon Mendoza here."

Right. Full government name. "Raymond Tindalo Castro Mendoza?"

"Ah, yes. Here we are. Raymond…Mendoza." The concierge nodded, skipping over his second name. It was fine. He never used Tindalo anyway, unless his mother was really, really annoyed with him. "Oh. Hmm."

"Is there a problem, A—" he asked, catching himself before he addressed her as "Ate." Different country.

"Well. The good news is that Leo Solano already checked in for you," she explained, still not looking up from her computer screen. "The bad news is that he has your keys. He said to expect him back around ten."

It was seven. Mon didn't have the emotional bandwidth to venture out into the streets of New York or leave his belongings in the lobby. He asked if there was a place he could hang out until then.

"I can let you up. Maybe you can wait for him there." The concierge seemed to take pity on him, standing from her spot at the desk to tap her key card against the elevator console. The doors almost instantly opened, beckoning Mon inside. "Good luck!"

How ominous.

The hallway was short, and scary. It was carpeted with a sage green that had seen better days, and Mon was surrounded by dark green paint, crown molding and soft, yellow sconces providing very minimal light. The hallway had exactly four doors, each marked with a number. He could hear noises, people living their lives inside, and hoped to God none of them suddenly needed to step outside.

But he was here. Sitting on the floor in front of apartment 23B, his luggage at his side, and his backpack on his lap. Maybe it was the jet lag, or the rising pressure of being here for thirty days with a life changing job opportunity, but he felt restless, overwhelmed and exhausted all at the same time. Even for a born and bred Manila boy, New York was too big, too bright, too loud and way too aware of itself to allow Mon to fully relax. He plugged in his earphones and decided to listen to some music, hoping the familiarity would be soothing.

Good luck!

The elevator doors pinged open, and all his senses laser-focused on manifesting Leo on the other side. He wanted to get started, he wanted to know how he was going to work, he wanted to find food. And sleep. Or all of the above.

Unfortunately, it wasn't Leo. It was, instead, a woman. Perhaps the most beautiful woman Mon had ever seen.

She had a lovely, heart-shaped face. Her long, dark hair cascaded over one shoulder, showing off the fine collarbones and the delicate shape of her shoulder. She wore a dark blue dress, the sparkles catching in the dim lighting of the hallway, stars in silver delicately sewn into the fabric. A scent he couldn't identify filled the air, but it was a lovely smell, something that evoked warmth and spiciness.

She was looking at her phone, her thoughts clearly somewhere else. Mon cleared his throat, to remind himself not to stare, that he shouldn't. Mon pressed the tip of his mask closer to the bridge of his nose, turning up the volume of his music. Ang Bandang Shirley was the perfect distraction—nothing like a good OPM song to clear the mind.

Whoever this woman was, she wasn't the person he was waiting for, so he had absolutely no business looking at her. Even if he was picturing himself holding her hand. Picturing an entire life with her without even knowing her name.

There was a familiarity to her face, and something in the back of Mon's hazy mind told him he'd seen her before. Maybe she was Pinoy? Or maybe that was just his general Pinoy radar pinging? He couldn't get over that nagging feeling of *oh, it's you*, like seeing a neighbor at the mall and momentarily forgetting their name. But anyway, they were strangers, her possible Pinoy-ness aside, and they had absolutely no reason to talk to each other.

Except she stopped in front of him. Almost exactly in front of him, the tips of her dark blue heels pointing at him, and Mon tilted his head back to look up at her.

She was even more stunning up close, and this view was terrible for his imagination. Her eyes were painted to make them darker, more piercing, and the full weight of that look was focused on him. She seemed like she was waiting for him to say something, or for him to prostrate himself before her feet. The hallway was suddenly warmer and cooler at the same time, and he wished he could explain that, but he really couldn't. Mon Mendoza was tongue-tied and a little embarrassed to be caught staring, and not for the first time he wished he was a Galápagos turtle so he could hide in his giant portable house. Good plan.

"Um. Hi," she said.

"Hi," he said back. Which was something a turtle could never say.

"Is that pancit canton?" she asked, pointing at the open backpack currently settled between Mon's thighs. And now they were both looking down at his lap, at the gigantic backpack, and the very bright, very green packs of Lucky Me! pancit canton peeking out from inside.

Quick, Mon thought. What was a witty, eloquent and charming answer to the question?

"Ah. Yes." *Perfection*.

"For me?" she asked, pursing her painted lips to point at the pancit.

"No...?" He was taken aback—because one, she was definitely Pinoy, and two, why would this strange woman with the deep cranberry lips and sexy collarbones think she had any claim to the pancit canton between his thighs?

"Oh!" She drew back a little. "Um, are you not a fan?"

"Of pancit canton?"

"No, of—" She cut herself off, shaking her head. "So you're not a fan, but you're sitting in my hallway. With provisions."

"What!" Mon's voice came out almost as a squeak, and he quickly cleared his throat. "I don't even know who you are."

"Then why are you wearing a—okay, fine, COVID safety." She sighed, pressing a hand to her temple, a clear indicator that this gorgeous woman had to deal with this kind of shit often, and that she was barely holding on to her civility at the moment. "I presumed, based on the mask and the beanie, that you had bad intentions, and that is wrong. I'm sorry."

"Don't be." Mon shook his head, taking off the beanie and running a hand through his hair. It was probably an oily mess from the flight. She blinked at the sight of his hair, of all things, like she was adjusting her vision, maybe? The hallway was pretty dark, and the lighting made it look like her chest was a little flushed.

"But you were staring at me when I walked in," she pointed out, which was really an excellent argument. And he could see why she would be cautious. A woman dressed as strikingly gorgeous as she was might catch unwanted attention from random gremlins sitting in hallways, and she had every right to be careful. Mon should probably explain that he thought she was—

"Oh," she said, as if plucking the thought right from his mind. "You were looking at me because you think I'm—"

"Arresting. Yes."

She gave him the softest chuckle, and Mon felt the sound pool in his chest and warm him up. "I was going to say sparkly."

Was it possible to capture someone's laughter in music? He wanted to try. He'd always been up for challenges like that.

"So you don't know who I am, and you're not a stalker."

"Are there other options?" He winced, because he really would like there to be other options, especially for someone who'd just landed in this country.

"I don't think you'll like the other options." She placed a hand on her hip and jutted it to the side, like she had all the time in the world to stand in that hallway with him, waiting for a proper explanation of his existence. "I didn't think I was big enough to have saesangs."

Mon's brow furrowed. "What is a saesang?"

"Stalker fans? I've only heard about Korean ones. Mythical to me, but incredibly dangerous." She tutted her lips. "I would rather not have saesangs."

"Oh. I'm not a saesang. Or a murderer."

"Wow. You know you're not really good at this convincing me you're not a criminal thing." She smiled, like she was...amused? Maybe making fun of him a little, but he was fine with that. Mon wriggled in his seat on the floor. "Tell me something reassuring. Like why you're sitting on a very musty floor with your stuff."

There were only four doors, and she was two steps away from the one on the very left. "I'm your neighbor, I think." Mon was assigned to the door right next to hers, ergo neighbors. He held his hand out over the display of his belongings, pancit canton included. "Or I will be at around ten-ish? There was an...ano." Fuck, English? Saan? "Basta. Malabo."

"Is mala-bo, like, kerfuffle?" she asked, wrinkling her nose for clarification. He shrugged. *Close enough.*

"My—workmate, work boss? I'm not sure of the dynamics yet—has the keys and he told the concierge he would be here by ten. Which means I will have been officially awake for forty-eight hours. And because the staff was probably suspicious that a Pinoy was standing in a tiny lobby next to a white woman with a bunch of maleta, they said I could wait up here, which was when the elevator doors opened and... well. You were there for the rest of it, I suppose."

"Sounds..." She wrinkled her nose, and he had the sense she really was evaluating his story. "Plausible. Long, but plausible."

"Brevity is the soul of wit." He shrugged. His old prof used to say that, and Mon had always been terrible at listening to his profs.

That made her smile again, her cheeks pressing up and her eyes almost entirely shut as she laughed. Mon had done that. And on his first day, too.

"Well, you still have your sarcasm intact. That's a good sign," she said between laughs. Mon wondered if he would have the chance to kiss her someday, but pushed the thought aside.

"I suppose the neighborly thing for me to do would be to offer you something," she concluded once her laughter subsided, crossing her arms over her chest. The sparkles on the dress moved as she shifted her weight to her other hip. She nibbled at her bottom lip, and he could feel her eyes raking over his rumpled clothes, his pancit canton, his hair, again. He was aware he looked a mess, but this was a little intense? "If you just flew in, you probably need a shower. Food. A nice bed. Until your work person, relationship to be defined, comes."

Mon's shoulders dropped and he sighed. All of that sounded absolutely heavenly.

"But it will cost you."

"Cost me?"

"Are you vaccinated? Boosted? Recently tested?"

Mon nodded. Now why did it feel like he'd lost control over the conversation? Had he ever been in control, really?

"Tested negative three days ago." He wouldn't have been able to come here otherwise. Probably. Nobody had exactly checked at any point of his flight out.

"Oh good." She took one step forward and expertly plucked the four pack of pancit canton from him in one smooth motion. Mon was very, very impressed, and maybe a tiny bit turned on. She greedily examined the package, and her smile got much wider, lovelier. "Yes! Original."

"Really? More than chilimansi?"

"Original flavors are the best flavors." Her deadpan delivery made Mon laugh. He had a sense she'd said this exact sentence to many people in the course of her life, in varying degrees of seriousness. She hiked the four pack over her shoulder like it was a luxury bag and walked to her door, her hips swaying. She tapped the back of her phone against the console and looked back at him. "Are you coming?"

"Oh, are you—I mean, I can come in?"

"That was the entire point." She shrugged. "Do you want pancit canton?"

Look. The thing was, if this was Manila, Mon would have probably said no. He would have lost his survival food (*just in case!* his mom had said) and he would have been fine. Because stranger danger was real, and who knows, the other person might be a Duterte supporter—shudder—or worse, a Marcos apologist—double shudder.

But he was in New York. Which probably meant he should be even more cautious. But then *again*, his new neighbor was offering the three things in the world he desperately needed at the moment.

Also she was definitely Pinoy, because not only did she kick off her red-soled heels at the door, she also slipped into a pair of Louis Vuitton slides as her house tsinelas, which was maybe the most bougie Pinoy thing ever.

"Hey, um, do you think Marcos is a hero?" he asked, holding his breath for the answer.

"Do you? Because you can't come in if you do."

Mon's decision was made. He pulled his phone from his pocket.

Hey Leo. It's Mon. Please ring 23A when you get here. Thanks.

That single text cost him twenty-five pesos, and it would take at least an hour for Leo to get it. But, to Mon's mind, it was a necessary twenty-five pesos. He gathered up his belongings and followed her inside.

Her apartment was large and spacious, all low furniture and dried plants. There were windows on two sides of the walls, framing a wraparound balcony that must cost an arm and a leg in rent. She hadn't turned on the lights, but the warm glow streaming in from outside made it look dark and romantic.

One of the sliding doors was ajar, and the linen curtain beside it whipped around in the cool, spring wind. Her view was stunning from where Mon stood, one side facing a building across the street, the other facing the corner and all the way down the street. He could picture her walking around the balcony, observing the life happening beneath her feet, sipping coffee. If he was honest with himself, he could imagine walking up behind her, stealing a kiss before he even knew her name, but…

No. She was being neighborly, and he was already taking advantage of her kindness. *And* just because he thought she was the most attractive person he'd ever met, didn't mean she thought the same of him.

"Cool place," he said, turning from where he stood awkwardly barefoot in the middle of her open plan apartment. She flipped a switch by the wall, and the kitchen lit up, the soft white light contrasting with the almost orange warmth from outside. But at least they could see each other clearly.

"Thanks. I've only been here a couple of days myself, and I definitely would not have picked out this decor." She chuckled, placing the four pack of pancit canton on the counter next to a large unopened gift basket. She flipped the card open and read it.

"Admirer?"

"Jealous?" she asked, raising a brow. Mon was about to respond (but really what could he say) when she shook her head and put the card aside. "It's from work. Anyway. I don't like the furniture. Bouclé couches look perpetually dirty to me. I know they're the thing, but it didn't look good in the lobby of the Ace Hotel, it doesn't look good here."

Did he know what bouclé was? No. Could he even *see*

the couch in the darkness? Not really. But he wasn't going to disagree, and said something like, "totally."

She walked to the balcony, leaving the door wide open for Mon to follow. So he did, and was given the full view of New York below. The entire city still seemed wide awake at this time of evening, and he could see into different apartments, observe people walking down the street. It felt immense and overwhelming, endless buildings and streets he couldn't name.

"You can't get a view like this in LA, though." She sighed, and Mon almost missed that because it was also really loud out here, sirens in the distance, and a low buzz that seemed to come with the orange streetlights. "What are buildings compared to hills and mountains?"

"I think Austen said that once." Mon lived near Timog Avenue, a part of Quezon City that was only just starting to fill with condos. Still, there were places that carried their quirks and let them show. Days could still be slow where he lived, and he liked that.

Suddenly Timog felt far, *far* away.

"Are you uncomfortable?" she asked. That little wrinkle just between her brows was cute. She was cute. Devastatingly attractive, and cute, and Mon was in such big trouble.

"Me? No," he said. "Why?"

She was close enough that he could count her eyelashes, enjoy how they fluttered. Enough that he could smell her. Santal. But it was softer and more subtle, and it reminded him of beaches and home.

"You're still wearing your mask," she told him, and the

way she said it made him feel like he was being scolded slightly. But then again, she was smiling, and it made his insides melt.

"Oh." He wasn't sure if he was reading this right. He wasn't even sure if what he thought was going to happen was going to happen, or why it was happening. They were all very different sensations.

"May I?" she asked, holding her hands up near his ears.

"I just came from a flight."

"I know. But I would like to kiss you."

"You would?" he asked, taken aback. His pulse was racing, like he'd run a marathon, a rush of adrenaline and thrill shooting through him.

"I really don't think I was being subtle?" She tilted her head, confused. "I invited you to my apartment. I asked you if you wanted pancit canton. Isn't that what the kids these days say?"

"I'm thirty-two?"

"Good for you?" He genuinely couldn't tell if she was about to start laughing or gearing to kick him out. "This isn't your first time, is it?"

"In America?"

"To...have sex?"

Oh. Oh! Okay, okay. So as it turned out, what he wanted hadn't been out of reach at all; he'd just been terrible at reading the signals. Which, to be fair, he had always been bad at reading the signals.

"It's okay if you're not interested," she said, and his heart melted at that. She was being sweet and gracious, and he was being an idiot. "I'm still happy to offer the shower and the food."

"I am, I am interested," he assured her, sighing and running a hand through his hair again. "My own thoughts are just in the way. It happens often."

She nodded, and he didn't feel like she was mocking him at all, which was nice. "I see." A rare sensation for Mon, who was constantly teased for being too smart. He was aware that needed unpacking. But right now, he was here, on this balcony on the other side of the world.

"So you invited me here to sleep with me."

She nodded. "I think you're cute. I don't know your name, and you don't know me. It's kind of sexy, don't you think?" She shrugged, like it was as simple as that. "May I?"

Mon nodded. He'd taken a test prior to arriving and was negative, but this was a risk. He knew it was a risk, and so did she. But still. Still. She was gorgeous. She was asking. And Mon wanted to stop thinking.

Her fingers looped around his ears, and he shivered at her touch. But it was very sweet and intimate, and he was holding his breath, even when the mask was lowered from his face.

"Hi," she said, her eyes twinkling.

"Hi," he said back, taking his first breath of New York air. Smoggy.

Then she kissed him, and Mon's already topsy-turvy world flipped all over again. Her lips were soft, and had a lingering sweetness. Mon chased it with his own lips, pressing against hers, pulling her in. But she cut the kiss off quickly, and it gave him an unimaginable thrill to see her cheeks flushed. He'd done that. Holy shit.

"See, I knew you would be cute under that mask." She grinned, and Mon kissed her again, feeling greedy for more. Her lips parted and licked at the bottom of his lip, as he slid his tongue inside her mouth. She tugged at the front of his shirt to bring him closer, his hands finding purchase in the sparkles of her dress.

"Did I tell you why I love this dress?"

"It's a beautiful dress," Mon acknowledged. "Does it have pockets?"

"It does!" She seemed delighted and showed him. "But it also zips down easily in the back. Could you…?"

"Yeah." His voice was dry in his throat, his hands on her hips as she turned so her back was to him. The expanse of her back was smooth and heated under his touch, and he skimmed the sun-browned skin as he tried (and failed) to find her zipper.

"Relax." She looked over her shoulder.

"That's not helping me relax," he told her, his voice tight. But he found the zipper, and he had all these ideas of exposing more of her warm brown skin, maybe kissing her there, but was taken aback when he instead saw…beige.

"What…"

"Shapewear," she explained, turning again, clutching the front of her now loose dress. She kissed his cheek, making it sound loud. When she pulled back, her own lips looked faded and smudged. Yeah, if his cock wasn't already hard, it was now. "My body is not going to be this perfect when I take all of this off."

"That's not the only reason why I want to do this," he said, lifting her chin with his fingertip. "You're beautiful."

"Oh." Her eyes widened as surprise and delight flared. She seemed pleased, and Mon knew he'd said the right thing. Thank God. "Good answer."

"I have a friend who would have said 'nobody's perfect.'"

"I am so glad you didn't." She giggled, reaching for his hand with her free one and pulling him inside. "I'm going to take off my makeup and the twenty million pins in my hair. But I like the enthusiasm."

"Um. Thanks," he said, shifting uncomfortably where he stood.

She giggled and walked toward the bedrooms. "Don't tweet about any of this."

"I won't," he promised. Weird request.

"Good. My God, what am I doing?" she said to herself before she disappeared into the bedroom.

He took a long, deep exhale, willing himself to calm down. Once he managed to feel like he wasn't floating on cloud nine, he noticed his reflection in the mirror by the couch and saw the lipstick smeared on his cheek. It was enough to make him want to laugh, or tell someone or write it in a song somehow.

It had been a while since he felt that way about writing a song.

"Your work friend's going to call when he gets here, right?" she said from the bedroom.

"I think so," he yelled back.

"Okay, come in!"

He walked into the hallway, into the first open door he found, and she was there, standing in front of the open window. She looked softer without makeup, fuller, almost like a completely different person. He spied the dress in a dark blue pool on the floor, shapewear in a heap next to it. And she was completely naked in front of him, only shadows hiding the parts of her body he longed to touch the most.

The tension between them was thick and buzzing with anticipation. She carefully watched his reaction to her, and he waited for her to take a breath.

"Come here," he said, his voice low as he held his arms out. She stepped in, and he wanted to bury her with his kiss, take her worries away. Take his thoughts away, too. There was only this, and this moment.

It was a long kiss, slow and sticky and sweet, the kind you wanted to drown in. He felt her knees go weak, and he caught her by the waist, lifting her up easily.

"This is a one night only thing," she told him, her eyes dark with desire.

"I know," Mon said, kissing her again, chasing a hit of something he wouldn't have for more than one night. She pulled her lips away, slightly dazed.

"If you tell anyone, I'm going to—"

"To?" Mon asked, interrupting her with another kiss. She pulled her lips away one last time, and placed her hand lightly over Mon's throat. It was hard to tell if it was a caress or if she was measuring his neck to chop.

"I'm going to destroy you," she said, kissing *him* this time, hard. She wriggled away from him, and he set her down on the wood floor. She pulled his wrist and led him to sit on the bed so he was gazing up at her.

"Okay." He nodded, fully believing it.

"Who taught you to kiss like that?" she asked, pressing her forehead against his, placing her knees outside of his.

"If I said it was natural talent—"

"Sure." Her laughter was like a song he hadn't written yet, a twinkling amusement he wanted to capture.

"Where did you come from?" she asked instead, sighing and resting on her heels.

"Quezon City."

That made her laugh. Mon ran his hands up her thighs before he squeezed, and she made a little moaning sound. She tugged his shirt up over his head, spreading her fingers over his chest. She seemed particularly fascinated by his pecs, taking a playful bite as her fingers toyed with his nipples.

"Fuck."

She giggled. "Fuck yes?"

"Yes, very."

She kept looking up at something over his shoulder, and when he turned, he saw it was a large mirror in the shape of an arch, their bodies perfectly framed within.

"You want to see?" he asked her, leaning back, his palm on the bed to give her room. She nodded, almost shy about having to admit to something she wanted.

So they moved. She'd unbuttoned his pants already, and he left them on the floor near where her dress was, his boxers following. And after quick consideration, he toed his pants over his boxers, which hadn't seen daylight since

Manila. She'd grabbed a condom at some point, the packet near his thigh.

He sat on the bed again, this time with her facing the opposite direction. The light hit them just right so their bodies were lit up in the arch frame, his hand splayed over her stomach, her breasts rising and falling with her excited breaths.

"Better?" he asked, lifting her chin gently so she could turn her head and kiss him. She nodded, nibbling on his bottom lip.

"Touch me," she said, leading his hand between her legs. The space was wet, and the confirmation of her want for him made him harder, made him want her to come. He curled his fingers inside her, feeling for the back of her clit. She moaned when he found it, grabbing the back of his head and tugging at the hair at the nape of his neck.

"You are very good at this, whoever you are," she breathed, and his hand involuntarily squeezed her thigh, pushed deeper inside her. The sounds of pleasure she made seared into his brain. Her thighs clenched, and her body arched, and Mon felt it, too.

But it was like they were on two different playlists. She was urging him faster, harder. His cock was perfectly placed low on her back, and she was using that to her advantage, rubbing against him so he would lose focus and hiss.

"Be good for me," he said, but there was no force to his voice, merely a gentle plea. Their eyes met in the mirror, dark and heavy, and Mon's heart leapt out of his chest. It was the most incredibly erotic sight he'd ever seen.

Then she came, calling the names of gods since she didn't

know his. He curled his fingers one last time inside her before sliding them away. She took his hand and sucked at his wet fingers, her dark gaze fixed on his through the mirror.

"Oh God. Puta." He cursed as his orgasm whipped through him, his hips arching up, his hand anchored on the bed, because he had no control over this, and he surrendered to the feeling. Even more so when she moved up his torso so she could have access to his cock and stroked him until he collapsed backward on the bed, completely spent.

He blinked, because he was seeing…stars? Or maybe his vision was blurring, but putang ina, that was…

"Fuck. That was embarrassing," Mon gasped, practically spread-eagled on the bed. Sticky, messy, hot and out of breath. But the smile on her face was a mirror of his, he was sure.

"It was hot," she admitted, easing herself off his lap. He had just enough strength to lift his head as she observed the mess he'd made on the sheets, then looked up at him. He was extremely exposed and vulnerable, but he was past the point of caring at the moment. "It's Olivia, by the way."

"What?" he asked, looking up. "Sorry, I came so hard my brain is leaking out of my ears."

"My name." She chuckled, crawling over his body to take another bite at the swell of his chest before she kissed him. "It's Olivia."

She collapsed on the bed next to him, using his arm as a pillow.

"Mon," he said, holding a hand up to shake hers, because shaking hands was the proper thing to do. "Nice to meet you."

They shook hands, and it was funny and sweet and so strangely surreal, this moment. She was curled up against him, hand on his chest, and Mon wanted to remember it forever. Maybe he shouldn't have given her his real name, but that was on him.

"Do you want pancit canton?" Olivia asked.

"I had assumed the pancit was metaphorical?"

"Well, if I came as hard as you had after a what, fifteen hour flight?" she asked, and he nodded in confirmation. "I would be really hungry."

"Ravenous."

"Poor baby," Olivia cooed, and ran a hand through his hair. "Go take a shower. I'll make pancit."

"Lucky me," he said. She got up from the bed, throwing on a silk robe that hung from the back of the open bathroom door, and left him to his own devices.

It was hard to explain the strangeness he felt walking back out to the living room. Like he was walking through a dream as his brain tried to fight off the effects of the international date line. Or was it the prime meridian that he'd crossed? He had no idea.

Olivia's back was to him in the kitchen, where she was humming to herself as she waited for the water to boil. He looked out at the view again and wondered how to explain to her—to Olivia—the sense of insignificance and smallness that suddenly overwhelmed him. Like he'd lived in a swimming pool all his life and suddenly jumped into the middle of an ocean.

That's what it was, wasn't it? There were a million other

songwriters, producers, people out there. How had *he* been chosen for this movie? He didn't have an agent, or a manager, and he didn't put any feelers out there. All he had to his name was a smattering of songs in a SoundCloud account.

Well, there was "Blue Period," but going viral on TikTok was a fleeting thing, and he was very aware of that.

But there had been an email, then a response, and a Zoom call, and another Zoom call, then a contract, then money. That was scary. Suddenly there were a million things to handle—his passport renewal, his visa, contracts, negotiations. The next thing he knew, he was here. He was here with Olivia, and he was still trying to wrap his head around it all.

"So it is your first time?" she asked when he padded to the kitchen counter. "In America."

"Yeah." Mon nodded, even if she couldn't see. "The US of Ah, as my titas said. That's not weird, is it?"

"Not at all," Olivia said quickly. "I mean, it's a thing isn't it, being here? It means something."

She understood perfectly, then. Olivia looked like she made pancit canton all the time, ripping plastic packs with her teeth, tossing blocks of instant noodles into boiling water. She was humming a song to herself (did he know that song?), pulling up the shoulder of her robe. She stood comically far from the stove, like she was terrified it would bite. It made Mon smile, in spite of his thoughts, watching her.

"I've been here a grand total of two hours, and I'm overwhelmed. Crushingly."

"By me? The country? Or just New York?" she asked,

shaking the slip of packaging with the spices so they would pool to the bottom.

"Yes, all of it." He chuckled. "There are too many factors. Different factors. This is supposed to be *it*, for me. I'm supposed to feel like a success, like I found a place at a table."

"But…?"

He paused, gathering his thoughts. "But I feel unwelcome," he finally said. "It's the third degree I got when I arrived, the questioning of my worthiness to be here, of how I could afford it. The way everyone asks how I am, when they never really want to know. The buildings are too tall, and everything is walkable, what kind of first world shit is that."

He couldn't read the expression on her face. She said nothing, continuing to shake the flavor packets before she added them to the simmering pot, using her other hand to fold in her sleeve.

"And the sense of danger is different. In Manila if I walk around flashing my laptop, it will get stolen. I can control that by not being an idiot. I know how not to be an idiot. Here, just my existence is offensive to some. Walking down the street has a risk I had never considered, and I don't know the rules."

He saw the wince she made then, but it was true. Everything he knew about xenophobia and racism, he learned from the US. Recognized those patterns in his country because this country had shown it to him.

"But at the same time, I'm here. There's something I'm taking advantage of, and there's so much possibility in the air. The whole city feels charged with it. Like I could turn a corner and find something that will change the way I see everything. Like everything could change when I meet the right person at the right moment."

He let those words hang in the air. Felt something under his skin thrum with excitement, like he'd spoken something into truth. He was met with silence, like the world was adjusting to the words he'd sent out.

"I feel it too," Olivia finally said. "Not exactly, of course. But that possibility here? I feel it too. That frustration, for sure. LA is…it's LA. No matter what I do, there will always be a list I won't be on, a place I won't be welcome, just because I'm not white."

Mon winced. When he was young, it was ingrained in him that "America Is in the Heart," that here was the greener pasture. That anyone who made it here was somehow better.

But as he grew older, he realized it wasn't greener on the other side at all. The problems were different, but they were still there, even more so when you were always going to be excluded. Yes, money. Money that you brought home, and maybe you could buy better things. But it wasn't for him.

"Anyway." Olivia sighed, wordlessly grabbing a bottle of fancy soy sauce and adding a bit. "That overwhelming feeling, I understand it, in my very different way."

Mon could almost see a spark of connection between them. He hadn't expected to feel so comfortable around someone he just met, but the fact that she had listened to his thoughts, acknowledged his feelings? It was rare. Rare and precious, and it made her even more beautiful in his eyes, that glimpse of herself she showed him.

"How do you get rid of it?" he asked.

"Saying it out loud helps." Olivia winced, like even she wasn't totally convinced. "My therapist says that words have power. Speaking things into reality makes you better equipped to deal with it, that kind of thing."

"Somehow I don't feel as relieved." Mon chuckled, running a hand through his hair.

"It will come," Olivia assured him, checking on the noodles. "I think I have eggs. Should we add eggs?"

The silence that descended between them was comfortable, a peaceful one where you'd found someone who understood you perfectly in that moment. It was unexpected, but welcome. It was the kind of silence that could grow into familiarity, and comfort, and something inside him ached knowing it wasn't going to last.

"Oh fuck, I'm out of battery. Do you mind if I borrow your—"

"The clock is a wireless charger." Olivia used her pursed lips to point in the direction of a clock on the counter. Mon left his phone on top for a second, waiting for it to turn on as she continued to assemble the pancit.

She was humming a song again, one he was sure he'd heard before, but eluded him at the moment. His phone chimed several times with texts, some from friends in Manila making sure he was in one piece and in New York, and one from Leo.

Be there in twenty minutes.

The text was sent ten minutes ago. Disappointment gnawed at him, at the thought of this being over.

Olivia turned from the kitchen to place the finished plates on the counter.

"Your dinner, my lord," she announced. There was something about the way she said it, the way her voice was smoother at the edges, the way her words were enunciated that sparked the familiarity he'd been feeling around her. Wait a minute. He *knew* her.

He'd seen her face on a billboard when he drove along EDSA. Three billboards in particular, the ones that faced the Pasig River, the biggest ones in the city on the most used national highway. He knew her because he saw her face every time he crossed from Guadalupe to Pasig.

He forgot, because on those billboards, she wore a crown of silver and gold, and blue contacts. Because she was Lady Tala Astralune Liwanag, Queen of the Magnavis Nation, commander in chief of the most powerful fleet in the galaxy.

Olivia next door was Olivia Angeles. Olivia Angeles the FilAm breakout star of *Conquerors*, the big budget space opera that was on everyone's lips. His internet exploded every time a new episode came out, half the people trying not to spoil it for the rest of the poor losers who hadn't seen the show yet.

Olivia Angeles was a person he should have recognized the moment he met her, because he'd binged the first season while he was packing for this trip. Mon was fuzzy on the details, but he was sure she'd been placed in an arranged marriage with Lord Aries at the end of season one.

And in season two, she maybe, possibly died in the finale because of Lord Aries. His Twitter feed was still a mess of people needing reassurance that their favorite space queen would live—she *made* the show, they said. They *couldn't* write her off like that.

Could they?

"Mon?" Olivia asked, tilting her head to the side, confused. And now that he was looking at her…how the hell had he missed it. "Are you okay?"

His throat was dry. Too dry. Uselessly dry. He was about to ask, just in case he was wrong. Because if he was right, he was fucked. Absolutely fucked. And he understood why she insisted this be a one night thing, why she would kill him if he told anyone about this.

But before Mon could ask, her doorbell rang. His phone started to ring too, Leo's name flashing on the screen.

Mon's stomach sank, because he wanted to know more about this. He wanted to tell her to stop, to stay, to make this moment never end. But just because he wanted to do it, didn't mean he would let his intrusive thoughts win. It was too late now.

Her doorbell rang twice, and Olivia hopped off the bar stool, peeked and opened the door with a flourish to reveal Leo.

"Olivia!" Leo exclaimed, giving her a friendly kiss on the cheek. Why was Leo friends with Olivia? How did they know each other? "How was the premiere? You looked gorgeous, as always. Colin didn't ruin your night, did he, with that comment?"

It took Mon a second to place the name. Colin Sheffield played Lord Aries on the show. His friends had gone into deep discussion about if it was still okay to like Colin Sheffield when he once Instagrammed a picture of himself and a random Filipina and tagged her as Olivia. Mon had thought it rude before, enough to never trust Colin in his *Conquerors* watch, but it was even more offensive now, knowing Olivia and her feelings about being excluded.

"Colin will be Colin." Olivia shrugged like whatever happened with Colin happened a lot. "And if the director really did coach Mia for the role, then…good for her, right?"

"Always so gracious, even in the face of racism." Leo tutted his lips like he was a little disappointed in her. "Now where's Mon? I've got a set of keys with his name on it. Well a card. But saying keys just makes more sense."

"Wait. Why are you—"

"Can I use your bathroom? Traffic was a fucking nightmare and I have needed to pee for about thirty minutes," Leo said, waiting for Olivia's nod before he headed off to the powder room with minimal instruction.

The sound of the door closing seemed to echo through the entire apartment. Mon physically braced himself, his hands clenched as silence cut through them. Olivia was still standing by the door, contemplating him like it was the first time they'd ever met.

"You never mentioned what you were going to do in New York," she said, brows furrowed in confusion.

"I didn't," Mon confirmed as dread crept up on him.

"Mon, hello! It's nice to see you from the neck down at last," Leo said with a big smile as he emerged from the bathroom, shaking his hands and spraying water everywhere. "Ol-

ivia, did I tell you Mon Mendoza here is going to produce
the music for *Overexposed*? I didn't?"

"You're Morningview," Olivia said, the two words coming out in a gasp, like he'd done something absolutely terrible. Disappointment hung in her words, but Mon didn't
know who it was directed at, and she took a step back from
him. "Oh my God."

Ah. That was why the song she was humming in the
kitchen had been so familiar. It was his. In fact, it was one
of his oldest songs, "Paz." Which meant that not only was
Olivia Angeles a fan of his music, she was a *big* fan of his
music.

"He's cute, right? Gorgeous eyes—lipstick on his cheek."
Leo paused, reaching up to rub his thumb on the stain Olivia's
lips had left. Leo's gaze moved from Mon's cheek to his neck,
and his eyes widened in surprise. "Aha."

"Aha?" Mon echoed.

"Leo." Olivia's voice carried exasperation and impatience.

Leo held up his hands as a show of innocence. "Look, I'm
just walking into this! So neither of you knew you would
be working together?"

"Well, I know now!" she exclaimed.

"I never mentioned it, did I, Mon?" Leo said, looking a
little sheepish and apologetic. "How we found you. It was
because our star, our leading lady, lobbied for *you* to be the
music producer for the movie."

And there it was. Mon's heart twisted in his chest, and
suddenly regret tasted a lot like instant pancit canton. On his
first night in New York, he'd had the most mind-blowing

orgasm of his life from the actress he was producing music for. His brain oscillated between his fears—that he'd just fucked up the biggest opportunity of his professional life and that he'd fucked up what he was considering the most perfect moment of his thirties. They roiled in his stomach, and he didn't know which he was more afraid of.

It sounded bad. Really bad.

"I'm sorry," he said, and the words felt flat and inadequate. "I didn't—"

"You really didn't know who I was?" Olivia asked him. He shook his head.

"Nothing you said to me today feels like the truth." Olivia sighed, and it felt like a hand had swept across his desk and tossed everything he owned aside, like none of it mattered. Now that was gutting.

"You liked that I didn't know who you were," he pointed out. "And I liked you."

She took a step back, crossed her arms over her chest, like the physical distance between them wasn't enough. "I can't believe you're Morningview, and I—we—"

"I can't believe you're Olivia Angeles." Mon said the first thing he could think of. Which was clearly the wrong thing, because she flinched. Yes, he knew the full weight of her name, knew what it meant that he was working for her. "I didn't think you would—"

"Listen. Guys. You flirted with each other." Leo's voice was a little loud, like he was reminding them he was still here too. "I'm being mild. Obviously you fucked. I'm not going to say I'm upset, because I'll be honest, it's cute."

"Leo!" Both he and Olivia shouted in varying tones of disbelief.

"In all our defenses, we didn't know!" Leo's attempt to calm them all was not going down well. "And honestly, if the universe has decided to place this conundrum in our laps, then we might as well deal with it." He lowered his hands, and when neither Olivia nor Mon said anything, his voice went softer and more serious. "Unless there *is* something we have to discuss?"

Leo said that to Olivia, and Mon's stomach dropped. He hadn't realized how much of a mess this had made, that the risks he'd taken had this kind of consequence.

She could have him fired, take him off the project before he'd even started. Anxiety rose inside him, and he felt like he could choke on it. He'd been thoughtless. It had all been surreal, but the thing with surrealism was that it rooted itself in reality. The persistence of memory, as Dali said. And reality had a tendency to be a cold slap to the face.

"We're fine." Olivia smiled at Leo, but looked away from Mon. A great start to their working relationship. "I think I should get some rest. Be bright and early for our meeting tomorrow."

"Olivia when have you ever—" Leo started, but Olivia glared at him in the exact same way Lady Tala stared down sand bandits and ushered them out the door in season one of *Conquerors*. Mon felt a lump in his throat, because now was not the time to think about how sexy it was.

"Come now, Mon. Your neighboring apartment awaits," Leo said instead, and Mon winced. They were going to be neighbors. Right. He followed Leo's lead, grabbing his back-pack while Leo happily tugged his luggage, talking about how much Mon would love the view, and had he ever heard of bouclé? He was going to love it!

Mon was tempted for a moment to leave his last two packs of pancit for her, but it felt petty somehow. He lingered by the door, wondering what to say. He wanted to…to what, apologize? Explain himself? Reassure her that he had no idea they were actually working together when they first met?

She didn't seem interested in hearing any of that.

Olivia stood away from the door, her arms still crossed over her silk robe. Mon could see evidence of his kisses blos-soming on her skin, and pushed down the ache that filled him. That he had lost something precious, and much too momentary. And yet she would still be around. He would still be around her, every day.

He started to speak, but found his throat too dry to say anything more than, "Olivia."

"I know what this means to you." Olivia shrugged, and it was more vulnerable this time, like she really wanted for him not to look at her right now. "And I know you'll be amazing at this. I want what's best for this movie, so I would appreciate it if we could keep what happened to ourselves. And not repeat it."

"Of course." Mon nodded. He wanted to stay here a little longer, talk to her a little more. He wanted this night not to be over yet. "I won't let you down."

"I know."

"Olivia," he said, again. Hoping.

She shook her head, cutting off anything else he wanted to say. "Good night, Mon."

The smile she gave him was too polite, too friendly. The exact same way she'd spoken when they first met in the hall-way. The secrets they'd spoken into reality vanished in puffs of smoke. Kissing her had been nothing more than a dream.

And when she closed her door behind him, he knew that was all it was going to be.

Two

@StarzSpotting Spotted @OliviaAngeles in Chelsea sharing a sweet moment with her non-celeb brother. Possibly telling him the fate of Lady Tala on #ConquerorsTV? We need to know!

[photo of Olivia pinching Max's cheek on the sidewalk]

@OliveNuts Olivia is in NY shooting a mystery project with Sol Stanley, CONFIRMED

@TalanisMorisette SO HAPPY FOR OUR GIRL. We all know how much she loves Hopeful Voice. I bet all the bitches are terrified of her at karaoke #PinoyPride [video of Olivia mentioning Hopeful Voice as her favorite movie in several interviews]

"I win," Olivia announced brightly the next morning, brushing flaky pastry crumbs away from her lap. Always a sign of a good pastry when half of it flaked on your lap. "Best order goes to me. Again."

Across from her, also brushing crumbs off his lap, her twin brother, Max, frowned.

People always did a double take whenever they saw the Angeles twins—Max was tall, mestizo, had criminally long eyelashes and was kind to all animals and children he came across. Olivia was also tall with equally long eyelashes, was morena, and on more than one occasion had been asked by a stranger to slap them across the face just like Lady Tala did her captors in the season one finale of *Conquerors*.

Tiny differences lang.

But what they did have in common, which they took with them wherever they were in the world, was the burning desire to constantly one-up each other in food choices. Max living in the Philippines made him a strong contender, but Olivia had always hated losing.

"Humph." Max frowned, holding up the same flaky pastry, but his had chocolate in it. "I disagree."

"I think you should know better than to disagree with your—"

Max's brow rose, and Olivia knew her brother well enough to know he was about to tease her for being older, and as an actress, she was *sensitive* about that.

"Do *not* even speak." She poked her brother with a manicured finger. "Also I keep telling you, just because it has chocolate doesn't make it instantly better."

"Well, if you actually enjoyed flavors outside of boring and vanilla, you could be surprised."

"Look, they are original flavors, and I cannot be judged because I like original! Suddenly I'm kind of glad you're leaving after this," she lied, using the fork to hack off a piece of his pain au chocolat. She was offseason for *Conquerors*; her trainer would forgive her. But only if she had just one bite.

"I'm going home," Max corrected her. "That's different."

"So you keep trying to remind me." Olivia sighed.

One would think she'd be used to Max living so far away—he'd moved to Manila ten years ago now—but the reminder still made her wince, like someone was telling her something untrue. She'd grown up feeling like it was the two of them against the world. Their parents were a unit, and so were the twins. Max really couldn't blame her for being selfish enough that a teeny, tiny part of her still hoped he would one day announce he was coming back home.

But then again, where was home for her these days? Certainly not in her temporary apartment on the Upper West Side, or the house she rented in Silver Lake.

She sighed and dramatically took a sip from her bowl of coffee, feeling like a heroine in a French film. They had the right setting for it, at least. Olivia always loved a good French bistro, and this one in the West Village did not disappoint. It had high ceilings with stained glass, white subway tiles, wrought iron tables, bistro chairs and a snort of laughter from the maître d' when she'd mispronounced pain au chocolat.

They did, however, get a free pastry from their waiter, who was from Zambales and a fan of Olivia's from when she starred in a phone company commercial years ago. It was about long-distance relationships, which she didn't get until someone explained that PLDT was the Philippine Long Distance Telephone company. Who knew? Who even said their full government name these days?

"Cheer up, Emmy," Max said later, after they finished their food and stood on the sidewalk. Olivia sighed, shaking her hair out, extensions and all, as if fighting off the sadness trying to creep up on her.

The spring day was clear, the city around her was loud and her brother was leaving. More than once she'd wondered what her life would have been like if she'd stayed Emmy Angeles, drama queen only in name. She liked to say in interviews that she'd fallen into acting—she and Max were child models before she'd been bitten by the acting bug, and it felt like a natural progression to her.

She liked playing roles. Stepping into someone's life and their way of thinking. She liked being consumed by the characters she played, finding out a bit about herself in the process. Real-life Olivia was still a work in progress. A constant whirl of thoughts, worries and feelings—about her career, her characters, the trajectory of her life and everything in between. And it never felt quite right to share them with anyone, not even her brother.

"I'm going to ask the girl I love to marry me," Max reminded her. "It's a happy thing."

Olivia's chest tightened and she nodded. It was why Max had come here. To tell her he was going to do this. To buy the ring. Of course she was thrilled for him—Max had always been a huge romantic, and his girlfriend, Martha, was the best—but it did mean Max was probably never coming back to America. He'd made his home somewhere else. And that made her feel even more alone than she usually did.

Big girls don't cry.

"Have you talked to Mom?" Max asked, and Olivia's stomach twisted, as it always did whenever her brother brought up their parents.

"Have *you*?" she asked, frowning. Marvin and Elisa Angeles were a team, just as she and Max were. "I don't think she'll pick up my call even if I tried."

"Just making sure," Max said. "I can wait, but—"

"But you're getting engaged." Olivia sighed. "You know you could just call them and tell them. It doesn't have anything to do with me, or why we fought. We don't have to be a team all the time, Max."

"I know," Max insisted. "But you should always have someone in your corner, Emmy. You need someone in your corner."

"I do," Olivia agreed. Oh fuck, her eyes felt hot, and she blinked away the sudden tears that had sprung up. If she brushed them away, someone might see. And while Max was in her corner, Max was half a world away, with a life of his own. She knew that. She was happy for him, really. But the happier he was, the harder it was for Olivia to imagine what happiness would look like for her.

"You okay?" he asked. "You never told me how your movie premiere was last night."

"It wasn't my movie," Olivia reminded him. "I think my publicist posted pics. It was fine."

She'd captioned the post with huge congratulations to Mia, who had been shooting the Alec Larsen movie and the last season of *Conquerors* at the same time. Mia's publicist extended the invitation, and Olivia was already in New York. It should have been just another work event, except it had left her feeling shaken, and more vulnerable than she was willing to admit.

She totally blamed Colin. Everything was fine. They had just finished walking the red carpet together, and come over to Mia to say hello. Mia had smiled and hugged Olivia, but had given Colin a cold look and moved on to her next admirers. Olivia was about to make a joke about Colin's reputation when he'd asked Olivia if she was worried she was being overshadowed by someone playing her handmaiden on the show.

Do you know Alec coached her for the audition? he'd said, acid dripping from his voice in a way Olivia couldn't scrub out of her head. *Her dad's in a fraternity with Alec and they coached her. You really should be worried about people like that, because I can picture the show choosing her as a lead after they just killed you off.*

Fucking Colin. She loved the guy, really, but he liked to indulge in pettiness and drama, even when Olivia didn't. And he'd just shot a dart straight to the heart of Olivia's fears, for what? To feel good? So Olivia would like Mia less?

"Are you still worried about *Conquerors*?" Max asked, twisting the knife he'd already stuck in.

"I can't do anything about *Conquerors*. I—" She craned her neck and glanced around to make sure nobody was close enough to hear her. "I don't even know if Lady Tala is still alive. Aries blew up that base pretty badly, and he was very determined to kill his wife."

"Lalala, spoilers!" Max complained, covering his ears with his hands. "Grabe, I haven't started with the last episode! What do you mean Aries wants to kill you? You're married! He said he loved you most ardently! You do not just tell someone that then want to kill them."

The thing with making a show on a streaming platform was that the platform's goalposts for success always changed. At first, all they needed was the vision. The platform was so hungry to make original content they funded the first season, pilot unseen.

Then, to everyone's shock, *Conquerors* became their most watched series of all time, so they were given a second season, just after COVID vaccines and boosters came out, perfect timing. The second season's reviews and ratings had just come out, and there was a significant dip in the streaming numbers. There were plenty of other space shows released in the interim, and it was tougher to maintain good storytelling and get new audiences. The dip in numbers might be too much for the network, because they still hadn't gotten their renewals. But dropping from number one to number three most watched wasn't *too* drastic, at least in Olivia's opinion. And their fans were amazing, doing half the work of promoting the show online.

But still, there was no word of a contract renewal. Not a peep.

Olivia's agent, Mercedes, wasn't *too* worried, because auditions and offers were still coming in. They were arguing over which roles to audition for, or even consider. Olivia insisted she still had enough recognition that she could afford to wait for those unicorn shows or films where she was neither suffering nor dying. She could wait to be cast as Filipino, not Latinx or Chinese. Mercedes thought otherwise. They needed to strike while she still had name recognition, even if it meant playing a Latina character in a superhero movie. Even if it meant passing for Chinese in an adaptation of a Japanese book.

Olivia's publicist had sat her down and informed her now was a crucial time in her career. She needed to make decisions that would make waves. But not too many. Enough that she still had somewhere to go, career-wise. Her advice? *Stick to Colin. People like the two of you together.*

Thus this movie, a Sol Stanley production being filmed in New York in the course of a month. Thus Colin costarring in it with her, after starring together in *Conquerors*. Olivia had always, always dreamed of starring in a Sol Stanley movie after *Hopeful Voice*, and had cried when she got the call. But her high was dulled when they told her Colin had been cast as her leading man. It was easier than pretending to date him. Thus meeting Mon last night, when she didn't know who he was.

Get Morningview, Sol had said, when Olivia pitched the idea of bringing in the artist/producer in one of their pre-meetings. *He's good. You have good taste, Olivia.*

She would have carried Sol's praise all the way to the bank. Even Max had commented how happy she was when they talked about it after dinner. But no. She had to pin her name on Morningview. On Mon.

"That bad huh?" Max said. "You're frowning."

"I am *not*," Olivia insisted, and felt her cheeks heat as she schooled her expression. She couldn't get it out of her head, that moment where Mon had stared into her eyes, made her feel like she was the only person in the entire world he wanted. The moment when they looked at each other in that arched mirror and she felt her entire body explode.

You're beautiful.

She'd heard that often in her lifetime, but never with that honesty. With that…God, with the reverence she craved. The man was accidentally charming and sexy as hell. It was endearing that he seemed completely oblivious to how sexy he was. How he managed to find the right things to say. It was why she'd decided to kiss him. He was sweet, and she wanted to taste it on his tongue, wanting to fight the bitterness that stayed.

Which now made sense, considering he wrote some of her favorite music.

"*Days are slow, home is a hard pill to swallow…*'" she sang absently.

"*When the world outside says it's time to go,*'" Max sang along. Because of course Max knew the words to the song on every Instagram reel from Manila to Manhattan. "Blue Period" made Olivia feel things on first listen, like someone had acknowledged how scary the world had become. No wonder it went viral. "*I'm still attached to being alone.*'"

She wished she was angry with Mon. But all her anger

had dissipated when he left the apartment. Leo texted her later confirming Mon didn't know they were working together, and it was Leo's fault for not telling her. It was her fault for not asking more questions, really.

Her publicist always advised caution. It was part of her media training. Fucking the music producer before she actually worked with him was definitely the opposite of caution.

"How long are you going to be in New York?" Max asked.

"A month? A month and a half?" She shrugged. "I'm an actress, darling, we must be flexible. And…it's Sol Stanley. I would volunteer all my time, and my future firstborn, to work with her."

It wasn't an exaggeration. There were few movies Olivia had seen that made her heart squeeze in her chest the way a Sol Stanley movie could. *Hopeful Voice* had shifted something in her when she first saw it, and finally meeting the amazing Black woman behind the camera was definitely the biggest highlight of her career so far.

Max snorted. He knew that, because she'd already told him. But when he said nothing else, Olivia was prompted to say more. Idly, she wondered if she'd ever had to explain this to anyone before. Had anyone ever asked? "I auditioned right after we wrapped season two of *Conquerors*. I sang 'Hopeful Voice' for it."

"You know I've never seen it," Max mused thoughtfully. She was aware. Her brother was tragic. "But at least one person sings it whenever we go out to karaoke."

"I saw *Hopeful Voice* a million times when it came out." Olivia sighed. The year was 2012. She was at a crossroads in her life, and she saw the movie. Her life was never the same. Because *that*. That was what she wanted to do. To pull an audience in, throw them into a story, make them feel for you. "You remember *Do Re Mi*?"

"Yes. The movie. You were obsessed with Regine's haircut."

"I was." Ah, nostalgia. "But it's kind of the same vibe, where people sing because they have to, and not because it's a musical?"

Max nodded. "Gets."

Sol Stanley was famous for making small budget movies where people sang, in a way that made it seem they were singing in real life, versus singing about their feelings in some fantasy sequence. She signed up for the audition as soon as her agent mentioned it. A lead role in a studio-backed movie was not something to sneeze at, small budget as it was. It was the perfect role that could help transition her from Ice Cold Space Queen to...what was it Satine had said in *Moulin Rouge*? A *real* actress.

"They want to call it *Overexposed*. And I honestly don't think I've ever been so excited for a project. Also, I'm working with Morningview on the music for the movie," Olivia announced, decision firm. "Mercedes managed to negotiate royalties and credit, so I'm going to be a singer." Provided she could be in a room with Mon without wanting to climb him like a tree. Well. She could. But him? She wasn't sure.

"Fulfilling dreams left and right, my sister," Max cooed, squeezing Olivia's cheek. A photo of that would probably end up on fan Twitter. "I'm really proud of you. Or proud for you. I know your career has nothing to do with me."

"Thank you."

"But if your song is anything like that song you wrote for Nick Carter in third grade..." At Olivia's confused look, he said, *"Nick Carter, I would barter my heart to you-hoo-hoo."*

Olivia's jaw dropped. She had forgotten about that. And the matching dance steps that she'd stolen from "Oops!...I Did It Again." "You. Are. The. Worst."

"Humph. You love me," Max said, as the Uber he'd ordered pulled up in front of them. She had insisted on using the car the studio provided to take Max to the airport, but her brother was as stubborn as she was and insisted he could make his own way back home. Which was half a world away from hers.

He had good timing, as she could see a small group of maybe three, four people waiting politely from a distance to approach her. She waved at them and signaled five minutes, and some of them actually shrieked excitedly, making her laugh.

"You really like this, don't you?"

"Like what?" Olivia asked, running a hand through her hair to look a little more casual. Stars, they're just like us!

"This." Max waved his hands around them. "Being Olivia Angeles."

She thought about her career in limbo, the hoops she had to jump through just to be noticed, to be seen. She thought about the shitty roles she'd taken in the past, the fact that she was still the lowest paid among the show's principal cast, despite being one of the main characters.

But then again, there were free pastries, the love of complete strangers and the totally surprising places her career took her.

There were also moments like last night. It was hard to deny that being wanted the way Mon had wanted her was… well, she adored it. She'd forgotten what it was like to be seen as Olivia, not Lady Tala or any other character. She'd forgotten how good intimacy with another person could feel when it was sincere, when there were no stakes outside of what they laid down.

"I don't think I could have been anyone else," she admitted to her brother.

She hugged Max, squeezing him tight. She could have followed him to Manila. She had been moments away from sending her application to Ateneo, after he announced his acceptance into the University of the Philippines. But in some ways, she was happy she'd stayed. She loved being Olivia Angeles, and couldn't imagine doing it anywhere else. There were dreams left and right to conquer.

"Come visit me in Manila," he said to her. "Martha's sister still doesn't believe me when I tell her we're twins."

"I mean…look at us, Max. We couldn't be more different."

"And yet…" Max didn't need to finish the sentence. Olivia got it. She extricated herself from the hug.

"Call me when Martha says yes."

"What about the time difference?"

"I don't care. Call me." Olivia gave her brother one last fond squeeze. "Now, layas."

"Labyu."

She gave herself one last minute to watch the car drive away before she checked her messages. There was an email from Mercedes, and she only needed to read the first part of the casting call to pass. Looking for Asian to play high school student/kitsune—a Japanese fox spirit. There was a text from her virtual PA, Ailee, reminding her she was meeting with Leo in Chelsea in about ten minutes, and should they call her driver to pick her up at the restaurant?

The last was a message from Colin—wanna eat before the shoot? Olivia wrinkled her nose and huffed. She wasn't too happy with Colin right now, but she was an adult and could handle it. Colin was like an annoying baby brother. Hard to get rid of, but occasionally fun to be around.

Stop trying to be subtle when asking for the schedule. You never eat before a shoot.

fine fine, was his reply. so i will see you later at...?

Ha! You'll find out. Olivia shook her head, chuckling. I'll text your PA. See you, my king.

ur a goddess! ☺

You misspelled queen.

After texting Ailee to send her the exact address to Leo's studio, and asking if she could also please share the shoot schedule for the movie with Colin Sheffield's PA, Olivia finally turned to the group of fans, which had grown into a slightly larger crowd. Nothing she couldn't handle on her own.

"Hi," she said brightly, walking over without a single wobble in her heels. If she'd intentionally worn a turtleneck with long sleeves to hide the hickeys, that was hers to know and them *never* to find out.

"My queen!" a few of the fans exclaimed, placing a hand over their chests and bowing, as all people of the Magnavis nation did to show respect for their royals on the show. Olivia returned the gesture, as she always did. She used to feel like an idiot, doing it outside of work, but now she thought it was fun, and it was a way to make fans feel less nervous. It worked…sometimes. "Are you here for FanCon?"

"Please tell me Lady Tala is still alive! That scene with Aries wrecked me!"

"Do you like lumpia?"

"Marry me, Olivia!"

"Are you dating Colin Sheffield?"

"Do you guys really call each other 'my queen,' and 'my king'?"

Olivia held her hands up, and the group immediately quieted, even if the excitement was simmering. She smiled. Max was right. She loved being Olivia Angeles. Lonely as it was, there were moments like this, where she could make someone else's day, that she loved.

"One at a time, please," she said. "You guys know better than to ask me questions about the show or my personal relationship with my king." She was pretty sure she heard someone trying to suppress a high-pitched scream. "Who wants a selfie?"

Three

Mon(e) Alone: Lost in New York Group Chat

Ava: @Moning, did you manage to get to your apartment last night?

Mon: Hey, @Ava. Yup. Thank you for sending the address.

Ava: Disaster averted?

Mon: More or less.

Scott: Mon's a mess.

Mon: HEY. >:(

Scott: I'm sorry, the rhyme was right there.

Tori: Oh my god @Mon use emojis, please. This is a group chat for 25 y-olds

Gabbie: Stop teasing the baby!
Moning, if you have the chance, try to get a table at Peter Luger. I went the last time I was in New York, it was divine.

Charlie: Who is Peter Luger and what makes his tables special?

Scott: I'm pretty sure Mon can't fit a table in his maleta anyway.

Gabbie: Oh my god.

Ava: @Moning don't get lost, and be a good boy, ha?

On his second day in New York, Mon got lost. He blamed his friends this time, as his college barkada had a tendency to orbit around a topic three times before someone finally managed to get to the point. It was pretty entertaining.

But then it did mean he'd gotten distracted, and now he was lost. Mon wasn't sure how he ended up in this particular part of the city. He wasn't even sure *which* part of the city this was. All he knew was he'd walked out of the apartment to grab a bagel somewhere the concierge said was nearish to where his meeting was supposed to be. The next thing he knew, the buildings started getting shorter and older, the concrete under his feet became a cobbled street, and he still had no bagel. There was, however, a river in the distance. Um. Okay...?

"Which river?" Teddy—business partner, collaborator, friend and pain in the ass—asked over video chat. It was 9:00 p.m. Manila time, which meant it was Teddy's peak working hours. Which also meant it was his prime Let's Tease Mon time.

"Does it matter which river?" Mon asked, settling into one of the outdoor seats at a nearby café. It was a nice spring day. By nice, the sun was out, but sitting in shade was like sitting under an aircon unit on full blast, and Mon was shivering in his jacket. "All I know is that it's big, and I can see another city on the other side."

"You should at least know if you're looking at Brooklyn or New Jersey," Teddy commented dryly.

"What's the difference?"

"No fucking clue." Teddy laughed, and Mon laughed along, suddenly feeling homesick. Agad agad? Yes, agad agad. "I don't even know how I know that. Colonization has done a fucking number on my music taste for the last thirty years."

"You're thirty-three."

"I diversified eventually," Teddy pointed out, crossing his arms over his chest before he peered at the camera. He must have seen something in Mon's expression, because he groaned and rolled his eyes. "Go on. Ask me."

"What?" Mon asked innocently, hoping the camera didn't

pick up the way he was a terrible actor. "I didn't say anything."

"You didn't have to." Teddy took a sip of his iced Americano—Mon doubted it was decaf. "Dali na, ask me. 'Teddy—'"

"Teddy." Mon finally sighed. Caught. "How's the move?"

"It's going *fine*. Just like I said it would."

"Oh really. And you're not sitting under your old desk trying to undo a mess of cables at nine o'clock at night?"

"It's stimulating my brain! At least it's not assembling furniture. I am *done* assembling furniture until Andi and I move in together, which is definitely not happening this year, because I am *tired of assembling furniture*." Teddy shook out his bleached blond hair and pulled out a cable from the tangle he was working on. Mon had no idea what that was for, and he was the one who set up all their equipment at the old studio. "Your stuff is moving tomorrow, but I'm prepared to stash it all in your office until you get back."

"Okay but the studio—"

"Will be fine. I told you I would take care of this, while you go out and live your Hollywood dream." Teddy chuckled.

Mon and Teddy owned Triptych Records. Formerly the Genius Archive recording studio (a fancy name for an old pantry they converted) now a full-on indie label. It was a work in progress, which included moving out of their co-working space in Pasig to Triptych's own lair in Marikina after securing an investment from a friend.

Neither Mon nor Teddy ever imagined they could eat,

live and pay taxes off of making music, much less do the same for other people. They were still wrapping their heads around the fact that their Little Label That Could *actually could*, when the offer for Mon aka Morningview to do *Overexposed* happened. Things were all still so new, and changing so quickly, it was hard to keep up. So much that Mon was going to completely miss the move-in because of the movie. And there was no way he couldn't do the movie. Not when Leo had assured him he would get full credit, which would trickle down to Triptych. Mon wanted to live his life making music.

But sometimes music took you to new places, that was all. And yes, he had been *close* to fucking it up because of his feelings. He was determined not to again, and talking to Teddy was an excellent reminder.

"You told me that you felt like there was something out there for you. That you needed it," Teddy continued, and the concern in his voice hit Mon hard, even from so far away. "Are you writing?"

"No," Mon grumbled. That was the thing. When "Blue Period" came out, the internet (or the side he saw) had been blown away. People actually made reels and TikToks, and posts and captions about his music. It was generally positive, and could make his ego swell three sizes if he wasn't careful. He was viral! Holy shit!

But one comment had terrified him. Followed him around for days, because it gave life to the thing he'd been feeling but hadn't wanted to admit to himself.

I can't wait to see what's next!

Short answer? He had nothing. The thing with writing a song about his feelings during the pandemic was that he was *still* grappling with his feelings about his feelings during the pandemic. Anything he wrote after felt trite, his desperate need to still sound deep but relatable but likable but viral, his own thoughts all getting in the way. What if he had just…run out of things to say?

So when the offer for *Overexposed* came in, Mon thought himself in circles and in knots trying to decide if taking the job was the right move. He had dithered about it so much Teddy had locked them both in their old pantry studio until Mon told him what was bothering him. Explained why it felt like the right step. Why he needed it now, of all times.

He was still relieved Teddy had only nodded and said, "Do you need a ride to the airport?"

"I haven't started," Mon explained now. "And I think I might have already messed it up."

"Wait! Let me push these cables aside." There was shuffling on his side of the video call, and Mon rolled his eyes when Teddy hollered, "Andi! Mon wants to tell us a story."

Mon groaned. "Oh fuck." Teddy practically skipped out of their old studio to the kitchen area where his girlfriend was clearly working. Andi, who kept the same working hours as her boyfriend, looked up from her iPad and waved at Mon, and the couple settled in to listen. "Seriously, do you have to bring Andi into this?"

"He would have told me anyway." Andi shrugged. "Hi, Mon."

"Hey Andi. How's the art?"

"It's arting." She laughed. "What happened?"

So he told them. About landing in New York, about meeting Olivia—glossing over the details of sex with Olivia—Leo knocking on her door, the *look* she gave him that made it clear the night was over. And throughout the retelling, Teddy's and Andi's eyes got wider, and wider, until he finished, and Teddy burst out laughing.

"Rude," Mon grumbled at his phone screen, jabbing at the volume button to spare the New York public the sounds of Teddy Mertola's maniacal laughter.

"I'm just..." Teddy seemed unable to speak. "Kasi naman! You didn't tell her you were Morningview! You know a few years ago it would have been the first thing you said."

"I was in my twenties, and I had unwarranted ego! You did too," Mon grumbled. "Andi knows."

"Yes, I know. There's a reason why you and I never went past the first date." Andi laughed. "But in fair Verona naman, it sounds like a very cute way to meet someone. I wouldn't say you're the asshole, but maybe talk to her, clear the air."

"But how?" Mon groaned. Talking was not his strong suit. Thinking was. But by the time he managed to sort out his thoughts, knew what he wanted to say, the person on the other side was usually tired of waiting. It had happened way too many times, and he had already made an ass of himself around Olivia.

"Bring her more pancit canton or something. Fuck, I don't know." Teddy chortled. "Do *something* to unfuck it up. Are you thinking of asking her out? You would be terrible at it."

"Helpful." Now it was Mon's turn to sound dry and sarcastic.

"You know you were about this helpful two years ago."

"Oh, you mean when you accidentally asked Andi out on a date, and now you're so in love you can hold her hand without having a midlife crisis?" Mon asked. He really was nailing Teddy's usual sarcasm. He could spot them holding hands now, the lovebirds. Ugh. He shivered in his coat. "Totally the same thing."

"I did not know this part of the story," Andi said, her brow rising as she turned to Teddy, who grinned and kissed the back of her hand. Alert the media, Teddy Mertola was a sweet kitten in love. Mon was…not jealous at all. He had too many things going on in his head, and zero words to show for it. This wasn't the time for love, or flirting, or kissing someone when they made you food.

At least that was what he told himself.

"Oh Andi, I have so many dating stories about Mon it could be a whole novel." Teddy laughed. "He once spent six thousand pesos *each* on a first date at this seafood tasting menu, when the man is allergic to seafood."

"I took an antihistamine before!"

"And yet you still needed to get nebulized at the hospital." Teddy shook his head as Andi pressed a hand over her mouth to stop herself from laughing. "Willing to do everything for love, this guy."

"Can we discuss my poor choices in love later?" Mon complained. "I just offended a Hollywood actress who lobbied for me to be here."

"I think you'll do great, working with Olivia," Teddy continued, as if reading Mon's mind. "You do really well when you're working with parameters from other artists. And you wanted to get Morningview's name out there, right?"

"Out where, though?" Mon mumbled. Perhaps these were things they should have talked about before he left, but, hindsight. "I haven't written anything since 'Blue Period,' and that's like, forever ago now. I mean, people aren't even wearing masks here anymore."

He'd written that song at the start of the pandemic. When nothing was certain, and he didn't know how much time he had left before he had to quit music—he wrote and wrote and wrote. Ironically enough it was the song that gave Morningview top spot in everyone's local playlists, with "Blue Period" still getting airtime and streaming numbers. The revenue was shit, but it was enough to pay for an occasional meal or two. In QC, not Makati.

He hadn't written anything since. There was just nothing to say. And what kind of label guy would he be, if he had nothing to say? So he came here, hoping for some space. Legitimacy. Inspiration. Words.

"It will come when it comes," Teddy assured him. And it was hard not to totally trust Teddy when it came to these things. "Jenny Holzer said that calm is more conducive to creativity than anxiety."

"I once saw a poster of Jenny Holzer truisms," Mon mused. "An Italian artist penciled in 'Believe none of this shit,' on the bottom."

"You always write better when you're not thinking about

it," Teddy added, as if he hadn't heard Mon. "Don't force it. And wear a mask."

"Try to patch things up with Olivia," Andi said. "Even if she insists she's fine. You owe her an apology at least, for withholding the truth. Who knows, she might even give you another chance."

"Yeah. Stranger things have happened," Teddy pointed out. And as Mon looked around at where he was, where he'd ended up, he agreed. He was feeling much better.

Until, of course, a bird shit on his shoulder.

"I've lived in Manila for thirty-three years, and not once has a bird ever shit on me," Mon explained fifteen minutes later, when he and Leo walked through the Swan Song Studio offices in Chelsea. "Five minutes in New York and it happens."

"Some people are just lucky that way." Leo shrugged, holding a palm out for his jacket. "Hand it over. We can get it dry-cleaned while we have the meeting."

"How?"

"Assistants, Mon. Assistants."

Leo Solano was something of an enigma. The man was excellent at writing musicals—he had a show on Broadway running at the Larsen Theater. Being chief producer for the Swan Song label meant he had his hand in every pie the studio was working on, and Mon definitely didn't expect him to be so hands-on with this particular pie. But he was, because he owed Sol Stanley "all the favors," and he was more than happy to work on "a little project once in a while."

In short, Leo was Mon's boss, but it was like, chill.

"You nervous?" Leo asked, as he and Mon wove expertly through the halls of Swan Song, easily three times bigger than Triptych, and with much more sophisticated equipment, for sure. The gloss and shine of the studio's scale was muted by warm red brick, friendly chairs and leather couches. But it was hard to deny that Leo's place had gravitas. Some of Mon's favorite artists had worked at this studio above Chelsea Market, and now he was here.

"Yes," he said. Easy enough to admit. "Scared."

"Of working, or of Olivia?" Leo chuckled, and Mon was about to open his mouth to reply when Leo laughed and shook his head. "Don't answer that. I think Olivia's great. Tough too."

"Her character is tough," Mon pointed out. "In *Conquerors*. Lady Tala wasn't supposed to be in line for the throne until her uncle died."

"Have you seen her glare? It's all her," Leo disagreed, as they passed a couple of offices, a pantry. "You have to be tough in this industry, obviously. But even more so if you want things to be fair. If you want to bring other people up with you." Leo pointed out the bathroom, the separate coffee pantry that had an espresso machine with a steamer wand. "It's her quality, even if she hasn't realized it yet. Olivia likes to make people sit up and pay attention. Which is how people in this production paid attention to you. She insisted on you, the minute she heard Sol still needed a producer."

Breath caught in Mon's chest. She was the one who'd brought him here. Had believed in his work enough to fly him in. It was an honor he wouldn't take for granted. Flashes of their night together filled Mon's mind, and how Olivia's toughness had manifested in her pinning him down, in how she took control from him. Yes. He could see that.

"This is your office!" Leo exclaimed brightly, effectively cutting off Mon's thoughts as they reached the end of a corridor, to a door marked STUDIO D, with "Morningview" written with a Sharpie on a card underneath.

Mon took a deep breath, hesitation, fear, excitement stopping him from opening the door. *Sometimes you have to trick yourself into believing you can do something, then you surprise yourself when you can actually do it.* His friend Scott had told him that. Of course, Scott had been referring to baking sourdough bread during the pandemic, but it was helpful.

Mon was excited. Thrilled. His hands were itching to make something, to get started, and where he came from, itchy hands could only lead to good things.

"Sorry," Mon said to Leo, who was clearly waiting for him. "It's a big moment."

"And you're just getting started," Leo reminded him, his smile kind. "Ready?"

"Ready." Mon nodded, and walked through the open door.

The studio was huge, or at least it was, compared to the pantry he used to work in. The floors were carpeted, with an additional shaggy checkerboard rug placed under a long, comfy couch on the side. LED strips hung along the recesses of the soundproofed walls, creating a soft, warm atmosphere. There was a microphone in the corner and a monitor on the desk waiting for a laptop to get plugged in. The other studio monitors looked brand-new, placed strategically around the desk. Mon peered at the nearby audio interface. Holy fuck, wasn't that the newest—

"Ah. They said you started without me."

Mon turned, and was not at all surprised to find Olivia leaning in the doorway, her hip against the jamb like she'd been in the room the entire time. Her hair was down, dark and fanning around her face. She looked tall, when an over-size denim shirt and loose jeans would have made any five-foot-something person look tiny. There was no trace of anger or disappointment from last night, just amusement.

Don't think about last night. It would do no good to think about that kiss on the balcony and everything that came after. The press of her lips against his, the soft, satisfied smile she had on after.

Ah fuck.

"Olivia," he said, the one word encompassing nothing and everything he wished he could say. *I'm sorry. I'm excited. I'm happy to see you.*

"Mon." Olivia's tone was even, polite and distant. Her gaze moved to Leo, who he had completely forgotten was there for a second. "You said we were meeting at ten thirty."

"I live by theater rules." Leo shrugged. "If you're early you're on time, if you're on time, you're late, if you're late—"

"Fuck off?" Olivia asked, making Mon chortle, but he hid it behind a cough.

"Well, you missed the tour, but you're just in time for my

hasty exit." Leo's smile was too wide not to be devious. "I know your schedule's packed today, Olivia."

She shrugged, but didn't deny it.

"But I really do appreciate you working closely with Mon on this," Leo said, squeezing Mon's arm. He felt a bit like a child, being passed off to the next minder. "Mon, I'll see you at my office in a couple of hours. I'll brief you properly. Schedules, studio time, that kind of thing. Give you back your jacket."

"Oh—" he began, questions at the tip of his tongue, but Leo was suddenly in a hurry, waving goodbye to Olivia and him, breezing through the door like a small typhoon had just passed.

"I have two hours before I have to be on set," Olivia explained, still standing by the door. "Until then, I'm all yours."

Air. Mon needed air. And he must have said that out loud, because the next thing he knew, he and Olivia stood outside Chelsea Market in the cold, being pushed together by tourists and locals streaming around them. Olivia's hands were tucked in her pockets, as Mon shuddered in just his shirt.

"So," she said, holding her arms out. "Air. Achieved."

"Yes." Mon nodded. Eloquent.

She must have sensed he wasn't ready to speak yet, because she briefly looked away, checking something on her phone.

"Actually, can we walk to the bookstore? There's a big one nearby. I need paper. And a pen."

"Sounds good." He nodded, and they started to walk.

He'd told her before about meeting the right person, about the possibility rife in the air. Mon could really feel it now.

He had the strange feeling this little walk would change everything. How, he wasn't sure. But worlds changed, relationships grew, from walks like this. And Mon would try his hardest to pay attention.

Four

"So, my character, Jessamyn—combined names of her parents, Jessica and Benjamin, naturally."

"Naturally."

"She's a pop star. The script specifically said, 'the biggest, now, ever, always.' I loved that. But she's at this crossroads in her career. She wants to shift the way she makes music, and she's unsure if the world wants to hear it," Olivia said, after they had walked a couple blocks in complete silence, letting her map lead the way. "Like Ariana Grande before she released *Dangerous Woman*. Or Carly Rae Jepsen before *Emotion* came out and changed my entire life."

Mon nodded and pulled his beanie lower over his ears. One would think it was the middle of winter, the way the poor boy was huddled and shivering sans jacket. It was April, the middle of a balmy, lovely morning. The sun was even out!

New York looked good in the sunlight. It had a magical quality, softening the city's harsher edges, making the tall buildings look a lot less like they were looming over her. She was used to wider, more open spaces, perpetual sunshine, artificial as it could get sometimes.

"'Cut to the Feeling' is still my favorite. But then *Dedicated* came after, and—"

"*Dedicated* was excellent," Mon agreed, nodding. "*Dedicated Side B* was even better."

"Oh wow, that is an *opinion*." Olivia laughed, walking slightly behind him.

Mon's strides were large, confident even as he was lost in thought. She vaguely wondered if he was even aware of the intimidating figure he cut, with his large chest, his pillowy lips in a straight line and brows slightly furrowed. His hair was cut short, and honestly the three lines buzzed on each side were so 2012, but they suited him, made him seem like he was all hard edges, even if right now he was hiding them under his beanie. His hair had surprised her, when she first met him, and when he ran it through his fingers, it felt like he was touching…her.

"So Jessamyn is a pop star, and she finds out she's been accidentally married to her ex-boyfriend for the last ten years. Something about paperwork when she needs to file a visa to have a concert in Taiwan. So she invites him to New York so she can serve him with divorce papers, but he says no."

Mon chuckled. "Is he *supposed* to be unlikable?"

"Colin pulls it off with his charm, his hair and his half-Canadianism."

He laughed, his hand brushing over the chest Olivia once had the pleasure of biting. Sigh. She looked at the shirt again, and noticed there was a fox embroidered on the front pocket, looking up at the stars as he wore a long, yellow scarf...oh.

She loved *The Little Prince*. Max had gifted her a copy when he first left for Manila, the sentimental softy, and she had read it, barely holding back big, fat tears on the way from LAX. She could relate to him somehow, prince of nothing on their little planet, only a prickly rose to care for.

She used to think she was the rose, thorny and prickly in her glass dome. But, as she grew older, she wondered if she was more like the boy who simply longed to understand what love truly was supposed to be. Seeing the tale woven in threads on Mon's body, broad and solid as it was, softened him. Softened her, really.

"What?"

"Nothing, I—" She quickly regained her focus. "I was admiring your shirt."

"Oh, thanks." He seemed a little embarrassed at the compliment, covering it up with a too big smile, his eyes almost closed as his cheekbones pushed them shut. "Ukay from Cubao Ex. Medyo mahal lang, but it was unique. I think it's hand embroidered."

None of those words made sense to her, even with her

Tagalog. It was fascinating to her, how different they could still be, when by most standards they were supposed to be exactly the same.

"Here," Olivia said, gently tugging at the hem of his shirt before he veered off in the opposite direction.

His eyes were light and observant, taking things in keenly. He was quiet, but Olivia could almost see thoughts forming in that funny little head of his. And knowing everything she knew about Morningview—the way he loved soft rain, the way he felt scared about going back out into the world, how he loved sunlit days and mornings in bed—it all seemed to fit the Mon Mendoza walking in front of her. She wanted to ask him about all of it, to slowly unpack everything that made the guy traveling with pancit canton the same man who touched her soul.

But she'd ruined it, hadn't she, having sex with him? She'd been too excited by the mystery, had craved the boost to her ego and had wanted it without consequence. And now they had to stay a good distance apart, keep their eyes on their work. That was fine. Hollywood was not bereft of attractive people. Honest people, however, were a different story.

"I'm sorry," Mon said suddenly, apropos of nothing, making them both stop in the middle of the sidewalk. A couple of people around them huffed at the sudden interruption and moved on with their day. Olivia gently took his arm and moved him to a quieter side of the street.

"What are you sorry for?" she asked, even if she had an inkling. Last night had been an honest mistake. She was embarrassed, but she was a professional. She could work with Mon, she'd wanted to, before all this.

"Last night. Lying by omission is still lying. And regardless of my intentions, or what we didn't know, I still didn't tell you who I was. I said all those things about New York, and how I felt, but I didn't say the important things." He sounded like he'd told himself this over and over, rehearsed it in his own head. Maybe he had.

Warmth spread in Olivia's belly, melting the cooler exteriors of her heart, even if she was doing everything not to show it. She appreciated this, Mon explaining himself, apologizing to her. They were in this strange situation, but he was doing it with sincerity, and not a notes app apology. That he was doing it so eloquently was just a bonus, really.

"Mon, come on." Olivia shook her head. "The things you told me were important too. Even if you skipped the highlights."

"I hope you forgive me." Mon wasn't looking at her, even as his sincerity radiated in waves. "I don't regret what happened, but I do regret what happened after. And I am really looking forward to making something great with you."

"Better than *Dedicated*?" Olivia joked. She appreciated his words. He'd taken her concerns seriously, reflected on them. She didn't owe him forgiveness, of course. But she was happy to grant it. More than happy.

"Um. I can't make any promises."

"Mon, I'm disappointed in you." Olivia laughed, walking ahead, letting him follow her.

"It's *Dedicated*!" he exclaimed behind her, and it felt like a weight had been lifted from between them, clearing the air. "And it's not you."

"I wonder what that sounds like." Olivia mused holding an arm out across his chest when Mon nearly jaywalked into a busy street. Oof. The man was a solid wall of muscle, and she ignored the itch to tuck her body into the expanse of his chest, because she knew how nice it felt.

She suddenly cleared her throat, needing a second to shake off the itch. Olivia was a professional, and she would remain professional. "The sound of a woman constantly trying not to spiral."

The sound of wanting love, maybe. Or maybe not.

"I've been thinking about it a bit," he announced. She had the sense that meant he'd been thinking about it a lot. "And I thought we would start with what you're listening to."

"Me? You mean Jessamyn."

"No, I mean you, Olivia."

"I'm an actress, Mon. I'm a vessel for a writer's voice. Maybe you should be talking to Sol, or Bash, they wrote the script. What does it matter what I like?"

"It matters because it will be your work. Leo said that was what you wanted." Mon's voice was perfectly calm, not at all fussed that Olivia was trying to argue. "You'll be singing too, so it's good that I know what you like. What happiness or melancholy sounds like to you. I want to know what the songs you love make me feel, too."

"Oh. Of course." Olivia nibbled her bottom lip, unsure of what to make of Mon's request. It wasn't that she was ashamed of her music choices or anything—there was no shame in what you liked, after all. But it was just…the letting him see it all laid out like that. It was her high school equivalent of holding hands. She'd collected this music, these playlists over the years, sang them in multiple showers. And to hand them over, to *Morningview*? To an artist who made her want "long nights doing nothing," and "sunlit days with you"?

"I'm sure you have good taste," Mon said, his dimples showing as he smiled with just his lips.

"You're just saying that because I'm a Morningview fan." Olivia wrinkled her nose.

"No!" Mon looked genuinely, endearingly embarrassed as a blush spread across his cheeks. "I didn't—"

"Kidding." Olivia smiled. They were one crossing away from the bookstore. She could see it right on the corner. She was still nervous, but she wouldn't let it show. More than her secret desire for Morningview to validate her music choices (because God, wouldn't that be amazing?), she wanted him to know how ready she was to take on the job.

"How do you know Morningview, by the way?" Mon asked. "Not a lot of people know 'Paz' enough to hum it while making pancit."

Nope. Olivia was *not* blushing. Because "Paz" was way, way below Mon's most listened-to songs, and she was pretty sure a third of those listens were from her.

"NY152," she said thoughtfully, ignoring Mon's confusion. "One hundred and fifty-two insights into my soul. It's from *You've Got Mail*," she explained. "That's what Morningview was—is, to me."

A pleased blush spread across his cheeks; she could just see it under his mask. He was trying to pull his beanie down over his face, but his eyes had pressed into happy little crescent moons. Olivia laughed and tugged his beanie back up. "Don't be shy, Mon. You should…what's the word, pandigan mo."

"Pan*in*digan, that's a good word." He chuckled. "You know Filipino."

"Is that different from Tagalog?"

"It's…" He paused. "Complicated. Linguistics aren't really my lane. But Tagalog is the original language that Filipino has since evolved from, if that makes sense."

Olivia nodded. "I think I get it. We used to go every year," Olivia explained. "To the Philippines. It was my parents' thing. Everything they saved went to the mortgage and to yearly trips to Manila in the summer to see my Lola Babes. My summers were all typhoons and thunderstorms, but my cousins sometimes got their classes canceled, and those were good days. But Lola Babes passed away years ago, and we stopped visiting. Then Max moved, but it got easier to just fly him wherever I was, visit the Philippines later. We finally made a plan to see Palawan, but then—"

"The pandemic."

"The fucking pandemic." Olivia nodded. "Also, that little fucker sends pictures of his every meal and I am so jealous. I know the food scene in LA is pretty diverse but Manila is *wild*. What is in a roka salata that Max has it almost every week? Gising-gising? And watermelon sinigang! Also your McDonald's has shake shake fries, what *is* that, even?"

It was one of the things her parents prioritized—making sure the kids didn't feel too much like strangers sa 'Pinas. Olivia admittedly hadn't enjoyed the heat in her youth, or the fact that she was missing out on summer camps stateside for typhoons in Manila. But it made Manila familiar at least, and not seem like the ideal barrio countryside some people still believed it to be. (What do you mean do they have carabaos on the road? Have you *seen* EDSA?)

Olivia knew a little better, but not much. Max told her that all the time. There was a lived experience of being Filipino that they didn't have. Her parents had given up some things so the kids could have others, but it was always up to the kids to reconcile that. Just diaspora things. But things Olivia was willing to work on.

"And Max is…?"

He should be back in Manila by now, in the safe, loving arms of his dog, Wookie. Olivia had never even *met* Wookie. "My brother." Olivia smiled, as she did whenever she thought about him, and how far away he was. "He lives in Manila, so he was the first to catch wind of the phenomenon your song created."

"And your brother is a fan of Morningview?"

"His girlfriend is," Olivia said. "She said she knew of Morningview. She posted a story of her with 'Blue Period' playing, and it sent me into this whole rabbit hole, which led me here to you."

"Lucky me," Mon said.

"Exactly." Olivia giggled. "I want to trust you, Mon. So. Let's do this."

Steeling herself with a breath, she wordlessly handed him one of her earbuds. Olivia ignored the rush of warmth to her belly when their fingers touched. He tucked it into his ear, those light brown eyes focused on her. His eyes were so gorgeous. Bright and so finely shaped, they were eyes that were hard to hide from.

And Olivia didn't want to hide.

They crossed the street together. It was a busy street, a busy day, the light was perfect, and Mon was about to listen to her music.

She was just about to push the door to enter the bookstore when Mon gently but quickly pulled her backward, and Olivia's back hit his chest with a little, "oof!"

She was about to whirl around and ask him what the deal was when another person burst from the other side of the door, clearly in a rush to leave. Totally unaware that he almost cost Olivia Angeles her face. Mon's quick instincts had avoided a collision, and now Olivia's back was pressed against his warm chest. She was off-kilter from the world, suddenly one second behind.

She was breathless. She'd been breathless, of course, several times—for screens, for other people. But this was a breathlessness that was just hers. Nobody else knew it or saw it.

Olivia physically shuddered. *The Little Prince* was chasing meadows in her head.

To you, I am nothing more than a fox like a hundred thousand other foxes. But if you tame me, then we shall need each other. To me, you will be unique in all the world.

Those were lines that stayed with her, that followed her. She didn't want to tame anyone. Not right now.

"Thanks," she said, extricating herself from Mon and walking into the bookstore like nothing happened. Nothing like the smell of old paper and controlled temperatures to clear one's head.

She chose a playlist—her favorite at the moment—and selected the first song. She didn't trust the shuffle gods with something this important.

The first song started with some kind of synthesized sound going up and down a scale, another instrument playing a countermelody. Olivia knew this one, of course.

"I love this song," Mon said, suddenly walking closely behind her. His voice was low, the kind that made her want to curl her toes, spoken softly into her ear. "Joji, right?"

"Yeah," Olivia said, letting him walk ahead of her instead. "Slow Dancing in the Dark" was such an intimate song, a lot more suddenly with someone on the other side listening to it. She'd always pictured the singer singing softly into the mic, creating as little space as possible between them and the person listening. The lyrics were about letting go of someone, pushing them away, and yet the music didn't echo the way others did.

She grabbed the first notebook and pen she could find— it was a little set, nice. For all intents and purposes, their errand was done. But she didn't quite feel like leaving yet.

They couldn't be too far away from each other, so Olivia followed Mon, walking ahead toward the books. He seemed to be in awe of the store, his hands twitching as he sighed longingly at everything. His eyes scanned the incredibly tall ceilings, every nook and cranny filled with books for sale. Eighteen miles of them to be precise, in multiple floors. The music swelled, and the singer sang, and it was the perfect soundtrack for the boy with stars in his eyes, looking out at the sea of books.

Then the music changed. A Filipino band, one she'd recently discovered. Well, not *discovered*. They had always been there, she just hadn't found them yet. Local (sorry, OPM—original Pinoy music, Max explained) bands were so cool to her. The traditional band + instruments = let's rock setup was so underrated in her world of pop stars and solo acts, and they dominated the Pinoy music scene. This band had two lead singers, and this song in particular put their voices and harmonies so in sync Olivia wanted to sing along. It was a good song, heart-wrenching, but she loved it. That crunchy guitar solo in the end, with all the band joining in? Amazing.

"What the fuck," Mon said, his voice a whisper as he dropped his jaw at Olivia. "You listen to Trainman?"

"They showed up on a suggested music list." She nodded. "I'm a little in love with Miki. You also know Trainman?"

"We've worked with them a few times. I mixed this song."

"Oh my God, what! That is so legit," she gasped, genuinely excited. "Can you introduce me to Miki? And Jill? *Wait*, does this mean you've met Shinta Mori—"

"Shinta Mori is not a member of Trainman."

"He *should* be."

"But wow. You listen to Trainman." Mon's eyes disappeared into happy curves again as his grin came out in full force. It was a pleased smile, this time. Olivia was trying not to melt on the spot. He was so legitimately *delighted* by the things that made her happy.

He walked ahead again, and God, she knew what was going on. She knew exactly what was happening because she'd played this scene before. *Drop Everything and Read* was an ensemble movie she'd starred in before *Conquerors* had cast her. In it she played the best friend of the main character (whose actress was now in an HBO drama with other serious actors), and played cupid to her bookstore meet-cute with The One.

Olivia had never been considered for the role of the main character, and at the time she had been more than happy to watch from a distance. Kilig was easy, after all, when she was watching from a distance. At the time, it was the peak of her career. This was it, she'd thought. *This is all I'm going to get.*

Today, she was suddenly asking herself—*what if I wanted more?*

"I found the art books!" Mon whispered excitedly when she turned the corner. Why were they whispering? He was still smiling. "Look at this, Olivia."

Shura's "What's It Gonna Be?" was playing, chosen by the shuffle gods this time. Mon was nodding his head along to the song, badly singing a line or two under muttered breath. It was incredibly adorable. God, her cheeks were in pain from all her smiling around him.

He held the book up to her, open to a particular page. It

showed a photograph of a Chagall painting, the one with the goat and the woman in a red dress, floating in a vibrant blue ocean.

"I know that one," Olivia said proudly. "'Happiness isn't happiness without a violin-playing goat.'"

When Mon tilted his head at her in confusion, she explained. "It's from *Notting Hill*."

Yes, she'd seen *Notting Hill* too many times. The irony was not lost on her, that she was just a girl, standing in front of a boy, asking him to love her. Asking him to make a song with her, at the very least.

"It's *La Mariée* by Marc Chagall," Mon corrected her gently, the reference completely flying over his head. "Depending on when you look, it's melancholic or euphoric."

She didn't think of it that way, but she could see it now, how the bride could be closing her eyes in peace or bliss, if the goat was playing a wedding march or a funeral. The song playing right now was a piano against the soft sounds of rain, and she could see the melancholy a bit more clearly.

"He also painted the ceiling of the Paris Opera, much later in his career," Mon continued, turning a couple of pages until he found the right photo. The colors seemed to leap off the pages. Surrounded by the gilded ceiling and the chandelier, it was still the art that drew her eye—characters of different famous operas performing against a shifting, colored sky. "I've always wanted to see it."

"I've seen it," she said, coming closer so she could get a better look at the photograph, using Mon's arm to anchor herself. "I did a commercial in Paris before the pandemic, and my hotel was near here, so I spent my free day at the opera, just looking at everything."

"We really are worlds apart," came Mon's whispered response, and the words sent a shudder down her spine. She looked up from the book, meeting his observant gaze. Mon with the eyes that could see everything, who was listening to the songs she held close to her heart. How far apart could they be, if he knew all this about her?

Then Morningview's "Lonely" came on. It was Olivia's favorite from his last playlist, a continuous stream of thought, his reflections on being alone. How good it was, how isolating it was. His voice in the track sounded far away, like the listener was wading through water to find him. And here Olivia was, invading his space to read the art book. She couldn't have scored this scene better herself.

"I'll get this for you," Olivia announced, taking the surprisingly heavy book from Mon's hands.

"You don't have to."

"I insist!" Olivia said too cheerfully. She needed to do something, to remind herself of her purpose here. To distract herself from her suddenly racing heart, and the violins wreaking havoc on her feelings. "Call it a 'welcome to your new studio' present."

"Like a reverse pasalubong?"

"Exactly like that, yes!" Olivia marched to the counters with the book and her little stationery set, ignoring the way the music was suddenly cutting off at random points like an old scratched up CD.

The music cut off completely before Imago's "Sundo"

could make her totally lose her shit. That song was too romantic for its own good.

The blast of cool air and sunshine hit her the second she stepped outside next to the bargain books. The world felt much bigger again, and the distance, while disorienting, was good. She was pacing suddenly. Why was she pacing?

"Hey, aren't you Lady Tala?" a stranger said, and while she wasn't quite ready, it was enough to get her back in the moment. They asked for a picture, and she complied, her world reordering itself to its familiar rhythms and beats.

"Damn, I thought she would be prettier in real life."

But then the outro to "Sundo" came out crystal clear and perfect as Mon emerged from the store, and it was like the world had fallen into slow motion, trapped in cooling amber, how Mon saw her and walked toward her, concern etched in his features.

She couldn't do this. Mon had said his apologies, this door was supposed to be *closed*.

"Are you okay?" he asked, a warm hand settling on her shoulder, eyes looking into hers, and it reminded her too much of arched mirrors and orgasms in the dark of the night.

"Yes," she lied, wordlessly holding a hand out for her earbud back. "Just wondering what you were thinking."

"Our tastes are a lot more similar than I expected." Mon seemed delighted at the thought. "I definitely think I can come up with something for you. But the theme, and what the song says…that's up to you."

She didn't know what she wanted to say, was the problem. Nobody wanted to hear what *she* had to say; it wasn't part of the job. "That sounds difficult."

"It's definitely a challenge," Mon agreed, starting to walk away, and Olivia had no idea where he was going. Did he? "It's almost like giving a part of yourself away for everyone to see. I think you can understand that better than most people."

"Like 'Blue Period,'" Olivia noted. "It felt like I was seeing you in lockdown."

"'Blue Period' was…well, it was the pandemic, and I thought I was going to disappear," Mon said. "Not literally, just that my voice would somehow vanish in the ether because I stopped using it. I didn't even know if I was still going to work in a studio, when the lockdowns started. So I needed to put it into music, into words. That part of myself I thought I was going to lose."

She understood, but she knew his experience of the pandemic was different from hers. She continued to work, had swabs stuck up her nose daily, stayed in her trailer between shoots. Her brother, Max, had told her about his experience—how murky everything had been, how many cases they had gotten, how little people who were supposed to protect them were doing about it.

"I'm just an actress, Mon. I don't think there's anything I can say that people would want to hear. I speak other people's words, you know?"

She was happy about that. What she truly wanted, though, was to speak the words of people she wanted to work with. Give a face to characters people could root for. She wanted to be a Filipina actress in Hollywood. Was that too hard?

"You're Olivia Angeles," Mon insisted. "You give life to other people's words, and nobody else does it the way you do. You've got a voice too, one I think people should hear. And from the music you've shared, and the things you're saying now, it's going to be great."

Mon's words were hard to absorb. She'd always felt like she was replaceable in this business. Lady Tala could have been just as successful if the role had gone to Mia Blanc, or any other Hollywood actress. But she had to give herself some credit. Lady Tala's scary confidence, her quiet sadness, these were all Olivia. Her. Mia could have played Lady Tala, but it wouldn't have been the same Lady Tala that everyone liked so much.

Olivia deserved to say those things out loud. Or write them down somehow.

They continued to walk, and the city contracted and expanded around them as they did. Olivia had always been amazed at the way New York played with scales. Spaces were aligned in grids, but the buildings shrank and grew depending on where they were. The chaos remained in all that order, and it was in that chaos where Olivia could come to terms with being asked for more. Being asked to open up.

"I don't know which parts of me are still me, or which parts I just held on to from the characters I played," Olivia admitted. "Their lives are certainly more interesting than mine."

"That's true. But we can't all be the long-lost princess and eventual queen of the most powerful space fleet in the galaxy."

"Oh my God." Olivia smacked his arm playfully. Now she

was laughing. The smack had been so loud a couple people turned to look, but whatever. "You've watched the show."

"Of course." Mon snorted. "I love your line, *'I will not be dragged into the childish games of kings and old men.'* You're magnificent. In the show, I mean."

"But you didn't recognize me right away."

"Well, you never expect to meet your heroines."

She had to admit that compliment sent butterflies whirling around in her stomach. Manufactured kilig was great, but surprise kilig? God, it was even better. She was magnificent; she was his.

"Where are we going, by the way?" she asked.

"I thought we were getting air?"

"Air. Psh." Olivia frowned, opening her maps app again. Where were they even? "Getting air means aimless walking. Going up a mountain to go back down. Circling a park for no reason. Running through a valley to 'feel connected to nature' when you're really doing it for the photos."

"You're from LA," he pointed out. "You make it sound so bleak."

"This city's rubbing off on me." Olivia chuckled.

"When you're alone, it's usually to settle your thoughts," Mon said. "Except in my case the park is a mall and I get distracted by things I definitely don't need."

She laughed. She would learn later that Mon wasn't kidding. There were very few parks in Manila you could just casually walk through—it was a mall or nothing.

"But when you're with someone else," he continued. "The point is this." Their fingers touched. "Talking to each other. Clearing the air, understanding each other a little better. Getting inspired."

The street opened up, and the next thing Olivia knew, they were in front of the Flatiron Building. It was a tall, imposing wedge in a city of mostly ordered rectangles, slicing the sky in half. Olivia had never seen the building from street level—she'd passed it more than once, in her comings and goings in New York, but it was still different to look at it from the street. Mon stood next to her in the same contemplative silence.

"You're good at this," Olivia noted.

"At what?"

"Saying your thoughts out loud. It makes me want to be better at this songwriting thing."

"That's what I'm here for." He gave her a wan smile, like saying that had bummed him out a little. But he looked at the view again, and how was the morning light so pretty? It was all diffused and soft, bathing Mon's profile.

Olivia took his photo.

"For my contacts," she explained when he raised a brow at her, very busily enhancing the photo just a bit. She saw the time. "Fuck. I should go. I have to be uptown in an hour for a shoot. Will you be okay?"

"I think so," he said with a tiny shrug, and something inside Olivia didn't immediately believe him. "I need to gather my thoughts before going back to Swan Song."

"When do we meet next?" Olivia asked, already texting her driver to ask how soon he could pick her up from here. "At the studio?"

Mon shook his head. "I'll come up with guides first, so we've got a starting point. You can start thinking of themes. Things you might want to sing about."

To sing was to speak, and to speak was to make things real. Olivia wasn't sure she was ready for the world to know how much she wished she was loved, how she wanted a relationship she was enough for, how it all scared her. She wasn't quite ready to sing it to the man who had evoked those desires in her, too.

"You can always message me if you have a question, or if you just want to 'get some air.'" Mon chuckled, his dimples showing as he said it.

He gave her a beso on the cheek. It was the polite version, where your cheeks touched. Air rushed out of Olivia's lungs and she squeezed his arm to steady herself. She looked down and saw her hand was clutched around an embroidered rose in his shirt.

"I'll talk to you soon," he murmured, and it was like a promise. He looped a mask around his ears, covering up his pretty mouth, and walked away.

She was still thinking of these things—shared music, walks, getting close—when she arrived at the shoot. She'd started jotting things down in her shiny new notebook. Sporadic sentences that made sense only to her.

It seemed she actually had words, things to say.

"Who is Marc Chagall? Is this research for a role or something?" Colin Sheffield asked as he waltzed into the makeup

trailer. Depending on the day, Colin waltzed or sauntered.
Either way it was dramatic.

Colin was very blond, very friendly, but also very nosy
when you let him have an inch. He picked up the book from
where Olivia had placed it just in front of the makeup mirror. She'd forgotten to hand it to Mon that morning.

"Oof. This seems like a lot of research. Wait. Oh my
God. Did you get that art heist film thing you wanted? Why
didn't you tell me, my queen! I mean I know I offered to
call the casting director for you, my uncle knows him, but
my schedule's been so packed—"

"Sit down, nosy." Olivia playfully kicked him and waved
her free hand at the empty chair next to her. The fun thing
about being cast in a movie set in the contemporary twenty-
first century was they didn't have to spend several hours in
a makeup chair. But it was in those hours that Colin and
Olivia's friendship had first formed.

Her phone chimed with a message.

Guess who got lost on the way back to the studio? Thank
God for kababayans patient enough to show you how Maps
works.

There was a photo included of Mon smiling and giving
her a thumbs-up (she could only tell because his cheeks were
pressing up against the top of the mask) with the correct
building in the background. Olivia smiled.

"Alert the presses, Olivia Angeles is *smiling*. God, your
face is luminous. Your publicist will have a field day," Colin

chortled, and she quickly got her makeup artist Pat's permission to pelt him with a makeup sponge. "That script must be a really good one."

Olivia stopped pelting him when he pleaded with her to stop. "Are scripts the only thing that can make me smile? Do you claim to know me that well, my king?"

"Well, my queen, we have been extensively exhausted talking about the things we want to do next when *Conquerors*—"

"If *Conquerors*."

"—doesn't get renewed. So is it a script or what?"

"It's nothing," Olivia muttered, grabbing the book from Colin and placing it firmly on her lap over her notebook. "Don't read anything into it. *Stop* trying to read anything into it."

Colin had more than once offered Olivia things. Contacts in the industry. Casting directors, publicists, friends of friends who could help with this or that. He always mentioned them, but never really did anything to introduce them. It was fine. She didn't want a reputation as Colin's charity case anyway. As it was, being cast in two big projects together was already generating speculation about their relationship.

She had to play it smart. She had to play it alone, because Colin was nothing more than a friend. And he wasn't going to help her with managing her image. A thought suddenly occurred to her, and she turned to Colin.

"Have you started your song yet?" She knew from the script that Colin's character sings exactly twice in the movie, just like her. Except Olivia had no idea what his song would be like. Somehow she couldn't imagine Colin Sheffield having an intense heart-to-heart with a producer he'd handpicked.

"It's done." Colin shrugged. "I recorded it like two days ago, and I start rehearsals for the number next week."

"Already!" Olivia exclaimed, making Pat tut her lips to get Olivia back in the chair.

"Yeah," Colin laughed. "Sol said you were insistent on going through this whole process for yours, rallied for this mystery producer—"

"Morningview isn't exactly a *mystery*—"

"Making things harder for yourself, again, my queen." Now it was Colin's turn to tut his lips. "That's the Olivia I know."

Five

Now Playing: OverexposedCreditsSongGuideFINALFINAL.wav

Leo's face remained pensive and unreadable throughout the entire listen, his foot tapping along to the beat. Mon stayed in his rolling chair, trying to stop reading into Leo's posture. His knee was shaking, even with his hand trying to steady it, and in the back of his mind he wondered if he had a predisposition for hypertension, because holy *crap* was he tense.

It was just a guide, after all. Leo was listening to it, deciding its fate. No big deal.

When he made it back to Swan Song that morning, suddenly full to the brim with creative energy, he got the entire picture of his tenure with the studio. For *Overexposed*, they wanted him to make two songs—a pop duet between Colin and Olivia for the closing credits of the movie (a Sol Stanley tradition, apparently) and Olivia's solo song.

After reading the script and hearing Colin's vocals (to be

fair, the man had been trained, and Mon could hear it), the guide track for the duet came to him easily, and that was what Leo was listening to today, three days later. It was in no way final (how can a song be final, really?), and it was mostly Mon's autotuned voice singing both parts horribly, but there was a general idea.

"I like it!" Leo exclaimed enthusiastically, slapping the table, his dark hair flying. "Retro pop is so in right now. And that little speaking part at the bridge? Olivia will kill it. I could kiss you, Mon, you're a genius."

"Not such a genius," Mon chuckled. "You heard my singing, right?"

"Details, details, Mon." Leo waved his hands. "Actually. Do you want Sol to give it a listen? I have a lunch with her in about..." He checked his phone. He was wearing a watch that probably cost three times more than all the equipment in the room right now, but he checked his phone. "Now-ish. I was supposed to pick her up at the shoot location."

Did he want the movie director to decide the fate of his song before it was finished? Sure, why not.

So there they were, sitting in a car on the way uptown in the middle of the day. Leo told Mon about how he knew Olivia, which was obviously through her auditioning for *Overexposed*. He was close to Sol Stanley because both of them walked out on a film class while attending Columbia. Apparently, the prof had loudly declared movies that won Oscars were winners based solely on merit—if people of color didn't win or get nominated it was just because they weren't good enough.

"Fuck that prof," Mon muttered.

"Exactly what Sol said when we left." Leo laughed, shaking his head. "We had tacos and we've been friends since. Lovers a couple of times, but we mutually agreed it was best for her to marry her wife, Edie, while I retain my freedom and single blessedness. It works."

Leo later went on to write *Swan Song*, a wildly successful musical about Truman Capote and the society swans of New York. Sol did *Hopeful Voice* and made a name for herself in film. *Overexposed* was officially the first time they'd worked together.

"She was hesitant to cast Olivia for this," Leo admitted, looking out the window like he wasn't divulging celebrity gossip in the middle of the day. "Mostly because of her *Conquerors* character. Lady Tala is seen as—"

"Cold?"

"I was going to say a bitch, but we can use your word." Leo grinned. "It's hard for people to separate characters from their actors now. People know Sherlock but not the guy who plays him. Most of the time they don't care. But we met Olivia and she was…" He tapped his chin as he searched for the right word. "Tenacious. She knew she wanted the Jessamyn role. She knew she wanted to make music with you, and she wore Sol down, and we loved it. It's the kind of tenacity Sol and I had when we walked out on that prof."

"Isn't tenacity a given, with the job?" Mon asked.

Leo frowned. "There's a particular kind. One that demands a seat at the table, when people don't want her there.

She wanted you here because she knew you would work well, but she also knows exactly what she's giving you."

Mon understood that Olivia's interest in him was just for his work, his talent. If he harbored any disappointment, he dared not acknowledge it.

"So while you're here, create as much as you want. Give her good work, make your best work," Leo told him, and Mon suddenly had a feeling this conversation and this lunch weren't as spontaneous as he'd thought. "I can set you up with meetings with some of our producers here, see if you're a good fit. Swan Song does production for film and stage, but I know a few music label guys, too."

"Wait, producers?" Mon asked, suddenly wary. He knew how the world worked. You weren't just offered meetings and allowed to create as much as you wanted. Guys like Mon had to make their own opportunities and maybe, if they were lucky, get to do this for as long as they could. Any more than that was a fever dream.

"Yeah." Leo laughed. His face was almost fond when he grinned at Mon. "Olivia took a chance on your talent, Morningview. Are you going to take the opportunity to make it big, or not?"

They arrived at the shoot location soon enough, and the traffic getting there made a little more sense—they were at the MoMA, which had been on a list of places Mon wanted to see on his days off. It was early enough in the day that the museum had just opened, curious museum guests observing the general chaos of a movie shoot. A couple of people wore shirts emblazoned with the Magnavis nation crest, the Federation star brand, or some other form of merch attached to *Conquerors*.

"They're shooting at the MoMA?" he said as the car pulled up across the street.

"I think they're in the sculpture garden," Leo said almost lazily, putting on a pair of sunglasses. "Let's go, Moncito."

They walked through the crowds and security like it was something they did every day until they came to a side garden. The intricate, blocky buildings of the Upper East Side around them were softened by trees, a perimeter wall. Even the noise had changed. Mon's head kept turning as he tried to observe as much as he could—the art nouveau Metro sign from Paris, a small pond with fountains, a bronze statue of a goat—until they came to a clearing, where Sol's personal assistant found Leo and assured him they were on their last shot.

A voice cut sharply through the set. "Quiet on the set! Three, two, one, action!" The crew was smaller than Mon imagined, about twenty people, still and in absolute silence, all eyes focused on the two actors waiting for their cue. He and Leo were too far away to hear or see what they were saying.

One of the production staff handed them headphones and invited them to sit near…some kind of sound machine and a monitor so they could see what the three cameras were focusing on, one wide shot and two tighter shots. The headphones allowed him to hear Olivia and Colin talking.

"Did Sol say the camera was coming in on the left or on the right?" Colin asked.

"Right," Olivia said brusquely, like she was thinking of too many other things to answer Colin politely.

"Ah you're getting ready to cry," Colin noted. "Sorry. I won't disturb you. But it's the right camera, so I should put my hand on your left cheek because you're crying out of your—"

"Right eye, yup."

He was pretty sure more than one person standing outside right now would pay an arm and a leg to see this. They were literally discussing which eyeball she would cry out of.

The cameras started rolling and Mon watched them on the monitor. Colin and Olivia looked good together—he was tall, blond and had a penetrating gaze solely meant for Olivia. She had a detached but fierce air, like she was well aware Colin was three heads taller than her, but she didn't really give a shit because she was the one in control here.

"Stop. Just stop, Jessa," Colin said, exasperation in his voice before he tightened his jaw. *Hmm, panga panga school of acting*, Mon mused. That jaw was doing half the work for him. "You *left* me."

"I did. Because you stopped believing in me," Olivia said sharply, irritation flickering across her face as she landed the blow. "You said you could wait, that you could hold on. You didn't."

"Coming in," they heard just ahead of them, and Colin's jaw tic took center stage in his shot. The wide view stopped, but it was the tight shot on Olivia's camera Mon was drawn to. As they had discussed, the camera came in from her right. Her gaze was arresting, transforming from determination to pain, and a sad resignation. "Take a breath, Olivia, then you can go."

The second she took for that breath had the entire room holding theirs. She looked at the camera, and Mon felt rooted to his seat by the force of her glare.

"I loved you, Ash," she said, and goose bumps ran up and down Mon's spine. "I loved you so much I was determined to make it all work. But you stopped believing in me. So I became the person I wanted to be, without you. And that's the part that kills you, doesn't it. That I did it without you."

The words were sharply delivered, harsh even. The much discussed tear was in her eye, but she seemed to exert more effort to make sure it didn't fall. Mon's fingers and toes were cold, like she had accused *him* of not believing in her.

He'd thought it was strange, the movie ending on this sad note—that the two characters' marriage had been a mistake, that they had both moved on. But the way Colin and Olivia spoke their lines, there was something electric, and familiar and...

He remembered the night Olivia kissed him. His first night here. Her touch had been featherlight, even as she kissed him with the heat and passion of a blazing star. Even he was having a hard time pretending it didn't happen, and he was only with her for one night. How could anyone stand to let her go?

Well, not Olivia, her character. Obviously. And Olivia herself wasn't interested in pursuing anything with Mon, not after what happened the night they met. That was done.

"Cut!" someone yelled, a slate clapped in front of the camera. Someone yelled at everyone else to pack up, and suddenly everything around Mon turned chaotic. The person from the production who had handed him the headphones yanked them away, explaining the museum was *not* happy they were still here.

The director jumped up from her seat and approached her actors. She gave Colin a proprietary pat on the shoulder, and the man smiled and nodded back like he hadn't just been inflicted with intense emotional pain. Then she turned to Olivia, and Mon nearly got up from his seat when he realized Olivia was fully crying from both eyes.

"Down, boy." Leo chuckled beside him. "She's a professional."

Sure enough, Olivia smiled and nodded at Sol, pressing the offered tissue to her eyes. She was glowing, her smile brightening at whatever Sol said to her. There was nothing but admiration in Olivia's eyes for her idol, and even Mon felt a twinge of pride for her at a job well done. Colin had already walked off to wherever. Mon relaxed slightly, and noticed Leo was definitely grinning at him.

"Yes?" he asked.

"Nothing." Leo giggled. Like full-on, schoolkid giggled, as if he'd just been let in on a big secret.

"Leo!" a voice exclaimed, and both Sol and Olivia smiled and waved at them, her assistant tapping rapidly on a phone behind her. "You owe me lunch!"

"Yan si Sol Stanley?" Mon asked, and Leo laughed.

"Si. Sol Fucking Stanley," he agreed, waving back. "I'll introduce you."

"Leo," Mon said, trying not to watch as Olivia was de-miked. "Do you still think Olivia and I would be cute to-gether?"

Leo's silence was palpable, even in the midst of all the hurried packing. His smile, however, was more revealing than anything he could have said.

"Acting is such a lonely profession, isn't it?" Leo said, like they were discussing the weather. "There are twenty people in this garden, and Colin was there, but Olivia was all alone in that moment. The movie isn't exactly Austen, but she's struggled with the emotions here, by herself. I thought you guys were cute, because you were both so damned awk-ward about getting caught. But she could use someone in her corner. Having that someone be the musician she picked to work with her was a good choice."

Like he was a knight, coming to the rescue of the prin-cess. Not that she needed rescuing. She needed a friend, maybe. The only thing she wanted from Mon was a song, and he would be content with that.

"Just sleep with her again if you want to." Leo snorted. "You're consenting adults, and everything is out in the open now, literally what is stopping you?"

I don't know if she still wants me, was on the tip of his tongue, but he didn't dare give it power by saying it out loud.

"Hmm," Sol said, her hand on her hip as Mon approached. "So this is the famous Morningview. I've heard a lot about you, sir. Now I will not name any names," she said, her lips caught in a smile as she glanced at something behind them. "But her name rhymes with Bolivia and she's talked my ear off about you. That presumptuous little sweetheart wants to change the way my movie ends."

"I'm just saying, it has more impact!" Olivia exclaimed behind them, and both Mon and Leo moved to include her in the circle. "With all due respect, of course."

"Respect noted." Sol's brow rose and Mon could sense Sol was more amused than annoyed at her lead actress.

"Olivia!" Leo exclaimed, turning to give Olivia, now sans mic, air kisses on the cheek. "That was a good scene. I wish you slapped Colin."

"Maybe on the next take," Olivia joked, wrinkling her nose before she smiled at Mon. Maybe it was because her eyes had been brimming with tears two minutes ago, but seeing her smile immediately made him smile too. "Hi."

"Hi," he said back. "That was…"

"Yeah?" she asked, as if she knew exactly what he was trying to say.

"Yeah." He nodded.

"Oh God," Sol said, making Mon almost jump back and blink in surprise. "Have they been like this the entire time?"

"It's been a week," Leo pointed out, his arms crossed but his smile all too knowing. "But yes. They have been like this. The *entire* time."

"I think I'm going to take our tourist here on a little trip to the museum," Olivia suddenly said, looping her arm around Mon's and tugging him in the presumed direction of the museum. "You like art, don't you—"

"I was going to—" he started. *Have lunch with Sol and Leo*, he almost said, but Leo waved him off with a hand.

"Just send me the file. I can be your errand boy for notes. Least I could do after setting you two up."

"What?"

"We'll be fine, won't we, Sol?"

And that was how Mon ended up walking around the Museum of Modern Art with Olivia Angeles on his lunch break. He'd waited about an hour for her to get changed, but it gave him time to wander around the sculpture garden. Sol's assistant had the good sense to send one of the security team with them into the museum. But aside from the quiet figure in a black suit following them around, speaking quietly into an earpiece every once in a while, they were surprisingly left alone. For the most part.

"That person just took a photo," Olivia announced beside him, her lips so lightly pursed he would have missed it if he wasn't looking. "I love their *Conquerors* shirt. I guess a lot of fans know I'm here."

"We don't have to do this, you know," he told her. "We could wait in your trailer or something."

"No, I want to show you something," Olivia insisted, walking past a Roy Lichtenstein piece without giving it a second glance, the actual *The Persistence of Memory*, Pablo Picasso's women of Avignon. Mon's mind reeled. "We were talking about inspiration, and I saw this and thought of you."

She squeezed his hand, which he hadn't even realized she'd been holding. A slow, warm feeling spread over him, like sunlight in the earliest of mornings.

"Hi, sorry, Lady Tala, Lady Tala!"

Olivia let go of his hand, even as the security guy blocked

the person's way, softly murmuring a request to please give Olivia some space, that this was her private time. The young woman was clearly a fan, donning a jacket with pins of the show's branding. She waved frantically at Olivia as if it were of the utmost importance that they speak.

"Ate!" she finally exclaimed, and that got both Mon's and Olivia's attention. The security guy looked at Olivia, and she made a gesture to get him to back down and let the fan through. The fan was almost trembling with excitement. "Ate Olivia!"

"Shh, quiet lang." Olivia placed a finger over her lips. "Hello po."

"Nag-Tatagalog po kayo?" she asked.

"Konti."

What followed was an impressive, singular breath in which the fan exclaimed her love and loyalty to Lady Tala, how Lady Tala's struggle to keep the Magnavis nation running under the strains of the Federation had reminded her of her own struggles to keep her family together as the eldest in an Asian household, and had been the escape she needed during the pandemic, and her anxiety over the fate of the show. Of Olivia's fate, in particular.

Mon couldn't see Olivia's face, but he could see the fan's. Her eyes were luminous, almost brimming with tears, and her sincerity was enough to melt any icy heart.

"May I hug you?" Olivia asked, and the fan nodded before Olivia wrapped her up in what looked like a very warm, politely tight hug. Mon looked away because he knew it was a private moment. Besides, he knew what it was like to hold

Olivia in his arms. He missed it. Wanted it again. "Thank you for telling me that, I really appreciate it."

It was an overwhelming amount of love to receive. Mon wasn't sure he could have handled it as graciously as she did. He stepped back, deciding to admire the Mondrian painting hanging on the wall near them.

"I can't believe you're in New York at the same time I am. Do you live here?" the fan continued. Mon made a little noise, and she turned to him like she hadn't noticed he was there before. "Who is he? He's cute."

"Short time lang," Olivia said, probably in answer to the first sentence, except the way she said it immediately made Mon chortle and the fan gasp in shock. "What?"

"Nothing!" Mon exclaimed, whirling around to see the fan look at him helplessly and Olivia look helplessly lost. "I'm just a friend. Do you want me to take a picture of you guys?"

He took the photo, and after one last hug and an awkward goodbye, they moved on.

Olivia's cheeks were red, and she refused to move from her spot when Mon started to walk away. She belligerently refused to move until Mon explained what short time meant. It was fucking adorable, and Mon was trying his hardest to keep a straight face.

"Short time is like 'afternoon delight,' I guess?" Mon explained. "There are a bunch of motels that charge you by the hour so you save a bit of money when you're doing... activities." Olivia's eyes widened when the meaning sank in. "All the good love hotels are in Pasig, and serve excellent pancit and crispy pata. At least that's what I've heard."

Good boy siya eh. And so when Olivia said, "Short time lang," the fan had assumed she was talking about Mon.

"Oh my God." Olivia groaned, covering her face with her hands. "That was so embarrassing. Now she'll think we're sleeping together!"

"Um. Would that be so bad?" he asked.

"That—" She stopped, as if to consider it, her eyes slightly wide like she hadn't before. Or maybe it was that she'd been thinking about it more than he realized? "No. It wouldn't be so bad."

They made it to the gallery, Olivia pulling at his hand more boldly this time, her gaze determined. Practically marching through the museum, she stopped in front of a massive painting. Most of the painting was covered in gold leaf, slightly bronzed over time. In the middle was Marilyn Monroe's face, painted in layers of black, turquoise, bright yellow and magenta.

Was this what Olivia wanted him to see? He was about to ask, when he saw the expression on her face. She looked… melancholic. Like the painting had struck a chord in her, and she was finding it difficult to move past it. He could understand the feeling, but why she felt this way, he didn't know.

"I read about this somewhere," Olivia explained. "*Gold Marilyn Monroe*. Andy Warhol made it to show how people never truly knew her. All they knew were the gilded parts of her life, the tragedy of her death. They saw the hair, the mole, the smile, and nothing more."

"It's beautiful," he said.

"Isn't it a little sad?"

"How?"

"Some days I love being known as Lady Tala," Olivia explained, leaning closer to Mon. "It's better validation than any award I could get. But that can't be who I am, if someone else can just take it away from me." She sighed, her shoulders dropping. "This role too. By the end of the month, I won't be a pop star working through her feelings with her estranged husband. Roles could dry up for me in a year, who knows? Everything feels stacked against me, and some days…"

"Some days?"

"Some days I wonder if I still have an Olivia, or an Emmy Angeles inside me. If anyone will ever see that."

Tension filled the air, hot and thick. His fingers twitched, and Mon was struck by the urge to hold her. To reassure her of the way he was feeling somehow, with his touch. *I would like the chance to see you more. You're lovely. Do you feel the same for me?*

There were worse places to tell someone how you felt. And he was from a country where you could dance around those feelings for years and it would be totally understandable. There was a whole topic of discussion he could start around sexual repression, how being shy and not so forward with how you felt was a cultural thing, but right now, at this very moment, he didn't want to think about that.

He wanted to stay here, in this moment, for a little longer.

"I see it differently," Mon said instead, taking Olivia aback, blinking as she waited for his explanation. "I think Andy loved Marilyn so much that he preserved her in his own way. Even if it was just a poor image."

"What do you mean?"

"Nobody in the world would have known about Vincent van Gogh's work if his brother Theo didn't believe in it," Mon explained, still looking at the painting. "Theo never got to finish that work, but his wife, Johanna, loved *him* so much that she made the whole world see Vincent's art. One of my favorite things about art is how it's a testament to how much someone was loved, enough that the world needed to see it."

And he could be totally wrong. Obviously, Andy Warhol had his own intent for making art from Marilyn's image, but Mon chose to think there was love and admiration there. A way for the artist to preserve her memory. He looked at Olivia in the light of the museum. Clear as day, and eyes wide with curiosity. That warm, honey feeling of affection bloomed in his chest. He reached for her hand and squeezed it.

"Marilyn was loved, and so she was remembered. Some people want to remember her the wrong way, but that's a matter of perspective." He shrugged. "You're loved too, Olivia. You'll be remembered, whatever you do."

The painting she'd wanted to show him, it turned out, was van Gogh's *Starry Night*. The painting was unassuming but arresting, hung on the wall in a room otherwise dominated by Monet's water lilies. But Mon could not tear his eyes away from it. The stars in the painting seemed to twinkle, the darkness moved across the inky blue sky in thick dabs of paint. It was just one night, a snapshot of a moment, but there was love in that paint, and Mon could almost feel it on his skin.

This is that I want, he thought. *I want to create music that makes people feel like this.*

But does that music mean diving in here, chasing the white rabbit of fame? He didn't know. And right now was not the time to think about it. His heart was full. Almost too full now, and he choked back tears. Beside him Olivia was looking at him, smiling.

"Thank you," she told him in a small voice. "I wanted to show you this because I thought you liked art, but now I want to show you this because you made me feel loved in the way I needed, back there. I don't have much, but I can give you this."

He placed a hand on the small of her back. She inched closer to him, and the touch was much more intimate than any hug she'd given out today. This felt earned, deeper. It was enough for now, to have her this close. To feel this much with her beside him. Seeing a van Gogh was an experience he would have never had if he hadn't come here. If he hadn't ac-cepted that maybe there were bigger things he could aim for.

"This is a lot, Olivia." Mon shook his head, determined to keep it together. "I never thought I would see this."

"You should have more," Olivia insisted. "You deserve more."

"So do you," he argued. Behind them, the security guard was politely turning away fans who had caught on to the fact that Olivia Angeles was viewing *Starry Night* with someone that might be Colin Sheffield, if he hadn't been wearing a damn mask and a bucket hat. Their curious glances were turned his way. There wasn't anyone else trying to crowd him for a picture of the painting.

He pressed his mask closer to his face and swallowed nervously. People continued taking photos, and he dropped his hand.

"Keep looking at the painting," Olivia reassured him, squeezing his arm. "I can handle the crowd."

"Olivia, I—"

"We'll talk," she promised him, giving him a wink and a smile. "Later."

Six

@StarSpotting Caught @OliviaAngeles admiring the fine art at the MoMA after a morning shoot for a Sol Stanley movie. Is that you @ItsMeColin ??

[photo of Olivia standing beside a dark shadow of a man in front of Starry Night. Her face is turned toward the light, and you can see her smiling. 10,613 likes, posted one hour ago]

Sunday nights were for reading scripts. When Olivia didn't have events, premieres, dinners or any sort of plans, she liked to hunker down and feel increasing panic about her career by poring over scripts and casting calls.

Wine helped. Also leaving the balcony door slightly open (for the hamog, her mom used to say, which she never understood, but old habits die hard) and having a bag of Cheetos and chopsticks on hand. Those helped. She also liked using a nice Sharpie to cross out scripts she didn't like. There was something about the smell that made her feel powerful.

Her agent, Mercedes, had even wrapped her favorites in little bows like Christmas presents, because she was hilarious like that.

Deep breaths. It was just Olivia's career. No big deal.

Tonight, as she flipped through a script for a movie where she would potentially be kidnapped at the start and be used as a plot point for her white husband to do cool things, (complete with multiple montages of her smiling and giggling like she had never been a whole person at all!) she vaguely wondered what scripts in Philippine movies were like lately. She didn't really catch up after the '90s, because nobody else understood when she referenced *Magic Temple* or *Do Re Mi* in school. So she got into Nickelodeon and the Disney Channel, and decided to shoot for the moon because she was already in the US.

It took her a while to remember she could have both. She could watch *Kiss Mo 'Ko* and *10 Things I Hate About You*, could be cast in either and she would still get what she wanted—the chance. The opportunity. She could have it all, and come back to whatever she wanted, when she needed.

"Are you seriously considering that, babes?" her agent Mercedes asked over the phone. Mercedes liked to be on call for Sunday Script Roulette. Just for emotional support. "Like, moving away?"

"No, it was just a hypothetical." Olivia sighed, putting down her glass of wine in the empty apartment that wasn't hers. What was it about this place that was so isolating? She'd been outside today; she'd interacted with people! And yet the silence of her room felt alien, even with the noise of the city outside. "Did we ever hear back from the art heist movie? The producers were really excited when we last met with them."

Generally, she trusted Mercedes' judgment, but even in a post–*Crazy Rich Asians* world, Olivia still had trouble getting Filipino American roles, let alone roles that got being Filipino American right. Every role felt like a fight, and with so much to explain when she got it. So it was always a matter of which fight she was happy to be in.

"They were, but there was an issue with the funding, and from what I know they were looking in...a different direction for the lead."

"The role is based on a book with a Southeast Asian heiress as the main character. How different a direction are they going to—" She suddenly got it. She should have gotten it much faster, really. "*Oh.* They're not casting a Southeast Asian, are they."

"Look, nothing's set in stone. If you really want it, we could talk to more people. Rally a crowd to make sure it goes to you. Didn't Colin say he would—"

"Let's not rely on Colin." Olivia waved a hand.

"Okay. But in the meantime, what do you think of the wife role? There's also a promising one as a nurse for a medical drama, although they're looking for a Filipino accent."

"Which accent? Bikolano? Batangas?" Olivia muttered to herself. "Do they know?"

After finishing her pep talk and career direction seminar

with Mercedes, Olivia sighed and put down the Cheetos. Chopsticks were fun, but it was nothing compared to reaching into the bag and getting the dust on your fingers. Her brother had posted a picture of himself and his girlfriend, Martha, enjoying dinner at a restaurant Max had described by text as "incredibly pretentious, but the food was so good, I hate myself for loving it."

It took a deep sip of wine to recognize the feeling brewing. It was loneliness. It was so constant she'd stopped recognizing it, but there it was. Large and painful and sitting on her chest. There was slight despair. Anger, frustration. She could pull all those emotions out in seconds. But right now, there was no camera to capture it, and all she was left with was this icky feeling.

She could go out. That was a usual remedy for the emotional blues. And with a whole city to explore, the sky was the limit. If she spoke to the right people, she could be watching a musical in ten minutes, bungee jumping somewhere else in an hour. Attending a secret Rihanna concert in Dubai. The weather was cool but not biting. There were doors that would be happy to have her walk through them.

But Olivia was not remotely interested in any of that at the moment. Tonight was a quiet night. A still and starry one. Wasn't there a poem about that?

"'The night is starry, and the stars are blue and shiver in the distance,'" she said out loud, the poem at the edges of her memory. Mon probably knew which it was.

Olivia: "The night is starry, and the stars are blue and shiver in the distance."

Mon: "The night wind revolves in the sky and sings.

Tonight I can write the saddest lines.
I loved her, and sometimes she loved me too."

Is there a reason we're trading lines from Neruda?

Olivia: I was getting last poem syndrome. U up?

Mon: Is this a booty call?

Olivia: What's that music you're playing? The walls are thin.

Lucky for you, I like the music, although I didn't picture you as a girl group admirer.

Mon: Are you willfully ignoring my questions?

Olivia: I'll order food and come over.

Mon: Something with rice, please. Had fried chicken without rice or unli gravy the other day and it just made me sad. Why is there no unli gravy!!

So she showed up at Mon's door on Sunday night, two glasses of wine in hand, carrying Vietnamese takeout, her notebook and pen like she did this all the time. And she would like to do more things like this, popping in to someone's place with food—because food was a good thing to share, and when was the last time she'd just hung out with someone? There wasn't really anyone to hang out with. Everyone back home had their own lives, their own people. And she didn't really have anyone with her who didn't constantly want to talk about the industry. There were some nights where it just wore her down.

The apartment door swung open, and Olivia forgot her entire train of self-pity because…

"That's not rice," Mon said, deadpan, when he saw the name printed on her Postmates delivery.

"Y-you're not rice," Olivia said distractedly, because what the *fuck*—Mon's body was incredible? "Mon."

He was wearing a…God, words were flying out of her brain. What were words, even?

He was slightly sweaty, and he was wearing a mesh sando that was loose enough to show off his collarbones. Turning just so, in the right light, it showed off the contours of his chest. *Hello, friends*, Olivia thought wistfully at his nipples. *Missed you.*

"Hi," he said, smiling in a way that made his dimples even deeper and his eyes like cute crescent moons, which was just unfair. "Sorry I can't beso, I went for a run kasi."

His top was sleeveless, and his arms where tightly muscled—larger than average, made from hours of work at the gym, and she knew because this was the same guy who had lifted her off the bed effortlessly. It took everything in her not to bite down on one of his pecs, to let her eyes move downward to his hips, where his sweatpants were *just* hanging on.

He was wearing Bench. Support local. Hot.

Olivia was a rational woman, okay. And she'd seen all of this before. But there was a big difference between seeing someone's body through a mirror in the dark versus in proper, LED lighting and she'd...forgotten this was what he looked like. This was how his body made her feel.

Damn it. She met hot people all the time. She worked with one of the sexiest men alive every day, and yet Colin had never made her feel this same intense longing. It made her cheeks hot, and warmth shoot up her spine and into her belly, made butterflies whirl around in typhoons. And she knew Mon could just pick her up and let her hug him like a koala, because she'd seen it! He'd done it!

"A *run*, my God."

"What?" Mon asked, blinking at her in confusion behind glasses. Glasses! Black brow-line glasses that made his already incredible eyes even more lovely. Whose idea was this? Olivia wanted a *word*.

"Hot professor fantasies," Olivia muttered to herself. "Who knew."

"Now you're definitely ignoring my questions," Mon huffed, and then he pouted, and God Olivia wanted to kiss him. The pho was hot against her thigh, and reminded her she did not come over for that.

"Can I come in? You can definitely ask me anything you want, after," she said, and he stepped aside, giving her room to take off her slippers and pad into his kitchen. "What did you do today?"

The sudden question felt odd on her tongue, just because it was such a domestic thing to ask. Like she asked him about his day all the time, like she was privy to enough of the comings and goings of his life that she *could* ask.

Her mom used to ask her that when she was a kid, the second Olivia eagerly sat at the kitchen table after school for snacks. It was always posed with affection, and would always prompt Olivia to tell her mother the most exaggerated stories about who wronged her, how it wasn't her fault, how she would hold a grudge *forever* if she had to.

"I went to Central Park and got into a fight with a pigeon," Mon started, immediately making Olivia laugh, because of course he did. "I was on a rental bike, and it just flew into me out of nowhere, and then it just kept…following me."

"Like hovering?"

"No, like…flying up then next to me. It was a little scary."

"More than squirrels?"

"Squirrels are cute."

"Squirrels are rats!"

"They're rodents." Mon sounded like he was correcting her, but she wasn't interested in finding out why she was wrong. "I made a narrow escape and arranged the tracks on the new Girl Crush album. That's what you were hearing, and I apologize if it was too loud. There's a particular order that fits with their concept, and—" Mon explained, and it was his turn to shake his head when he saw Olivia's face light up. "No spoilers."

"Boo." She wrinkled her nose. He'd sent her the Pinoy girl group's first album, which Triptych was producing, and she might have a crush on Sab, the leader. It surprised her that Mon could produce such poppy earworm music without being cringey, but really, what else could she expect from someone so talented?

"Leo introduced me to a few guys in Capitol and Universal," Mon continued. "No idea where that's going."

"But that's good, right? You're getting your name out there, letting people know you exist?" Olivia asked, unloading the food on the kitchen counter. Her back was turned to Mon, so she didn't see his reaction, but she was sure there was something in the silence she wasn't able to read yet.

"Do you have snacks?" Olivia asked, wrinkling her nose. "I'm suddenly feeling snack-y before dinner."

"Merienda is a meal, and I eat out."

"And you never invited me? I'll consider that an oversight." Olivia tutted her lips and shook her head. "Anyway, I got beef pho for me—"

"You're not vegan? Gluten free?"

"Okay, hello, judgy much?" She raised a brow at him. "Besh?"

"Sorry. Was that bitch or besh?"

"I said besh! Max taught me. Short for best friend, right?"

"I guess? Bestie is closer. And you totally skipped over 'beshikels,' and 'beshie,' but I guess the gays won't be too mad that the straights appropriated gay lingo. Again."

She stuck her tongue out at Mon, who was clearly teasing her. "Anyway, I have extra hoisin and basil, deep fried spring rolls, fried tofu with mushroom, and I got you the Vietnamese chicken rice. Do you know how to—"

"Eat with chopsticks?" Mon asked, taking a pair of chopsticks with a smug smile. "Who's being judgy now?"

He made a show of pulling them apart, except he must have pulled too hard because the chopsticks almost completely disintegrated in his hands, some pieces flying off, falling on the countertop. The two of them looked at the wreckage with shock. Olivia had actually jumped back.

Then they both started laughing, the sounds echoing through the apartment. Olivia was laughing so hard she needed to bend over and grab the countertop to support her upper body.

"How did you manage to break it like that?" she asked between wheezes, coming closer to inspect Mon's handiwork. He was laughing too, but his cheeks were flushed and he was trying to hide his face with his hands.

"I've never seen chopsticks...disintegrate like that."

"Mon, you are so clumsy, I can't believe—"

"They're bad chopsticks, it's not my fault!"

"Let's put those destructive hands away..." Olivia took his wrists in her hands and pulled them apart, and suddenly she was looking into Mon's widened eyes. They really were so pretty, these eyes that could observe the world. His lips that sang about loneliness and isolation, that sang right into her soul. There was a little mole just below his lip. She'd never noticed it before.

"Can you tell me about Neruda?" she asked, her voice soft, as if speaking louder would scare him away. And she didn't want to scare him away.

"I can't tell you much." Mon seemed fixated on a strand of her hair by her cheek, gently tucking it behind her ear. She could almost hear him thinking, formulating words. "Beautiful poetry. I'm sure it's even better in his native Spanish. He could put love into words. All the pain, and all the happiness and longing it comes with. *'Rest with your dream in my dream.'*"

"*'And you are* pure *beside me like a sleeping ember,'*" Olivia recited, plucking the words from a distant memory. "I once heard a recording of that. I'd never imagined simple words evoking that much feeling. That you could change the meaning of a sentence with how fast or slow you say something, how soft, how gentle."

She sighed, remembering the moment as a younger girl, hearing the recording and playing it over and over. Heard how the words shifted in meaning because he'd read them the way he had, the tenderness and love it carried.

She didn't move from her position, instead resting her forehead against Mon's shoulder, thinking.

"It's a real skill," she continued. "That you can pull someone in and make them feel something. I think I'm still chasing that. And I remembered that from listening to you."

"You give me too much credit."

"You don't give yourself enough." She shrugged.

She'd promised she'd talk to him about...this. About the way his words had wriggled into her heart. About how hot and bothered he made her feel, and how much she enjoyed spending time with him. The way she wanted to be this close to him, and touch him. Even if she had no idea what they were doing.

But she was terrible at talking. She always had been. She never knew what to say, never knew how to describe how she felt. She felt things, felt things strongly. But it was always easier to act on her feelings than to explain them.

"Olivia," Mon said, his voice barely a whisper. "We said we would talk."

"Talk is cheap."

"It's really not."

Olivia blinked and took a step back, giving Mon his space, even if she was frowning. He sighed and closed the gap, pressing a kiss on her forehead. Friendly. Sweet.

"Olivia." His voice was a plea, and it tugged at her. "Please don't test me. We said we weren't going to do this."

"Did we?" she asked. "I don't recall either of us saying anything about not doing this. I remember you apologized to me, and I accepted the apology. I remember you saying you didn't regret what happened between us."

His eyes were dark, his jaw clenched tight. She knew she shouldn't push him, but God. What were they doing? Why were they waiting?

"I need to know what you're thinking, because I've been thinking myself in circles about you. Natotorete na ako."

She didn't know what that meant. But she approached him anyway, careful and watching him as he watched her. She was ready to jump back the second he asked, but...

Olivia's fingertip touched his collarbone, and he inhaled sharply. She positioned herself closer, skimming her fingers along the rest of the bone, until her hand rested on the base of his throat. His eyes were dark and serious, but the heat contained in them was hard to miss.

"Do you want me?" he asked her.

She tugged the neckline of his shirt to beckon him lower. She kissed him and a wave of...relief? comfort? peace? washed through her as her lips found home against his. His body was warm and solid, she knew that, but he wrapped his arms around her, kissed her harder and rested his hand on her cheek. It made Olivia's knees weak.

"I want you, Mon," Olivia said when their lips parted, and she licked the bottom of hers, not missing the way Mon's eyes studied the movement. "I want this. I don't know why we told ourselves to stop."

She kissed him again, harder this time. It was the kind of kiss that wanted more, that could easily ignite something inside her she'd kept kindled since Mon first walked away from her.

"Are you wearing lip balm?"

"Peach iced tea." He nodded. "It's too cold outside. My lips are dying out there."

"Poor boy." She teased, pushing him backward until he hit the counter. She kissed him again, allowing herself to fully melt into it, absorbed by the way he kissed her hungrily. His hands wrapped around her waist, and she felt delicate, and special, and she didn't want to let go until she had to. "I didn't think we were going to do this."

"Really?" Mon asked, genuine shock on his face. "So you weren't making a booty call?"

"I brought food!"

"Food can be foreplay," Mon argued, and she could not believe those words were coming out of his mouth.

"My pen and notebook are here!" Olivia tapped said objects on the counter. "I did not come here to have sex with you!"

"I am choosing to believe you." Mon shook his head, catching her chin with his fingers and lifting it before he kissed her again. Whoever taught this boy how to kiss, Olivia wanted to send them a thank-you note. He was good at this, at displaying his desire for her so openly. She should be terrified of how much he wanted her.

But it only made her want him more.

"Wait," he said between kisses. "The food."

"I assume you're familiar with the wonders of a microwave?" Olivia asked, splaying a hand over his right pec. *Hello, yes, I am here again.*

"No, I…I don't want to have sex in front of the food?" he said, and yes, he was definitely shivering at her touch, at the not so accidental brush of her fingers over his nipple. "Unless we're not having sex?"

"Ah, Mon. I think resisting you isn't an option for me." Olivia giggled, because it sounded like a line she would say for a movie. "And I've never been patient."

"Okay." Mon sounded distracted as his hands slid around her hips, and he deepened the kiss. His tongue traced across her lightly parted lips, and playfully nibbled on the bottom one as he grinned. Olivia liked this version of him too, the one who was a little smug, confident in his sexiness. "I don't want to resist you anymore, either."

He flicked on the screen of his phone a few times, and the bright, poppy sound from Girl Crush changed into something else. Something that stretched, with deeper bass sounds, an easy, chill beat. The song was incredibly sexy, but casual enough to still be fun.

"You made a playlist," she teased, swaying her hips in time to the music, humming along to the familiar vocalizations. "Nerd."

"It sets the tone," he insisted.

She had to admit, he was right. There was just something about a really good song, the *perfect* song, that made her want him more. Made her kiss him harder, feel zero fear or shame about flicking a tongue around his nipple, about sucking. Mon was getting hard, his erection pressing against her hip, until she touched it, and it became even fuller, hotter in her hands.

Thank you, joggers.

"Oh fuck," Mon hissed, arching his hip into her, clearly enjoying the sensation. Olivia squeezed him lightly, and he took off his glasses, hastily placing them on the counter beside him. "Fuck. Olivia."

"Mon," she said, her voice low as she kissed his collarbone, making her way lower. "What's going on in that head of yours?"

"I'm trying to remember what comes after 3.14. In…in pi." His words were stilted, like he was trying to remember how to use words, too. "Six? Five?"

Olivia slipped her fingers into the waistband of his briefs and tugged them down.

"Upsilon?" Mon spluttered as his cock sprang free. Olivia wrapped her hand around him, her fingertips just managing to meet. The absolute trust he had in her was freeing, and she trusted in return that he would tell her if he didn't like something. Like she could pull the plug on this, if she wasn't comfortable.

But the thing was, she was comfortable. She wanted to do this, and do this well. Wanted to make Mon stop thinking so hard, to make the man who made her see love in art see her, too.

Mon's free hand, the one not gripping the counter behind him for support, was under her shirt, stroking the skin on her waist. The man who remembered the word *upsilon* before 0.0015 still had enough sense to slide his hand down her pants too, kneading the skin on her bare bottom to bring her closer, to get a little friction. Olivia held on to his arms to brace herself, but the motion ground her against Mon's thigh, and God... He was distracting her.

"Don't distract me," she scolded him, playfully biting his pec, making Mon jump.

"Trust me, Olivia. Anything I do right now is accidental," he groaned, kneading her flesh again. His eyes were dark pools of desire, and Olivia felt it in her stomach, settle even lower. Enough to lead her down his body. She nuzzled against the soft skin of his belly, nipped at the inside of his now exposed thighs, resting her hands there. Mon's body was almost vibrating with pleasure, moisture leaking from his tip.

"Olivia, are you sure you want to—"

"Yes," she said without hesitation. "I do."

Then she took him in her mouth. There was no time to think about when she'd last done this, if she knew what she was doing, because *God* Mon was bigger than she was used to, and she needed a second to adjust, to suck him without getting greedy. But greed was a heavy sin, and Olivia threw herself into it, hollowing her cheeks, digging her nails into Mon's thighs.

"Oh fuck, Olivia," Mon groaned, his hand sliding into her hair. The touch was still careful, as if she would break, as if she would wriggle away from this at any second. Olivia took him in deeper, as if challenged, adjusting around him.

She pulled out and glared at Mon, whose skin had flushed pink. She liked the dazed look on his face, the sweat he was building just from keeping himself together.

"Has anyone told you how pretty you are, Mon?" Olivia asked, giving the tip of his cock a dainty lick, and his hand tightened its grip just a little. He shook his head.

"Well, you are," Olivia helpfully informed him, wrapping her lips around him again, taking him into her mouth, feeling the contours and ridges, the slight saltiness of him. Mon's hips bucked, and he tugged when Olivia took him deeper.

"Oh my God," he said, looking up at the ceiling, where she could see the line from his cock, his stomach, his chest, his throat. It was an extremely erotic sight, and it made her so aware of the power she had over him, even as she had him in her throat. "Olivia. Olivia, tang ina. Fuck. Fuck!"

She hollowed her cheeks and sucked, enough to make Mon stop thinking, to make him let go. She could see he needed something else to lose it completely. And God she wanted to make him lose it. Wanted it to be by her hand. He was panting hard, but he seemed restless, caught in the force of a hurricane.

Olivia dug her nails into his thigh. Mon moaned, bending at the waist, control finally lost. He was saying her name, groaning as she pulled him out, wrapping her fingers around his cock, murmuring soft words of encouragement as she helped his release along, not giving a fuck that he was making a mess on the borrowed tile. Mon was spent, panting against Olivia's shoulder as she spread his cum across his stomach, catching the stray, absent-minded kisses he planted on her.

"Sarap," Olivia cooed into his ear as Mon held her close, nosing at her neck like he sought her comfort. She gave it easily, even as he held her hand in his, licked at the cum remaining there. He held up the hand she'd assumed had been holding on to the counter, and it turned out he had been holding on to his glasses instead. The poor things were practically ground into dust.

"Oh no." Olivia giggled as Mon groaned at the inconvenience. "We'll fix it."

"This was not how I thought this would go," he murmured, still breathing hard into her neck. "What about you?"

"Hmm, what about me?"

"Let me take care of you," he murmured into her skin, and she turned away, her back to his front. His fingertips danced across the skin of her stomach, slightly exposed from his touch. Olivia shivered and felt her toes curl when he moved lower, slipping into her sweatpants, pushing aside her underwear and—

"Oh. Baby, you're so wet." Mon's chuckle was low and rumbling, and Olivia's knees buckled at the sensation. "You were this wet for me?"

"Touch me," Olivia said, her breathing already getting rapid as Mon curled his fingers lower, swirling around her clit. "Oh, Mon. Harder."

"Mmm," was all he said in response, his voice making her spine tingle deliciously. Or maybe it was his fingers? Or that his other hand had wrapped around her middle and held her more securely than a roller coaster safety bar? Olivia arched her hips, making him go deeper.

"You like this?" he asked, even as he was fully stroking her now, as Olivia angled her hips to get it just right. She gripped the nape of his neck, too aware of her sighing and gasping. Mon sucked a kiss to her neck.

"Yes," she gasped. "Yes, oh my God. Mon, harder."

He obliged, and Olivia saw stars, coming so hard she wasn't sure if she was floating because she had to be. And Mon had taken her there, fuck.

"Next time, I want you inside me," she gasped, as Mon slowed his ministrations, riding her through it. He raised his hands to Olivia's lips, and she sucked his wet fingers. The little sound from Mon made her chuckle. "Next time."

"Next time," he repeated, and it sounded like a promise. Olivia turned back to face him and snaked her arms around his neck, and it was her turn to catch her breath.

"I didn't expect this."

"Neither did I," she admitted. "But I'm used to surprises."

He kissed her this time, and Olivia leaned in. It occurred to her that spending Sunday nights like this was infinitely better than what she was doing by herself. That it had been a while since she'd had a Sunday night like this.

The kiss was interrupted by an insistent buzzing coming from Mon's pants. Olivia tried to ignore it, she really did, but she just ended up giggling, then laughing.

"I think you should get that," she said, pulling away. Mon made a noise that was almost a whine and kissed her again, but whoever was on the other side of that call really wanted to get in touch with him. "I'll heat up the food. I can't trust you in the kitchen. Seriously, who is calling?"

"It's..." Mon peered at his ringing phone while he cleaned up the mess on the floor. She couldn't read the expression on his face, completely confused by whatever he was seeing, until he seemed to remember something.

"It's Monday in Manila," he said, sighing. "I forgot."

"What's Monday in Manila?"

"My parents are calling," he groaned, washing his hands. "Well, not my parents. My friends. But they might as well be my parents. They're going to know. I shouldn't feel guilty about what we did, but they're going to know, and..."

"They're not going to know," Olivia said, washing her hands after him.

"They will. But I don't want you to think I'm ashamed of what we did, or—"

"But you need boundaries with your friends," she pointed out, pulling now cold soup and noodles from the delivery bag. "I get that. That's healthy. Establish them. Sit in the living room so they don't see me."

"My friends have powers I can't even explain," Mon muttered, and Olivia laughed, watching him trudge to the couch like he was being sentenced. She kept her eyes on the task at hand, opening containers and checking that everything was microwave safe. Yet she couldn't help but be morbidly curious as to what Mon was like around his friends.

She wasn't eavesdropping. She just…happened to be in the room while he was talking.

"So, Mon, are you taking a big juicy bite out of the Big Apple?" Scott Sabio asked, as his girlfriend and live-in partner, Ava, winced beside him.

"How long did it take you to come up with that, Scott?"

"The whole day." Scott preened, and it was hard for Mon to miss the love in Ava's eyes as she patted the top of her boyfriend's head.

Mon smiled back, like nothing was up. Like Olivia hadn't sucked him off in the kitchen and he'd fingered her in return. She seemed to enjoy it. And he definitely enjoyed it. And he'd barely had time to process it, and what it meant, when his friends called. Which meant that even if he wasn't ready to talk about it yet, they were probably going to find out, and want him to talk.

While Olivia heated up Vietnamese food in the kitchen.

"I think the better question is if it's everything you want it to be," Ava said, direct to the point as always, even if she was snuggling against Scott on-screen. Mon smiled. Their barkada liked to joke that Scott and Ava were Mom and Dad, and they exuded those vibes long before they even realized they had feelings for each other, which was a whole other story.

"It's different," he admitted, hoping his bad lighting hid the blush on his cheeks as he thought of what he'd been doing (what was done to him?) not fifteen minutes ago. "I'm savoring the experience."

"And you're being a good boy?" Scott was clearly teasing him now. "Playing nice with the other kids?"

"Uh...you could say that."

Mon didn't miss Olivia stifling a laugh. She was sitting on the lounge chair next to him now, reading a script out of view. He poked her thigh with his big toe. She stuck her tongue out at him in retaliation.

"Is there someone there?" Ava asked, intuitive as always. Mon froze. "There is. Who is it?"

"Raymond Tindalo C. Mendoza." Scott tsked and shook his head. "Are you hooking up?"

"Uh..."

Olivia covered her face with the script. Her shoulders were shaking.

"You are!" Scott exclaimed. "Wait, I feel proud, why do I feel proud—"

"Do you need to process?" Ava asked.

"I don't—" Mon started.

"Tori's going to love this." Scott was practically vibrating out of his seat. "I'll tell her I have a secret, it will drive her bananas, then I'm going to make her treat me to lunch at Amano before I tell her. It will be *so* overpriced, but it will be worth it."

"Guys!" Mon exclaimed, sighing deeply. Even Olivia jumped at the sudden authority of his voice. But, boundaries. "It's all very…recent. So there's nothing to tell yet. Trust me, I will tell you if there's something. You guys will be the first to know."

Scott and Ava looked at each other, and Mon wasn't surprised Ava was the one who smiled and nodded.

"All right. Tell us about New York," she said, and those words reassured him the boundary was set, that it would be fine. "Have you been to Times Square yet?"

The call went on a little longer, just until Ava finally groaned and announced she had to leave for work. Olivia had put the script aside and was stirring pho with chopsticks, steam rising in clouds in front of her face. It took a second for Mon to readjust—his friends always treated him like the baby of the group, and he always needed a second to get out of it. He wasn't embarrassed by his friends' clinginess, he just had this idea that maybe it wasn't…normal? But really, what was normal.

"I'm sorry about that."

"No, it's fine," Olivia assured him, shaking her head. "I thought it was sweet, how they were teasing you."

"I just don't want their thoughts to cloud mine," Mon explained. "And they will definitely have thoughts. I'm still trying to catch up to what happened earlier. What we did. Can you remind me?"

"Do you want to talk about it?" Olivia asked, pouring sriracha out of packets and onto a little plate. "What word did your friend use? Processing?"

"Not yet. Eventually, I will, but…not yet."

"Okay," she said, and Mon was surprised at how quickly she'd said it. She wasn't going to ask anything else? Wasn't going to tell him what *she* thought about it?

It was oddly refreshing.

"So do your friends do video calls often?" Olivia asked, sucking the ends of her chopsticks, which she'd used to pour hoisin sauce onto the plate.

"Not video calls, but we've got a group chat that runs daily." Mon went over to the kitchen counter and took a bit of the fried tofu with his fork. The tofu was perfectly fried, and the thick sauce had a slightly sweet quality to it. Yum.

Olivia was still stirring her pho, picking out the fatty pork slices.

Mon held up his phone and showed her the group chat, currently called "Ava Ginoong (Ilog) Maria: Group Order" since Ava was placing an order with Ilog Maria. Their throat spray was really good. "It was my lifeline during the pandemic, and when lockdowns ended, we just kept using it."

"That's so sweet."

"Yeah. We share most of everything on that chat—what we're eating, where we are, cats on the street. And it's a nice, safe place to admit when you don't know what 'deins pare' is supposed to mean, or analyze the timeline of how 'girl boss' became pejorative." Mon quickly locked his phone and placed it on the table. "They're all in committed relationships right now, mostly with each other. But still. They make time to reply and talk to me. It's everything."

It was hard to articulate how much he loved his friends. How much he loved that they were in love too, but still made him feel included.

Olivia dropped some basil leaves into her soup.

"They love you a lot."

"I love them too," Mon said. "It's easy to love."

"And you're the baby of the group." Olivia nodded. Mon was aghast until she patted the top of his head like he hadn't had his hand between her legs less than an hour ago. "It's cute! You're cute."

"Thanks? It's not always fun being the bunso. Especially when they're being stubborn, and you have the right answers and they just don't listen."

"Virgo," Olivia singsonged. "Your Mercury must be a fire sign. Or is it your Venus?"

After Mon took a quick shower, they moved to the coffee table. He was playing songs from his playlist on his phone (a different, nonsexy playlist, he assured her) while Olivia was only just starting to eat her pho. She got a boring one with just meatballs, and Mon found out she had a passion for all flavors…plain. Sorry, *original*.

Did it kill him a little inside? Yes. But good pho was good pho, he supposed.

The moon was high and bright, peeking up over the buildings outside. It added to the soft ambience of the scene. There was a cool spell in the room, the kind that made you want to cuddle up in a blanket and read a book, or watch a movie. Mon lived for days like this. Wrote his favorite music sometimes in those quiet, cool moments.

Maybe it was the chicken, which was perfectly charred and really good. Or maybe it was the pho, warm and perfect, even if Olivia had added too much hoisin for his taste. He continued to enjoy his soup and chicken rice while Olivia continued to read the audiobook script she was prepping for. Judging from the way her soup was on the way to cold and still half-full, Mon assumed it was a good one.

"And how do you read this one?" Olivia asked, holding up the word to him. "Bard-ah-gullan?"

"Barda-goo-lan," Mon corrected her gently, smiling when he saw her circle the root word, *barda*. "*Bardagol* is the root word, I think. But people mostly use it to refer to social media drama these days."

"Oh, that makes sense with the rest of the book." Olivia nodded thoughtfully. "I know it's disingenuous to want to read an audiobook knowing only half the Filipino words."

"Hey, you're asking for help." Mon shrugged. "It's a good thing. But you couldn't ask the author?"

"I did! But you're here, and faster." Olivia squeezed his nose with her fingers, making him frown. "And there's really not anyone else involved in the process that can tell me if I say it wrong, which is all kinds of screwy. But hey, I know how to say the author's name, and her character's name—Makisig."

"Kisig. Formal." Mon nodded. "Good."

"You know the electrical tape on the glasses only helps the professor vibe, weirdly." Olivia wrinkled her nose and Mon tickled her for revenge.

Who was he kidding? It was her. Sitting next to him, telling him the story of the time her fans decided it would be funny if they asked her to marry them every chance they could—it was in response to something she'd said in an interview, apparently about dreaming of settling down, probably in the Philippines.

"I can hear you thinking," Olivia announced, pressing her finger into one of his dimples. "Even when I was blowing you, I could practically absorb your thoughts."

"That would be a medical marvel," was his instant, dry response, making Olivia playfully smack his arm with the back of her hand. But he wasn't quite ready to tell her what he was thinking yet, because he still hadn't quite settled around the panic in his head.

He was in a situationship with Olivia Angeles, officially. With a kiss—with a little more than a kiss—he'd put himself in this position that felt temporary yet irrevocable, like driving along a cliffside, vaguely aware of the drop below.

"Hey," she said, reminding him, "this honesty thing goes two ways, Moning. Let me hear it."

Her toes were tucked under his thigh, a throw blanket

draped over her shoulders as the light cast shapes and shadows across her face. She was lovely in the dimness.

"I adore you, Olivia."

The tofu dropped from the tip of her fork. Mon frowned, trying to gather his thoughts. Because he had been thinking about it, in his journeys from the studio to the apartment, in his attempt to orient himself to the country that demanded his adjustment.

In between the subway rides (the subway was terrible, and he said this as a person who lived in Manila) and the walks down the blocks, he thought of how he felt for Olivia, and *adore* seemed to be the correct word.

"I've concluded that I don't like this city, but I adore you," Mon explained. "That meeting with the music people. They said my music wouldn't appeal to a broad audience. Can't imagine it going viral."

That was a gut punch, one he could still feel. He should have expected it, right? Hearing that he needed a following to get a following, that he didn't make the kind of music they were looking for. He'd walked out of the meeting and felt like the entire city had been stained gray. This coming from someone who'd told himself not to expect anything (but he had, stupidly enough).

He would recover. Remind himself these labels didn't always do the right thing. But right now, he just wanted to wallow, and a part of him just wanted to go home.

"Excuse me!" Olivia gasped, incensed for him, which made his heart swell. "Do they know 'Blue Period' has millions of listens already? Not to mention the numbers it's doing on TikTok, and—"

Mon shook his head. "It's okay."

"It's not," she told him. "How stilted are they that they can't see how good you are? I mean, you're *here*."

"I know." Mon nodded. "I rode a ferry to see the Statue of Liberty, and I was accosted for ruining the experience."

"What do you mean...accosted?" Olivia repeated the word carefully, her frown deepening at the implication.

"I mean a man roughly grabbed my arm and yelled at me for wearing a mask and said my phone was in the way of his view." Mon shuddered. The fear hadn't hit him until after, until he was walking with jelly legs out of the ferry building and looking at an unfamiliar part of the city. It took him some time to calm down, to keep going instead of turning around and heading back to the apartment. The powerlessness of the moment terrified him—mostly because it had never happened to him before. Microaggressions, sure, but outright xenophobia? He couldn't do anything about that.

"I met a Pinoy on the way back, and talking to them helped a little. They said, 'okay lang. Uuwi ka naman.'"

"God, Mon. I'm—"

"It's not your fault," Mon assured her. She couldn't control anything any more than he could. And he worried about that, about her, not being able to leave, having to live with this. "It's not even my fault."

"It isn't," Olivia said.

Mon nodded. "Cities are living things for me. New York doesn't want you there. Seoul is bright and shiny. Manila is—"

"Home?"

"A fucking mess. Hellscape and trashfire. But yeah. Fuck. It's home."

"So why are you still here?" Olivia asked, taking his hand and squeezing it. It wasn't an accusation or disbelief. Just a question. He wondered if she understood what he was trying to say, how shattered the glass was for him, this country that was supposed to be his end all and be all.

"I made a commitment. To Leo, and Sol, and to you." He was resolute in that. He came here to do a job, and he was going to do it well. It was almost a relief, knowing he didn't want more from this place than what he had. "I enjoy that part. And I adore this part. Getting to know you, spending time with you."

She burrowed her toes under his thigh, and he liked the contact, even if he wasn't used to it. He was overwhelming her, maybe, with his thoughts, and she didn't have to say it for him to know. It usually happened.

"It's a lot."

"Now who's willfully ignoring what I'm saying?" she teased, pressing her finger into his thigh. "I like you too, Mon. I haven't examined my feelings, sought out the Force like you have—"

"I watch *Conquerors*, not *Star Wars*. I'm not a nerd."

"You are a nerd. A big nerd that I have warm, affectionate, sexytime feelings for." Olivia pulled her feet out from under him so she could turn and lie on his lap. Mon's fingers raked gently through her hair as he rested his arm on the seat of the couch. "I don't know what I can say beyond that. What I can give you, when you already gave so much."

It occurred to him how far apart they actually were, even with Olivia snuggled up against him. How different their lives and their paths were, even as they wanted the same things—recognition, opportunity, a life with their craft. This time they had together would be short-lived. It was just the way it was.

"I'm okay with that," he told her. Honestly, any time he had with Olivia was good time, he thought. And it was fast. It was *so* fast, how strong his feelings had become. "I just need to know where you are."

"I'm here." Olivia nodded, closing her eyes. "This is very good."

"And this?" Mon asked, brushing a fingertip down the bridge of her nose, the bow of her lip, the tops of her cheeks.

"Makes me sleepy." She giggled, and it was sweet and it made her seem more...herself.

It was hard not to separate the Olivia on his lap from the Olivia on the screen. It magnified everything, like a fanboy dream come true, except it turned out the person you stanned had her fears, her insecurities, her unwillingness to compromise, too.

God, Mon was going to fall in love with her, he knew it. He already adored her, and he was being allowed into her thoughts, her day. He could fall in love with her in the next minute, the next second. It was an inevitable slide for the ones like him with their hearts on their sleeves.

"Now let me see your lyrics."

"Who told you I have lyrics?" She gasped like he'd asked to take pictures of her feet.

"You brought your filler," Mon pointed out, holding up said notebook, placed on the couch, and gently waving it around. "That means you have something you're ready to show me."

"Maybe. I *maybe* have something to show you," she muttered, sitting up and nodding when Mon asked if he could flip through it. He knew how personal a notebook could be, and hers was more than halfway full, a feat considering the number of pages. "What the hell is a filler?"

"Filler notebook? Like Cattleya fillers?" He was greedily turning pages. "You know you really shouldn't be writing with a fountain pen on paper that's less than 80 gsm."

"What?"

"Paper has weight, just like words do," he said simply. He believed in the power of good stationery. "And you aren't giving your words enough weight."

"It works, okay!" Olivia snatched the filler from his hand and cuddled it to her chest like a precious puppy. "But I think I have something. It's not complete, and it might not suit the music…"

"Let me worry about the music," Mon reassured her, grabbing her fountain pen. It was probably loaded with a cartridge, and it was plastic. Medium nib. Mon shook his head. He had better gel pens in his backpack. "Can I…?"

"Wait," Olivia said, turning pages and checking meticulously like she was going to be quizzed on the subject. Mon chuckled, and she smacked a hand to his chest. "Stop laughing. I bet you were like this when you started, too."

"I'm still like that, honestly," he said, twirling her pen in his fingers. "But with better pens. And proper paper."

"Here, snobby," Olivia said, folding the notebook back and handing Mon a specific page. "I think that's the one."

The air in the room went still as Mon read the lyrics. Olivia was doing an incredibly poor job of pretending like she didn't care he was reading words from her own hand, but he kept that thought to himself and read.

It was an intensely personal song. There were lyrics about specific moments in someone's life—running away when things got hard, shutting out parts she didn't want, wasn't ready for. She wrote about enjoying the solitude yet feeling the loneliness following her. But the chorus was about wanting—wanting to let someone in, about being brave enough.

I want to be unafraid, she'd written. *Let me open myself to you.*

"It's Jessamyn's issue, at its heart," Olivia explained, although she couldn't seem to look at Mon when she said it. "She wants to open herself up to him again, to forgive him for what happened. But she's scared, and she can't figure out if how she feels is stronger than what she's afraid of."

"What is she afraid of?" Mon asked gently.

"Being alone."

Two words. And the heartbreak it gave him was almost visceral.

Mon could hear the melody. Somewhere in the back of his mind, the chord progression slowly formed itself, waiting for Mon to put pen to paper (brain to piano) and make the song. It wasn't going to be a huge, explosive number. No fireworks, big instruments or belting. But it would be a good song. A hopeful one. That was what Olivia—Jessamyn— was looking for. Hope.

It was good, especially for someone's first try.

How do feelings grow, he idly wondered. *Exactly like this.*

"You like it," Olivia gasped, wrapping her arms around his neck and kissing both his cheeks, his forehead. "You really like it, Moning?"

"My friends call me that," he mused, suddenly missing them all. God, their input on this situation would be…complex. Loud, maybe, with thousands of exclamations. Would probably revolve around twelve other topics before they got around to saying how they felt.

But would this last long enough for him to even tell his friends? *God, don't go there yet, Mendoza.*

"Well, we are friends, aren't we?" Olivia asked. "Friends who adore each other. That's a thing."

He knew it was a thing. But was it going to be their thing? This was all too new, and as many times as he'd turned it over in his head already, it seemed there were more questions on the other side.

He kissed her, hoping to quiet those thoughts. And they did, replaced with something closer to a melody. A chord progression. Words. His, this time.

You feel like a city I know. You feel like a place I can be.

Seven

[selfie of Colin with Olivia at an outdoor bistro table, presumably on the upper west side. She's looking up from her phone, smiling while holding a piece of paper, from which the word "Overexposed" is clearly seen]

@ItsMeColin From outer space to the upper west side, would go anywhere with you @OliviaAngeles !

@NoContextConquerors "Wow. That is one big ship."-Lord Aries

@Colinopolis omg babe blink once if she made you post that photo because of that TikTok

@MagnavisTala Cant decide if I ship them or their characters

@Tala_Star91 Aw remember when they were first cast and Colin totally posted a pic with the wrong Pinay? Growth!

Oh God.

He was so cute.

Two days later, Olivia watched Mon through the glass on her side of the recording studio, fighting every feminine urge to sigh into a heap of kilig on the floor.

As much as she enjoyed spending time with Mon, listening to him talk and think himself into circles, it was a completely different thing to see him at work. He seemed in control of whatever situation was happening on his side of the recording booth, nodding, gesturing, laughing when Leo laughed.

Then he looked up and gave her a smile through the glass. It was a cute little smile, the kind where he seemed to be too embarrassed to give her anything less than his eyes squeezed shut and his cheekbones pressed up in a grin. She couldn't see his lips because of his mask, but his eyes were hard to miss.

Oh you dear, romantic boy. One of her favorite little quips from *The Importance of Being Earnest*, the kind of sentence that was the nineteenth-century English version of a sigh.

What did he say again, when she was making him come in her mouth?

"What is happening, you're looking so beautiful, my queen," Colin said, walking into the studio, ten minutes late and staring at his phone. "Hey Sol!"

He waved at the group behind the glassed-off area. Because

Sol was meticulous in her work, she attended most of the re-cording sessions. She said it helped her get to know her actors better, but over a Korean barbecue lunch she admitted to Ol-ivia that it really was just because she enjoyed the process of making music. Plus, it was always nice to have extra footage.

The studio was what music dreams were made of—yellow lighting, soft carpets you wanted to sink your toes into, headphones, music stands, microphones, the works. There was even a camera set up, ready to take video for promo-tional purposes once they started recording. Both Colin and Olivia had gotten a minimum amount of grooming, just to make sure they were camera ready. They were finishing the setup, people coming in and out of the recording booth to adjust this or that.

"You're late," Olivia pointed out, looking over Colin's shoulder at his PA, Macenna, who smiled sheepishly at Olivia. "What happened?"

"I had to stop him from getting kombucha!" Macenna exclaimed. "Bad for the throat."

"It's probiotic!" Colin argued, but Macenna simply shrugged and shuffled off to the corner where she was ex-pected to sit and wait. Mon came out of the room, and Olivia felt herself sit straighter, smile wider. He smiled back at her, his cheekbones popping up from behind his mask. She'd been around him long enough to know it meant he was slightly embarrassed, or trying to hide what he was re-ally thinking.

Olivia winked at him.

"Oh hello, Mon." She tapped Colin on the shoulder to

get his attention. "Colin, this is Mon Mendoza. He's the producer I brought in for the movie. He's working on my song, but Leo apparently roped him into doing more work."

"It was consensual!" came Leo's voice from the speaker, making everyone in the room laugh.

"Hey." Colin nodded at Mon, not incredibly interested in the man Olivia hadn't stopped talking about since she first heard "Blue Period." She was sure she'd sent Colin the link, and had assumed he liked it because he posted it once on IG. But judging from the way Macenna looked up from her phone with wide, fangirl eyes, Olivia had recommended Morningview to the wrong person. "Your name's an alliteration. Nice."

Colin said that with the same amount of flaccid enthusiasm as fish cake in boiling soup. Olivia was confused, mostly because she didn't remember Colin being a jerk. At least not to people he just met. But then again, this was the same guy who couldn't tell her apart from another Filipina cast member when they first met. Suddenly, it didn't feel quite like the "honest mistake" he'd said it was.

She was questioning everything.

"A skill to aspire to," Mon muttered. Then to Olivia, he asked, "We're still going to that exhibit at the Whitney, right?"

"Of course." Olivia nodded. She'd gotten an invitation from the Whitney, and normally Olivia wouldn't have attended, but Mon was way more excited than she was. Olivia could be an art lover, why not?

"Okay, sige. Leo wanted to go for drinks after, but—

anyway." Mon cleared his throat. "There are a few lyric changes I was hoping to run through with you guys before we start recording. We're not quite done setting up, but I wanted to make sure you got these."

He handed them both sheets of paper. The song title "Overexposed" printed neatly, with the changes written in red pen, including the addition of "Final Ultima Final" next to the title on top. Olivia giggled.

"Final Ultima Final? Sounds like a *Final Fantasy* spell."

"What can I say, Flare Final just doesn't deal enough non-magic damage," he said without missing a beat, and there was a moment where they just looked at each other, and that connection brought Olivia back to last night. Specifically, to the moment when all the Vietnamese takeout was gone and she showed him how to use her vibrator. She smiled and whispered, "nerd," under her breath.

"Says the one who was very specific about her balls."

Olivia cleared her throat, suddenly needing water. She thanked the staff member who caught on and handed her the thermos she'd brought in with warm water and lemon. She waved off Mon's concerned look.

"Wait," Colin said, his brow furrowing as he studied Mon's face. "You're Morningview. From the Philippines. Olivia's favorite."

"Yes."

"Oh wow. So you really brought him in, Olivia? That's great." Colin seemed delighted, a complete change to his utter lack of enthusiasm earlier, and reached a hand out to shake Mon's. "Your English is great, dude."

Olivia groaned, rolling her eyes and mouthing *sorry* to Mon. It wasn't that hard to believe a Filipino could speak impeccable English. America was literally their colonizer. They were a part of the Commonwealth until the twenties!

"Thanks." Mon's smile was subdued as he shook Colin's hand, and Olivia wanted to bury her head under the ground. "I've been told I'm articulate. Eloquent, even."

"I think you mean fluent."

It was hard to miss the sudden tightness in Mon's jaw, the flash of irritation he quickly tamped down. But instead of saying anything, he smiled at Colin. It didn't reach his eyes at all, which made it a little terrifying, but perhaps that was the point.

"Hmm. I'm really looking forward to working with you, Colin." Sarcasm. God, she could hear it, buried as it was in layers of sweetness. "You too, Olivia." The words were reassuring, but Mon hiked his mask up a little higher, pressed it more firmly over the bridge of his nose. "I'll be right back."

"We'll be here," Olivia assured him. Mon said nothing, but gave her one last look before he turned and walked back into the sound booth. She debated going to talk to him. To maybe apologize for Colin, even if it wasn't her job at all. But he'd asked her to work. So she was going to do a good job, and keep Colin in line.

Olivia looked down at the lyric changes. There wasn't much that would trip her up. The guide she'd had on repeat the last couple days was helpful. It also helped it was Mon's voice on autotune, which made her laugh every few listens.

She didn't miss the little "oh God what the fuck" he'd left in toward the end.

"Olivia."

"Colin?"

"Should I be worried about this?"

"Worried about what?" Olivia didn't look up from her lyrics, humming through the song and the changes, testing them out.

The song was fun and poppy, perfect for the end of the movie. It was the kind of song she could picture being played at a friend's wedding, where all the adults and the younger people in the room could dance without making anyone uncomfortable. The blending was beautiful, the melody was a bit coy and cheeky, but the lyrics were sad.

Even with the changes, it was all about regrets and loneliness, how "hey, maybe in the next life we'll have sorted our issues out enough." Not exactly the happy ending Olivia was hoping for. It was like a Fleetwood Mac song, regrets and breakups included. And she knew from conversations with Sol that it was because life was messy, people were complicated. But didn't people also deserve their popcorn-selling, seat-filling, movie theater ending? Those could be as real as anything. Those were celebrated because they were real, because people were complicated, and life was messy.

I'll be better then, we'll be okay
What's one more life, it's only been three
See you at four, let's fall in love then
Consume all we've grown

But hey, it wasn't her movie. She was just happy to be here.

"Olivia. Aren't you worried about this?"

"Worried about what?" She still didn't look up. That part seemed a little tricky.

"This reel I keep getting tagged in," Colin grumbled, handing her his phone. "And you know when it's on reels, it's been on TikTok for much longer."

She was not remotely interested in Colin's parasocial relationships online, but the phone was shoved in her face, so she took it from Colin's hand and unleashed the reel of concern.

A K-pop song was playing. There was a picture Olivia posted when she went to the MoMA, text covering most of the screen. An electronic voice read the caption out loud, "Tell me why Olivia Angeles is still hanging out with Colin Sheffield when her bodyguard looks at her like..."

The photo disappeared and the sound changed to a deep, thumping bass, a voice crooning about sexy vibes to the equally sexy song as photos of Olivia and Mon at the MoMA flashed, one after the other, so simultaneous it looked like a video.

And then there was an actual video.

A lot of the clips were from when they were looking at the van Gogh, Olivia with her arms wrapped around herself and smiling, looking up at Mon. He was wearing a black turtleneck and a jacket, his face hidden behind a bucket hat and his mask. But yup, he'd taken his hat off at some point, so you could see him run his hands through his hair, gently lead Olivia toward something with a palm on her back. And in all the shots, he was looking at her with such intensity, it was hard to hide, even with a mask on.

"Sir, I am looking respectfully at your tiddies," the caption read, which *was* funny.

There was no mistaking him for Colin Sheffield—Colin did not have the same build as Mon at all, plus he was blond as the California sun. Mon was darker in contrast, more intimidating from afar. But there was a sweetness to the photos, like Mon was trying to keep his distance, even as he was unable to take his eyes off her. She knew that look, that intensity. Had it focused and completely zoned in on her in moments of passion and desire. It made her shiver.

Olivia had always been a visual learner. And seeing the evidence of the two of them together made something click in her head. Just like when she first walked into her Silver Lake house, like the first time she'd held a script in her hands. This was right, and the thought of it being right made blood rush to her head and butterflies dance in her stomach.

I adore you. The words were intoxicating, and made him hard to resist.

She handed Colin his phone back. Made a mental note to ask Mon to wear the black turtleneck from the photos again. It was funny how different Mon seemed, depending on what he was doing. There was Mon, downright sexy, confident and cool, who could write lyrics into her soul, make her shiver with a look. Who glared at men who assumed things about him, and took them down with a few words and a clench of his jaw.

Then there was Mon, nerdy and quiet, who could whisper things like *I adore you*, or *you're lovely* and make her feel like the only girl in the world.

"Should we be talking to your publicist?" Colin asked. "Who is this guy?"

"What do you mean who is this guy?" Olivia chuckled. "He's right—"

Colin huffed. Olivia knew that huff of indignation, one that brooked no further argument. It also meant he was about to say something she was definitely not going to like. In the corner, Macenna looked up, immediately sensing trouble.

"You know, a lot of your career is built on the speculation that we're secretly dating," Colin said as a matter of fact, not giving a shit that she was on the other side of this, picking up what he was saying. "People think we're together. They like casting us together. Going viral with someone else isn't going to help, because you need *me*."

Olivia refused to let her jaw drop, refused to let Colin get under her skin. But the pressure of her boiling blood needed to go somewhere. She glared at him instead, turning over the sheet with the lyrics as if she was trying to hide Mon's words from Colin. Which made absolutely no sense. But, God.

"I need you?"

"Yeah. Like this role, right? They wouldn't have cast either of us if we weren't together. Sol Stanley's standards are notoriously high, but she chose us anyway."

Olivia's jaw dropped. It was rare that Colin could catch her off guard with the shit he said, but this was a new low. Even for him. Because that was the part they never talked about—many looked at Lady Tala because Lord Aries looked at her, because on the show she was Magnavis and not... white. That she was connected to Colin meant she was "more acceptable" to some. For Colin to bring it up like this? Asshole.

Olivia had always considered Michelle Obama to be a wise woman, and so kept her advice close to her heart. When they go low...

"You know you're usually better than this, Colin." She lectured him instead, turning away from the cameras so they couldn't see her expression. Thank God neither of them were miked. "But still. Fuck you all the same."

Maybe working in such close proximity with someone for three years wasn't such a good thing, because Colin had been on the receiving end of Olivia's glare so often he didn't flinch. The man honestly, truly believed neither of them were talented enough for the roles in which they were cast. Not talented without the other. And it was fine for him, but why did he have to drag her into it?

He might not be intimidated, but he did look surprised, as if Olivia had revealed a truth he hadn't been ready to hear.

"Oh fuck. You're in love," he gasped. "God. Why? How? Why didn't you tell me?"

"How is this about that?" Olivia asked. Not that she was agreeing with him, but what the hell? "You just called me untalented."

"Olivia, please don't put words into my mouth." He sighed as if she were the exasperating one. How sad was it that Colin seemed to truly believe he wasn't good enough?

It made her pity him a little. "Just tell me who this mystery bodyguard is, and I'll fix it, okay?"

"Colin!" Olivia stood up from her seat. She was suddenly very aware the whole room had gone quiet. Sound carried, clearly. And Colin had once again lived up to his reputation of just being…Colin. A little pushy, the placement of his heart kind of questionable. Most of the time Olivia could stand it. Not today.

"I'm going to step outside," she told him, holding up a hand for Colin not to follow her. She glanced briefly at the sound booth, and they seemed busy and unaware of what happened. Good.

She walked out to the hallway, letting the door close by itself. Fucking Colin. He'd just caught her so unaware, and making these assumptions about her and what she was getting out of her career. He made it sound like she should be grateful they'd hitched their proverbial wagons together, that people liked seeing them.

Your career is built on the speculation that we're secretly dating… You need me.

It was bullshit. Yet despite everything Olivia worked for, everything she'd done, there was a part of her that actually agreed with him. It was true, the opportunities she got after she and Colin started to show up in places together had changed. People looked at her, recognized her more. Colin being white *had* done something for her career. But she thought the unspoken between them was that they were equals, or at least they considered each other as such. She was wrong. Clearly. Because Colin thought she was untalented.

What a fucking asshole.

"Olivia?" Sol's voice tugged her out of her thought spiral, the director looking at her curiously. "Hey. You escaped too, huh?"

"You could say that."

"I forgot how much of a micromanager Leo can be sometimes." Sol chuckled, eating a mint from a tin, and offering Olivia one. She accepted. Why not? "Thought I should leave two guys to it. I did not think it would take this long for two grown men to decide which buttons to press."

"Kinky." Was Olivia's witty response, but the wit was somewhat dampened by her weak smile. A look of concern passed Sol's face, and Olivia inwardly cursed. She didn't like showing weakness, especially not to her boss. How was she going to get any respect otherwise?

"You want to talk? You look like you could use a talk," Sol said, leaning against the wall, arms crossed over her chest. A Black woman could be an immovable force, especially one who just wanted to help you unpack your shit. It had surprised Olivia at first, how generous the BIPOC women in her industry were, how legitimately they wanted her to do well. It made her want to step up, do well, so she could help others too. Working with Sol was definitely a highlight of Olivia's career, but getting to know her, talk to her, was a gift, and one she wouldn't take for granted. But Olivia shifted and squirmed where she stood.

She didn't do this. She'd grown up in a house where it was always, "sunod muna." Don't ask questions. Do as I say first, mentally unpack your trauma with your therapist later.

With Max in Manila, and with all the other things that were easier to do (move on, move up, find the next thing, model this, post that), Olivia had gotten used to either processing things by herself, or not processing them at all. It was hard to find someone she could talk to without worrying about context, or language, or privacy. All those things were hard to come across in one person, and she was tired, okay? Was this the right time? The right place? Was it okay to dump this all on Sol?

"I'm fine."

"You are. Talk to me anyway." Sol shrugged, and that door to Olivia's feelings was gently pushed open. Just a sliver. "I don't think anyone caught everything Colin said to you. But then you walked out in a huff. Your boy was worried, so I made him sit down and keep pressing buttons so I could check on you."

"I don't huff," Olivia huffed. "And...my boy?"

"Dimples. Mon. Morningview. Your boy. He's one of the rare ones. The world easily swallows up sweet boys like that. But he manages." Sol shrugged. "Now do I need to talk to Colin?" The implication was clear. Had Colin crossed a line?

"No." Olivia shook her head. "I just...I wonder sometimes."

She leaned against the wall, her hands behind her back as she formulated her thoughts. Processed them into words, ones she hoped Sol would understand. There was no script here, no road map. And Olivia had never been good at "yes, and..."

"What I'm doing here. Whose story I'm telling at this

point. I've fought to be here for a long time, but the 'why' eludes me. And Colin is very good at reminding me of that. That I still feel replaceable."

Sol chuckled and made a noise that sounded dismissive to Olivia. She narrowed her eyes at Sol, who shook her head.

"First of all, have you ever tried to be selfish?"

"Sol, I'm an actress. My existence is inherently selfish."

"Psh." Sol rolled her eyes. "It's a powerful motivator, admitting you're doing this for yourself. It helps to not feel like you're carrying the weight of generations on your back. I mean, you could be. We are. But you don't have to let it control you. I think after living through a pandemic, after working as hard as you have for your career, it would be unfair to call 'living for yourself' selfish."

It was hard to explain to Sol why that was hard. Olivia was still a first generation Filipino from an immigrant family. There were still expectations of being a good Filipino girl. Sunod muna. Don't ask questions. Be grateful. Close your legs, close your mouth when you chew. Be like Maria Clara. Pray. Saying you were here for anyone other than "the little girls who never saw themselves on TV/books/music/ movies," or "for my family" just wasn't done.

But the thing was, Olivia *had* grown up seeing herself in those things. She saw it in the summer, watching Pinoy rom-coms from the nineties, and movie musicals on VHS. She heard it in Mon's music, when he sang about traffic, historical revisionism, monsoon days. Who a good Filipino girl was, was supposed to be defined by the Filipino girls themselves. Not someone playing the part of what people assumed a good Filipino girl was supposed to be.

She didn't need the validation of Hollywood for her representation to matter, because it had always been just at her fingertips.

And her family? Well, her family was happily living their lives for themselves. Surely, she could make them proud by living her life for herself, too.

Sol was right. At this point, she'd come too far not to admit she was doing this because she wanted it. Because she should be able to. Because she could.

"Second of all," Sol continued, and Olivia was surprised there was a second of all, because Sol had already given her such a freeing truth. Had she been the kind of person to write things down, she would write this down and remember it. What did Mon say about fountain pens and filler notebooks? "We might have rewritten the pop star character into Jessamyn after you auditioned."

"What?"

"I had all these lofty dreams of casting a certain persona. I wanted someone untouchable, who wouldn't be at all fazed when she finds out she's still married to her ex-husband. Like Beyoncé in *Lemonade*."

It made sense. It was there in the script, that perfectly controlled anger, the rage smoothed by a veneer of courage and calm. It was what Olivia had been drawn to, when the script first fell into her lap.

"But you walked in, read the script, and I knew we needed to make a Filipino pop star." Sol chuckled. "I mean it makes sense, don't you think, that a Filipino would be one of the biggest pop stars in the world? And you brought it together, for me. You were so sure of who you were, and who you wanted to become. And you were happy to be that person. Like Beyoncé in Coachella."

"I could never be Beyoncé in Coachella," Olivia disagreed. "I have zero Virgo placements."

"Still. We rewrote the part for you. Not to inflate your ego, or anything."

Olivia laughed, even as the high praise left her a little dizzy. She didn't read reviews, and validation for her came from likes, comments on posts, in view numbers and posters of herself on Sunset.

"Colin came on board after you, at the insistence of the studio. They said it would be 'too much' to cast a Black lead alongside you, in the year of our Lord Twenty Twenty Something." Sol rolled her eyes. "I made compromises. Well, not compromises. Choices. They're choices I don't regret, because I had the opportunity to work with you. And I got to choose something else to push back on. I think you've got good instincts, and you have a long career ahead, if that's what you want. Give yourself those flowers."

Olivia's heart felt full suddenly. This was the first time she felt so professionally validated, and to have it come from someone she respected so highly? It was everything. Sol had given it freely too, without the expectation of anything more than Olivia's talent. She didn't want to take it for granted.

"Thank you, Sol," she said, holding a hand out, and

squeezing when Sol held hers back. "I think that's the nicest thing anyone's said to me, professionally."

"You need nicer people. Actually." Sol sighed, squeezing her hand. "This business is a selfish one, Olivia. You need to surround yourself with people to keep your head afloat."

"Who?" Olivia asked, the laugh bitter on her tongue. She wanted to give Sol the entire list—her brother wasn't here, her parents were ready to follow him any day. There were her three golden retrievers back home—Artoo, Three-pio and Bibi—but cuddles weren't exactly the best therapy. Then there was Colin, who understood Olivia's struggles, but wasn't good at the empathy part. "Who do you have?"

"I have Leo, unfortunately." Sol shrugged. "When you eat at Los Tacos No. 1 with someone, it's for life. Or so he told me. I have my wife. Our three cats. My struggles to learn how to knit. It's oddly soothing."

"Not a lot of friends in the biz, huh."

"Not a lot of true ones. What about you?"

What, or who indeed. The question seemed to wrap around her throat and get tight.

"I'm working on it," Olivia admitted. "So…tacos tonight?"

"From your lips to God's ears." Sol winked at her. "We can always meet up after your little museum date."

Ah yes, her museum date with her man, the one who adored her and made her look at art differently. But could she ask that of him? Did he want it, even?

"Good," Sol said, seemingly satisfied. "Now are you ready to go in there and sing?"

"Well." Look. She was already here, and Sol was already listening, and she'd just gotten bolstered. She might as well go the full kapal ng mukha. Was she using that phrase right? "There is one more thing. Just—"

Sol must have recognized the look on her face, because she rolled her eyes. And as much as Olivia didn't really know Sol, she saw some fondness in her eye roll, and sometimes that was all Olivia needed. "Oh here we go."

"Sol, that ending."

"Olivia. My patience." Sol groaned, shaking her head.

"Just hear me out!" Olivia said quickly, because she knew Sol wouldn't wait. "We've been through so much already. The pandemic isn't over for everyone, and a bit of hope that you can have everything, if you work for it, if you say it out loud, and want it, and fight for it... Even after everything's been stacked against you. It's powerful. I know you know that."

"Oh, I do."

"Jessamyn shouldn't be punished for fighting for what she wants," Olivia added, as they both made it back to the door of the studio, where she could see Mon and Leo waving them in. "Just my thought."

Sol paused by the door and looked at Olivia. She held her breath in anticipation, because she could almost feel her resolve crumbling.

"I'll think about it," Sol said, and Olivia squealed in surprise and clapped a hand over her own mouth. "Stop that."

"But, Sol, you're the best!"

"That I am."

"You're the nicest."

"Don't tell anyone. It confuses people when I'm nice."

"But you are nice," Olivia said. And she was comfortable enough, thrilled enough, that she said out loud, "You're my favorite now." And how amazing was it, to be recognized by someone you admired, to be welcomed into a part of an industry that sought to exclude you? It made her little moment with Colin insignificant.

Again, that fond eye roll. Sol was a master. "Oh my God, relax. Now go inside and sing, will you?"

"Gladly," Olivia said smugly, walking into the studio with Sol behind her. Leo was in the staged area with Colin, and Olivia could hear them practicing the blending.

"He's…struggling a bit." Mon sighed, shaking his head. "I knew the lyric change might trip you guys up, but it's so much better this way. It's almost a folksy sound, and if you don't get it right away, it's hard to…" He must have seen something in Olivia's expression, because Mon's glance turned curious. Those light, observant eyes of his shifted from her to Sol, as if trying to determine what happened. "Is everything okay?"

"I think we're in for a couple more lyric changes." Olivia grinned. "Right, Sol?"

"Why do I keep listening to you?" Sol huffed.

"You said I had good instincts!"

"Lyric changes, what?" Mon asked, adorably confused. Olivia giggled and crossed the room, wrapping her arms around his neck as the retro pop music continued to play in the background.

And without caring who could see, she kissed him full on the lips, making him drop the papers in his hands. And there was nothing else she could see, or hear—not Leo clapping his hands gleefully in the background, not Colin's jaw dropping or Sol rolling her eyes and willing God to give her strength. All Olivia could see was Mon, and the blush on his cheeks, and the endearing smile he gave her.

"I'm not changing the lyrics just because you kissed me," he announced.

"I know." Olivia grinned. "But I think there are other ways you could be persuaded."

By the end of the session, there were a couple of lyric changes. Just enough so it didn't feel so tragic (*and I'll never wake up by your side* became *I can wake up by your side*, which was as much hope as Olivia needed) and could go with whatever Sol decided, when she and Colin got their blending down.

The recording was, in short, a success. Both Colin and Olivia thanked the crew, waved to the cameras that saw everything, and absolutely nothing, that had happened. They were packing up, Olivia slipping on her jacket and scarf, picking up the tumbler of lukewarm lemon water she'd brought. She carried that thing everywhere. Singing and crying out of specific tear ducts took a lot of moisture.

"I'm sorry," Colin finally muttered, as he pulled her hair out from under the silk of her scarf. "Macenna said I was being a brat."

"Are you sorry?" Olivia asked. "Or do you need something else from me?"

The man at least had the tact to look embarrassed.

"I need a break, Colin." She sighed, shaking her head. "Can it wait until tomorrow?"

"Tomorrow?" Colin glanced behind Olivia, where she knew Macenna was probably nodding her head. God, that girl was not being paid enough to be Colin Sheffield's PA. "Okay. Tomorrow. I'll treat you to breakfast at Peter Luger."

Naturally. A place where they would be seen. Olivia didn't blame him.

"Do they serve breakfast at Peter Luger?"

"I'll make sure they do." Colin winked. His face then softened as he smiled at Olivia; she would almost say with fondness, if it had been anyone else. But as much as he was forgiven for what he said, it was always going to be in the back of her mind now. "I like us together."

"Professionally."

"Sure. That," he said, nodding.

"Olivia?" Mon asked, emerging from the sound booth, his smile cautious as he approached them. "Edward Hopper awaits."

"Can't wait." Olivia smiled, because she liked seeing him so enthusiastic. Even during the recording, it had been infectious, when he got excited. "I'll meet you outside, Moning."

She exhaled slowly, watching him leave, completely forgetting Colin was there until he flicked the edge of her scarf.

"Colin." Her tone was flat.

"You asked for a break. I'll talk to you tomorrow, my queen." He gave her a wan smile and left the room. Olivia watched him go, watched Macenna give her a glare before she followed him out.

Olivia waved goodbye to the staff still packing up before she left and found Mon waiting for her in the hallway. He leaned against the wall, shifting his weight from foot to foot, lost in thought as he contemplated the shapes the windows and the setting sun made on the floor, tracing them with his toes. Olivia watched him for a moment, and she smiled fondly until her cheeks started to hurt.

She wanted more days like this. Wanted more moments where she could catch Mon lost in his myriad thoughts. The sun was golden, and he was cast in that light, with the city outside and waiting.

She could keep them waiting for a little longer.

"I was just thinking about stillness," Mon announced, no prompting needed before he looked up at her. "How paintings capture moments that were alive and vibrant, but the moment in time is frozen by the stroke of a brush."

"Is that a good thing?" Olivia asked. "For things to be made still?"

"I think humans are inherently nostalgic, but we're creatures who also need to keep moving forward," he said, holding a hand out like he was cutting the light, one eye closed. Olivia watched the shadows fall over his face, felt herself falling, too. "A paradox."

"So we're selfish."

"We want things," Mon said, dropping his hand and smiling at her warmly. It made Olivia feel comforted, settled, that somehow this was the right thing. "Good things, good moments last longer. Forever, if we could."

You need to surround yourself with people to keep your head afloat.

This seemed a good place to start.

"We should go." Olivia looped her arm around his. "If you're feeling contemplative now…"

"I can stop," Mon said, pulling away as if embarrassed.

"No, no. I like it." Olivia assured him by squeezing him tighter, keeping him close, where she wanted him to be. "I like you. And I like hearing your thoughts about things. I can't wait to hear what you think of Edward Hopper."

"Oh."

"And to clarify, he is not named after the villain in *A Bug's Life*?"

Eight

Now Playing: "I Can't Make You Love Me"—Kinda Blue feat. Hwasa / "Cuida" (Live)—Ebe Dancel / "Too Much"—Carly Rae Jepsen

Olivia: Moning, are you here yet? I bribed one of the grips to buy us CHEESECAKE—!!

Mon: What flavor?

Olivia: There is no better flavor than P L A I N I keep telling you this

Teddy blinked at Mon over the video call, his face betraying absolutely nothing of his thoughts. Mon liked to tease and call Teddy a cat, all calm and quiet and unemotional until the feline demon swiped an entire vase of flowers off the table, for some reason. You could never tell what a cat was think-ing, just like Teddy Mertola.

Until, of course, he started laughing.

"I leave you alone for a month and you go fall in fuck-ing love with Olivia Angeles," he said, crossing his arms over his chest as he continued to laugh. "Fucking typical."

"What do you mean typical? There's nothing typical about this." Mon frowned, holding up a shirt against his front to look at it through the video screen. "Yes?"

Teddy wrinkled his nose in distaste, as if he didn't wear a black shirt and cargo pants every day. His hair was also getting long, curling at the edges like he was a J-pop star. "That's too formal for a midnight cheesecake booty call."

"It's not a booty call," Mon protested, tossing the tie-dyed button-down shirt among the other rejected tops on the bed. How many shirts did he bring on this trip? "It's a live recording in Times Square, and she wants to have cheese-cake. It's perfectly normal for people who are…"

Are *what*? More than friends but not quite lovers? Was sex the only requirement to call someone your lover? Would she be comfortable with Mon declaring to the world that he was in love with her? That he thought about her constantly, that he'd spent his entire day with the music for her track because he couldn't find the right hook? That she inspired music in him, made him happy to see her be herself?

Teddy nodded his approval at Mon's final choice—a denim vest over a white T-shirt and his usual jeans. Mon worried it teetered a little too close to TikTok farmer or beekeeper.

But then again, a stranger *had* asked yesterday if he was a horticulturist when he was walking through Central Park. Unironically. It was hilarious. They ended up in a brief conversation about Philippine native trees.

"Stop. You look good." Teddy pulled him out of his thoughts. "So you admit it. You're in love."

"Why do you say that like it's a bad thing?" Mon asked, hunting around the room for a clean pair of socks. He didn't love living out of a suitcase, but it wouldn't be forever. "It's a good thing. A many splendored thing. It's all you need."

"So you're leaving on a jet plane?" Teddy snorted, sarcasm dripping in his voice. But when the silence stretched too long, and Mon hadn't said a word, his business partner's eyes went wide. *"Oh babe."*

"I don't have plans, and we haven't discussed anything," Mon explained, and saying "we" made his heart skip in his chest at the idea. A good skip, he knew, but still, it made him stop, his fingers brushing over his fragile heart. "I was just thinking. Picturing what it could maybe be like, to be here for…longer reasons."

"God," Teddy huffed. "In this economy? *There? Now?*"

"Some would argue it's the more beneficial move."

"Mon. Look." Teddy sighed, clearly sensing he was being defensive. And he was.

It wasn't like Mon was seriously considering *anything* at this point. And he knew, he knew more than most, what he would have to give up to stay here. What he was taking on by signing up to be a perpetual second-class citizen just because of where he came from. His original point still stood. New York, the US? Was not for him.

But if Olivia asked him to stay?

He didn't have an immediate, firm answer. And it bothered him that he didn't have an immediate, firm answer. So he started thinking about it, writing about it. Here he was, three songs into something that didn't make him cringe, wearing a denim vest and heading to work in Times Square. Here he was, getting closer to someone, wanting more, thinking about putting an Uno reverse card on his own life because she made him happy. Because she gave him the love he'd longed for.

"I'm happy you're happy, Mon." Teddy was using that tone of voice for when he was trying his hardest to be patient. "I know love is something you wanted for yourself."

Mon said nothing, because nobody knew more than Teddy Mertola all the strange things Mon had done for love. Dated people he knew didn't really want the same thing, opened his heart up to others while trying to respect boundaries. Failing.

"I worry you're diving in too deep," Teddy said. "Doing—"

"Too much." Mon sighed, collapsing backward on the bed to stare up at the ceiling.

He'd heard that before. When he talked to a date about the wonders of stan culture after she asked what time it was. When he googled fifteen different Philippine native trees after a date with Andi, pre-Teddy, because she liked trees, and ended up unable to talk about anything else.

"It's great," Teddy assured him. "Your heart's out there, and it draws people to you. I just don't want you to come back from this dream job all sad and mopey. It's like watching Charlie Brown try to kick the football over and over again."

"JobJams wants one of my tracks for KST," Mon announced, just to remind himself this was what he was supposed to be doing here. Working. Making opportunities.

"KST? Fucking KST? Mon, that's amazing!" Teddy exclaimed, because of course he was aware of one of the biggest K-pop groups in the world, the name of their producer, what that meant for Mon and his career. "How did you even meet JobJams? Is his name really JobJams?"

"His name is Kim Sungjoon. He was renting one of the studios at Swan Song, and we just got to talking," Mon said, sitting up. "We bonded over a love of banchan and Tiger Balm—the rapper, not the ointment."

"I fucking know who Tiger Balm is. I told you about him, you jerk."

"The next thing I knew, he was calling the people in Korea, and things were happening."

"That's the fucking dream, yeah?" Teddy said, shaking his head in disbelief. A proud kind of disbelief. "That's what you came there to do."

"It is," Mon agreed, smiling at Teddy through the video. The sunlight in his office was nice. It made the giant orchid print Andi risographed for him look like a museum piece. Things that were homey and familiar, and yet new, in an office Mon didn't recognize from the old preschool it had once been. But still he missed it.

"I should go," he announced. Now wasn't the time for these thoughts. He had a song to record. "Will you—"

"Get the Dela Cruz estate to agree on Tipsy Log's cover for the album? I got it."

"—be okay?" Mon finished his question. "You should talk to Joe in marketing. He goes to those drag brunches in QC, and I think he met one of the grandkids there."

"On it. You've got a big heart, Moning." Teddy's sincerity was unexpected. But not unappreciated. "Big hearts bruise easy."

"I'll be fine," Mon grumbled, but he wasn't angry. He understood Teddy's trepidation. Even he had his doubts. But he'd given the words power, and now that they were spoken, he couldn't help but start wondering...what if? "I'm used to it."

"And we'll be here," Teddy added, continuing to burrow words into Mon's heart and give him all the reasons not to stay. "Whatever you decide. The music, the studio, me and Andi and everyone."

"*If* there's a decision to be made," Mon reminded him. "I'll talk to you soon."

It was a thirty-minute walk to Times Square. Even this close to midnight, it was a lovely, long stroll that took Mon past Lincoln Center, Columbus Circle. He could stuff his hands in his pockets, listen to his music and not think about everything he and Teddy had just discussed. He could give himself time to stop holding on to his whirling thoughts too tightly, and enjoy the KST album he'd added to his playlist. He was heading to work, that was all.

"You look warm, but suspicious," a stranger said as he passed, to which Mon shrugged and pressed the tip of his mask more into the bridge of his nose. It helped with the cold too, okay.

Time to himself was hard to come by, even when he lived alone. As much as he loved being with people, walks like this, moments like this, were rare, and times he savored.

You would have more of this if you stayed.

Which was true. There weren't a lot of places to just walk and think in Manila. There was no time, in a place where survival was of the essence, and he needed to hustle. A walk through New York in the spring was a luxury. If he stayed, it would be his norm.

He knew he was near when the lights started to change. When the tall buildings seemed to shrink because the flashing, street-level lights were enough to hide everything above in the inky black night. When he could see in clear detail the chip bag that flew by because the brightness made everything clear as day.

Times Square stopped his breath. Everything was ginormous, larger than life! Bigger and better! Nothing in front of him was smaller than life-size, especially not the colorful but silent ads telling him to shop here! Watch this!

It lit something up in his hindbrain, the same part of him that loved shiny and new things. That knew which popular restaurant people flocked to in Manila, which café was generating buzz. Sakto, Lizzo's new song "About Damn Time" started playing, and it was just the cherry on top of the moment that made Mon pause and take it all in.

He snapped a photo and sent it to the group chat.

Ava: Yatta!

Mon: My thoughts exactly.

He had a weird sense of accomplishment, that he'd made it here, in a place that not even he imagined he'd ever get to see. Mon deserved this. He deserved his time, and deserved to entertain the idea of staying in the US.

But he still didn't know what to do about it.

There was a small crowd gathered around the center of the square, and Mon instinctively knew that was where he needed to be. He spotted Sol in the middle of the chaos, telling people what to do in a way that was authoritative and only a little bit scary. Leo was there too, chatting up the drummer as staff worked around them. He knew the sound guy, who had helped him with his headphones at the MoMA, and he even spotted the same bodyguard who'd accompanied him and Olivia through the museum.

They were recording live today, as Sol wanted Olivia's song to be "the emotional one" of the tracks in the movie. That it was more a pop song than a ballad had very little to do with her decision. So they were all here—live band, cameras, recording equipment. Leo had taken the lead on the recording since Mon didn't have much experience, but it was all-hands-on-deck, so here he was.

"Psst. Huy."

Mon looked up to where the call was coming from, surprised to find Olivia sitting alone on the topmost rung of
the bleachers looking out into Times Square. Her head was
resting on her arms, which in turn were splayed over the
railing, her smile soft as she looked down at him. It would
have been a normal sight, if not for the crowd that pressed
around him, clamoring for her attention.

"You're late!" she yelled, and a few people in the crowd
looked around, confused. Mon simply shrugged in response.
No need to tell her he'd been absorbed in making mental
notes on the mastering of "Overexposed" and got lost for
a bit.

She jerked her head to the entrance to the set, leaving him
to his own devices as she smiled and waved to her audience
below. Mon pushed through the crowd, moving past a lot
of bystanders and more than one fan. He was pretty sure
someone recognized him, catching a gasp and someone saying, "It's the bodyguard!"

He'd take it.

"She's been waiting for you," the crew member manning
the door commented as he approached, speaking softly into
the headset before she waved him in.

Without stopping to process *that*, Mon jogged over to
the bleachers, up the steps to reach Olivia, who had moved
closer to the center and out of view.

"Hey," she said, nodding as if she didn't know he was
coming. "Come sit."

She looked the absolute epitome of cool—wearing a magenta jumpsuit, complete with flared pants. Her hair was somehow longer and wavier (more extensions?), her eyes painted with an incredible magenta eye shadow that sparkled even from where he was standing. The entire effect was made even cooler with a pair of rose-colored glasses, sitting prettily on her button nose. Olivia frowned and pushed them up a little. It was amazing because Olivia still looked very much like herself. No way was she letting all these clothes wear her.

"I told them I was too pango to wear these, but I couldn't explain pango to the wardrobe department," Olivia complained. "Flat nosed? Does that sound right?"

"You look cool," Mon assured, sitting next to her. That was when he noticed the bright red box. "Cheesecake?"

"Illicit cheesecake," she said gleefully, pulling a pair of recyclable forks from the side of the box. Mon peeked into the box, and as explained, the cheesecake was pure white, almost unassuming in its promise of whatever was inside.

"You know Burnt Basque cheesecake is a thing," Mon started. "Strawberry. Matcha. Ube, even."

"Not interested. Well, Burnt Basque *maybe*, but I keep telling you, I like my flavors original. So when you eat something good, it's really good."

"And when you eat something bad, it's just sad."

"Hush."

"I feel like, as your producer, I should tell you that sweets are bad for your voice," he warned her. "Especially when you're about to put on a vocal performance."

"Mon, I have been chugging warm water and honey all day. *Please* let me have this creamy, sweet, perfect, original New York cheesecake," Olivia begged into his ear, as she pressed against him. Mon was trying his hardest not to look, but she was clearly pouting at him. "I'll be good later."

"Be good now," he said, turning to look at her, which was absolutely a mistake, because Olivia's eyes were dark with desire, and he felt it too, pooling in his stomach as she pressed her lips together.

"Fine," she said breezily, breaking the contact by looking away. Mon nearly stumbled forward, even though he was sitting down. "We'll have cheesecake later."

She was still pouting and leaning against him. Mon felt her body shudder.

"Cold?"

Olivia nodded, huddling closer to him. "This jumpsuit is all sequins, zero insulation."

"You could always go into one of the holding tents."

"I'm asking you to cuddle me, Moning." Olivia rested her chin on his arm. "In case it isn't obvious."

It hadn't been obvious to him, *obviously*, because he didn't mind wrapping an arm around her and letting her use him for warmth. Especially when she pressed her thigh closer to his, as her hands snaked around his body.

"I like this jumpsuit on you," he told her. Awkward, but he wanted to compliment her. "Does it have a zipper?"

She grinned at him. "Dirty."

He shrugged in response. He couldn't help himself.

"They wanted to do a thing where I had a cape with Baybayin on it," Olivia told him, wrinkling her nose. "I vetoed it, but I didn't have the vocabulary to explain why it made me uncomfortable."

"Because people would recognize it, but not be able to read it. Nobody uses Baybayin."

"I told them I should get to decide how to represent my own country."

"I think the fact that you're Filipina, that Jessamyn is Filipina, is a big enough homage." Mon shrugged. "Not that I'm an expert. But personally I would have found it more validating if you spoke Filipino, or did that backbend thing Pilita Corrales does. Even a step or two from 'Tala.'"

"The Sarah Geronimo song?"

"It's practically the national anthem."

"What's the difference?" she asked. "Between that and the cape thing?"

"Sincerity? Or just the acknowledgment that there are singers and performers in the Philippines, that they should be part of your vernacular. I think the great thing about being who you are is that you will always have the best of both worlds."

His thoughts were met with her silence, and perhaps Olivia was trying to digest. But Mon had to deal with this all the time. Half-hearted representation that had no heart or sincerity behind it, just someone's desire to appeal to an audience that would find them "fascinating" at best, "exotic" at worst.

It absolutely fucking sucked. It was part of a long list of reasons why he wouldn't want to stay. But at least she *asked*, which was more than what he got a lot of the time.

"You know, I thought I was going to be a Broadway actress when I started," Olivia said, looking at the massive poster of *Hamilton* beside them. "I looked up all the shows, and I convinced my parents and Max to skip going to Manila one summer so I could watch as many shows as I wanted. It worked, mostly because Max wanted to see the lions at the public library, so sulit na."

"Why didn't you?" Mon asked. He supposed it wasn't as impossible for her as it was for others. "Do the Broadway thing, I mean."

Olivia shrugged. "My Dad said I wasn't Lea Salonga, and even Lea has a hard time getting lead roles. And I had too much faith in myself to not want the lead."

"That must have crushed you," Mon said, imagining a younger Olivia, with the world she wanted to be a part of just at her fingertips, but still out of reach.

"I didn't let it." She shook her head. "Or maybe it had, but I didn't realize?"

"Just parental trauma things."

"Exactly," she agreed, nodding at the revelation. "I kept my head down for a while, did the school thing. Took acting jobs when I could, but I kept telling myself not to want more. That what was in front of me was enough. I'm still convinced that one day all this will end in disaster and despair."

Olivia avoided pressing her cheek against his clothes— she didn't want her makeup on him, he supposed, but she did hold him tighter, a silent signal for him to listen, to pay attention.

"I think that's one of the reasons why I enjoyed playing this role so much," she mused. "In so many ways, it's vindication. It's *fun*." She smiled to herself, looking up at Mon with the stars in her eyes, the lights of the city on her face. "I'll miss it."

"Me too." The words were almost a whisper because saying them any louder would break the moment.

This shoot was one of Olivia's last for this production. Certainly the final big one. They were doing a few reshoots to fit in a new ending (or so he'd heard) but this was the last with the full crew, the last one Mon would be involved in. The month had flown by faster than either of them were ready for, but it was happening all the same. And still, Mon said nothing about what he wanted after. He didn't want to be the one to start the conversation. Maybe he was too much of a coward, or it just didn't feel right to be the one to ask if he could stay. Maybe it was all in his head.

"There will be more roles like this," he assured her, because he knew Olivia, and she wouldn't settle for anything less. And she deserved it, to do work that made her feel fulfilled and happy. Vindicated, if that was what she wanted. She was going to be fine.

"Is it weird that I still want to play Inez Duhatan from *Luna's Landing*?" Olivia sighed. "Everyone keeps telling me they want to cast in another direction, but there's something about playing a Robin Hood type art thief who falls in love with her bodyguard that resonates with me."

"Is that why you posted that picture from the MoMA?" Mon asked. He knew *Luna's Landing*. He'd seen the cover show up on his stories so often he could probably redraw it from memory if he had the skill.

"I posted that picture because you were in it." Olivia chuckled. "Subtle jowa reveal."

"Who taught you *that*?"

"TikTok! I found the Pinoys." She looked proud of herself. "But I have to admit, I'm a little more interested in you lecturing about Anita Magsaysay-Ho and...post-Cubism?"

Mon nodded, just happy she remembered the term. He liked it when she brought up things he'd said before, little facts that floated around in his head that he'd passed on to her. He liked that she listened and remembered, and even better, she seemed to enjoy it too. Add it to the list of reasons why he would consider staying. God.

"Anyway. It's fascinating, but I am more fascinated because I'm interested in the role."

"Have you asked?" When Olivia looked confused, Mon continued. "For the role. Like directly lobbied for it. Imagine if the people standing out there all tweeted the director or something, and they saw you? You're so good—"

She cut him off with a kiss, pressing her lips against his as she tugged on his denim vest. He could feel her smiling just before she pulled away, her lipstick smudged slightly.

"Hey Mon," she said. "Let's have sex."

"Now?"

"No." She laughed, and there were sparkles in her hair. "Later."

He nodded. And when his thoughts settled, and the panic alarms faded, he took her hand and kissed her palm. He could almost hear music. With acoustic guitars and brass instruments, slowly swaying palm trees and soft breezes under twinkling lights. He could hear it tonight, in the touch of his lips against the back of Olivia's hand, in her kiss, in the way she smiled at him and blushed with her sparkly eyes.

It was a moment he wished he could keep still, and have for much longer. Like a painting, like a song.

"Excuse me, m'amsir." Leo's megaphone-aided voice cut through the moment. Mon...kind of regretted teaching him that shorthand, because Leo had quickly adopted it to his vocabulary. There he was, standing at the base of the bleachers, one hand on his hip while the other held the megaphone, looking not very pleased. "Could you grace me with your presences for sound check and blocking? And don't think I don't see that cheesecake box, Miss Olivia."

"He's mad." Mon winced.

"I might have been gatekeeping the cheesecake," Olivia explained, and at Mon's shocked face, she explained. "I didn't want you to not have any!"

Mon's heart fluttered. He was easy like that. And he'd lived with the urge to kiss her since the day they'd met in the apartment hallway, but this time he didn't fight it, and pressed a quick kiss to her lips.

"Are you ready?" he asked.

"Am I?" she asked, a nervous chuckle following. Her face cooled into contemplation as she looked at the crowd, which seemed to grow the deeper they were into the night, looked at the band and the stage they set, looked at Times Square lighting everything up in its own way beyond that. They were all waiting for her.

"Olivia?"

"Just..." She exhaled. "Kind of regretting everything I put in my lyrics now. What was I thinking, writing about wanting love and feeling lonely? It's so personal, and now I have to sing it *here*, of all places."

The words were said softly, as if he was not meant to hear them. Well, he had. And he wouldn't let her go down there and regret what she'd written, because it was good. She was too talented to hide herself away. And she'd never admitted to the lyrics being personal, because they fit her character so well. It was a sneaky way of speaking things into truth, without fully admitting them out loud. But Mon knew what the truth was, because he was one of the few allowed into that part of Olivia's life.

"Putting how you feel into words is powerful," he said, "because someone out there might need the words, too."

"Like you did for me," Olivia told him, sighing deeply. "You really got me through some difficult moments, you know."

"You found me when you needed me."

The universe was way too random for some powerful being not to be in control, and he saw that in coincidences, in moments where things that changed your life fell into your lap. When at the peak of your loneliness you found something precious that you loved and cherished. Something to give your heart and your time to, because you felt safe and happy around it.

Just like love.

"But I needed to say the words out loud too, when I was

writing them," Mon continued. "Words are powerful. Songs even more so, I think."

Olivia was still listening. He saw her bite her bottom lip, but stop. Saw her wrinkle her nose, but stop again. She was quiet, and he took that as a sign to say what he really wanted.

"Those people out there will love you, or they won't. The important thing is that you do the job, and feel good about it." He slowly stood up. Olivia looked up at him wordlessly, her face unreadable. "You're wonderful, Olivia."

He held a hand out to her, presumably to help her stand. "And if all else fails, I could always autotune you."

That made her laugh, playfully smacking his hand away before she stood up and drilled her fingertip into the divot of his dimple while he laughed.

"Oooh you are *so* going to get it," she told him.

"Later? I hope so."

"Just grab the cheesecake box, will you?" Olivia asked, marching down the bleachers to Leo, who clearly found them adorable, but really just wanted to get on with work.

"Yes, and cut a slice for me when you've got the time," he said through the megaphone, making Olivia stick a tongue out at him and head to the stage. Mon carried the box down and followed Leo. He was on the clock here, on the job he was brought here to do. And while he didn't want to even think about this job being over already, he had to do it.

And he was going to do it well.

This was the dream.

When Olivia allowed herself to picture life as a Hollywood actress (after the Broadway thing didn't work out) as a child, this was exactly what she saw. In fact, it was so close to what she'd pictured in her mind that this moment felt like déjà vu. She pictured a crowd calling her name, a smile on her face, a camera, and lights as bright and sparkly as they could give her, as pop music played from the live band behind her.

"Cut!" Sol called, and the dreamy sequence ended abruptly. "Lighting, can you adjust, I think the drummer is squinting. Olivia, I need you to look at the camera. The crowd isn't actually your audience for this one."

"Let's take it from the top of the chorus?" Mon suggested, focused on whatever he was monitoring, and Leo nodded.

There was agreement from the rest of the crew and Sol. When Olivia returned to her blocking position for the top of the chorus, Sol gestured for the cameras to roll again, and Mon cued the band. She was embarrassed, and felt it burn, but was determined not to let it show.

But Olivia fumbled a lyric, and they started from the top. She could feel the frustration in the air, pooling around her feet. Nobody enjoyed being outside at night past midnight, given most of the crew were past their thirties. She needed to focus. This was Jessamyn's song. Her confession to the man she still loved. Olivia could channel that. Sing that, even, without losing herself completely in the process. Olivia closed her eyes, inhaled and exhaled slowly, releasing the tension in her hands, in her limbs, in her neck.

It hasn't been easy, having you
I was going to be tougher and stronger
But you eroded the edges over
Made me want you too

She opened her eyes, and...well. There was Mon. Mon who was quickly feeling more and more like hers, who looked at her so softly, and filled out that shirt and vest so well. He was just so handsome, it caught her off guard sometimes, when he looked at her like she was brighter than all the studio lights, than Times Square itself. She enjoyed spending time with him, listening to him talk about art, eating with him.

So open up they said
Put that fear to bed
You could get hurt but god, let it hurt
There's no strength to being strong
Open your heart

The music he made fit her words so perfectly, starting with a soft touch on an electric keyboard, her voice leading the way for chimes, drums, bass, building up and up into a big, hopeful anthem about love. She wanted to match that energy, but still have the emotion. Vulnerability doesn't have to be sad, it could be joyful and radiant, no matter how afraid you were.

She was terrified and worried about being judged, but right now, it mattered very little when Mon was mouthing along with the words. And in this moment, Olivia Angeles was in love.

Olivia sang her heart out, danced around the stage they gave her, and smiled at the cameras. She even managed a Pilita Corrales backbend, thank you, Google. The crowd couldn't hear her sing, but they were dancing along to the music, and seemed to enjoy her performance.

You've turned me into love
and I love you

Olivia and Mon had decided to let the song end on a last soft note, lingering like there was supposed to be more. Learning to live and surrendering to your fears was a constantly evolving thing, one that didn't quite have a definitive end. Which was probably the scariest part. But Olivia could do it. She was a big girl.

The song ended, and Olivia counted to five. Sol was cutting there, and the five seconds were a buffer for just in case. She needed to stay for five, even as her entire body felt like a live wire, thrumming with joy and excitement.

One, two, three, four...!

She thought she heard the call for "cut." So she ran like hell, in shoes that weren't meant for running like hell. She was a magenta blur that moved past Sol, Leo, all the crew and the equipment. Had they yelled cut? The song was already over, she was done.

It didn't matter that nobody knew what she was doing,

or where she was going. Because Mon knew, and his arms were wide open for her. Olivia took the leap.

And Raymond Tindalo Mendoza, the man who disintegrated chopsticks with his bare hands, who nearly dropped a rare vinyl at a music store and who lost an ice cream to a pigeon, caught her easily. He held her firmly, arms around her body as her legs wrapped around his waist. Olivia buried her face in Mon's neck, and God, she was crying. She was crying and laughing as Mon held her close, telling her how proud he was of her, how good she was.

"Are you okay?" he asked, when Olivia pulled away, and she couldn't speak, but nodded before she buried her face in his neck again. Sorry na lang to her makeup. She would be fine. She just needed to hide her face for a little while.

His arms felt safe, and Mon felt like home.

"Cut!" Sol called behind them. "That's a wrap!"

Now Playing: "Gondry"—Primary & OHHYUK feat. Lim Kim / "Ghost"—Lianne La Havas / "Tabing Ilog"— Barbie's Cradle

"Have you been with...many people?"

They were back in the apartment, a couple of hours later. She leaned her head against the back wall of the elevator, her face tilted up to the light as she smiled. She was Olivia again, dressed down in a soft cardigan and her lips still slightly stained magenta. She was idly playing with Mon's hand, playing a half-hearted, lazy game of sawsaw sa suka with him. It was closer to dawn, but sleep was the last thing on his mind right now.

"What is many?" Olivia sighed wistfully beside him, but he was sure she was smiling, getting a kick out of his nerves.

"Olivia…"

"Mon." She tried to sound reassuring, but he wasn't soothed, not while they stood in the building elevator, too close and still too far apart, with only the CCTV camera between them. "Are you making tampo?"

"Medyo." He hated admitting it, weakly catching her finger in his palm. "I just know I'm not as experienced as—"

"Generalization."

"Right. I'm sorry, that wasn't, I mean, I'm just…" *God, why the fuck were words so hard?* "I just don't want you to be unsatisfied. I don't know what you want, and—"

She kissed him. And Mon really could get used to Olivia cutting off his thoughts with a kiss, because it stopped *all* his thoughts, made his knees melt and his entire body want to sink into the kiss. Olivia chased it with a lick on his bottom lip, and Mon pressed harder.

He opened his mouth to ask her what that particular kiss was for, and could they maybe talk about what they wanted out of sex, but she placed a finger over his lips, her eyes dark and hungry in the harsh light of the elevator. Olivia turned her body to face him, pressing her stomach and thighs against his.

"If only you could feel how wet I am for you," she said, lashes fluttering, the words spoken low into his ear. "How much I want you."

The finger on his mouth traced the shape of his bottom lip, the silhouette of his chin, his throat, the dip of his denim vest. Mon could hear his own breath quicken, could feel his cock stir. She was so beautiful. So beautiful, and she wanted him. It made him feel good, too.

"What I want," she continued, "is for you to take charge of me. Just a little."

"I can do that," Mon said, all the breath in his chest leaving his body in a whoosh. Or maybe it was his soul?

"What do you want, Mon?" she asked, the tip of her nose brushing against the side of his. She was smiling, and he could tell from the feel of her lips, her skin.

"You." He turned his face fully to hers. His hand rubbed the arm looped around his neck. "I just want to be with you."

The elevator dinged, opening to their floor. The familiar sight was almost soothing.

"I'll meet you at my place in five minutes. I need to get this glitter off," Olivia said, before bending down and sinking her teeth into Mon's chest. Not enough to hurt. Clearly Olivia was acting on a long held, intrusive thought. "Mmm."

God. If Mon hadn't been fully erect then, he definitely was now.

Ten minutes, a moment of anxiety and a quick change later, Olivia opened the door for him. Her cheeks were flushed, hair a mess and her lips still stained pink. She was absolutely staring at his body, unshy about the way her eyes lingered on his lips, his collarbones, his chest. And Mon drank it in, enjoying how she seemed to enjoy him. His decision to keep his shirt off seemed to be a good one, and

he felt ridiculously sexy, showing himself off to her, showing her how hard he was for her. That she appreciated all of
that only made him feel even more cocky. Pun intended.

"Hi," she said.

"My eyes are up here, Olivia."

"I knew that," she huffed, and yet she still spent a moment looking at his chest. "You're just so…"

He waited. Instead, she sighed (or maybe she swooned?)
before she tugged him by the waistband of his sweatpants
to kiss him. Mon stumbled through the door, thanking the
gods and his ancestors for the invention of slippers he could
just kick off while the rest of his body held on to Olivia's.
That he didn't stumble or trip on his own slippers was an
Olympic feat, but there was little time to appreciate that
when Olivia still pulled him backward, still kissed him like
there was no tomorrow. She'd already tugged the tie loose
on his sweatpants.

Mon started to chuckle against her lips as he caught her
wrists. Olivia pulled away and frowned at him.

"Hey!"

"Huy. I thought you wanted me in charge," he gently
reminded her, placing her hands on his hips as he swayed
along to the music playing over the speakers. Then he slid
her cardigan off, kissing her bare shoulder. "How did your
shoulder get glitter on it?"

"I was born in glitter. Dipped in it like, like…an ice
cream," Olivia commented, wrinkling her own nose when
Mon laughed, pressing his nose into her shoulder. "Mon."

"Yes…?"

"You're so distracting." She sighed, using her hands to lift his chin so she could kiss him, like she couldn't get enough of him. Her fingers ghosted over his nipples, and her touch sent heat shooting to his stomach and down his cock, hard in his sweatpants. "You don't even have to do much and I think you're hot."

"I try very hard, actually." He scooped her up by the thighs, and Olivia's legs wrapped around his waist. He moved in until he pressed her against the wall, until she arched her hips against his, and his entire lower body tightened, his hands flexed on her bottom.

"And yet all this feels so effortless." She teased him. He was aware, but he couldn't bring himself to bite back or say much when Olivia was grinding herself on his cock. Then it was hard to think altogether.

Mon didn't usually come into things with a plan. He grew up wanting to be a lawyer, and he ended up running a record label. He wanted to write a song or two, and here he was making music for a movie. He tried, but things never went the way he wanted them to. Tonight was no exception. Because while he wanted to take his time and go slow, there was too much desire, too much heat, and he wanted it. He wanted her to melt under his touch.

So he brought her to the couch, the ugly bouclé couch that was too weirdly shaped to sit on comfortably, but gave him just enough room to lay Olivia on her back and tug on the ribbon of silk around her waist until her robe slid open to reveal her body. Her eyes darkened with desire, her warm brown skin slightly flushed.

"I can't believe I'm here." He chuckled, as Olivia's hands smoothed over his bare arms, sending goose bumps up his skin. "You're so beautiful."

"Hmm, right back at ya, stud." Olivia winked. "Oh God, that was cheesy."

"I like cheese." He kissed her lips, moving down to her throat, her collarbones. "Kesong puti, Cheez wiz…"

"Parmigiano-Reggiano?" The name came out in a breathy gasp as Mon showered kisses on her breasts, licking around her nipples, sucking at their curves. He squeezed one, making Olivia arch and throw her arm over the back of the couch to keep steady.

"Queso de bola." He snickered, and his nose touched her stomach, nipping lightly at her skin. "God this is—"

"Making you want cheese?"

"Among other things," he agreed, then quieted her laughter by kissing her lips. Olivia brushed her fingers over his jaw. But Mon was determined to do what he wanted, to take charge, as she wanted, and found himself between her legs. He opened her thighs with a light touch along the inside, smiling in satisfaction.

"Mon, what comes after 3.14?" she asked suddenly. He was already at her thighs, his lips hovering so close to her skin he was sure she could feel it, but—

"One." He kissed the skin there. "Five." He sucked on the skin, and Olivia sighed blissfully above him. "Nine." He moved up, closer to where she needed him to be. He nosed the hair around her labia. "Two."

He spread her open with his fingers and gave her a little lick. Olivia's hips rose in response, and he did nothing to stop that urge as he continued to draw out her pleasure, using her voice and the sounds she made to guide him in his exploration of her body. He enjoyed this, enjoyed being able to make her moan and hold back her sighs. He needed to get deeper, wanted more of her.

"Up," he breathed. He tapped her hips and Olivia complied, as Mon grabbed one of the ball pillows (seriously, pillows shaped like a ball, *why*) and used that to angle Olivia's hips just right. Her voice was louder, every moan she held back released, encouraging Mon even more. He looped his arm around her thighs to keep his position, letting her writhe and move as he explored the inner folds of her body.

The audible sounds of her pleasure had an unexpected effect on him. The higher her pleasure went, the more he wanted her. His hips were grinding into the couch, his cock seeking anything to rub against.

"Mon," Olivia chanted, her hand raked in his hair and tugging. "Fuck, Mon, I'm so close, just, just—"

There was another ball pillow that managed to wedge its way into the perfect spot between his legs, and Olivia's hand freed from his hair and fell on his shoulder with a loud smack, her nails raking his skin as Mon absolutely did not let up. His own thrusts were vigorous, and as Olivia's heels dug into his back, Mon pushed himself up to take a breath, and God was he seeing stars, because he was...he was...

"God...damn it," she said, between pants, cheeks still pink. "Did you just come?"

"Tang ina. I—yes." Mon lifted himself up and completely

off Olivia, where sure enough, a huge stain marred the inseam of his sweatpants. Yeah, that was not fun.

Both he and Olivia looked at the evidence of the completion of his desire. And while he wanted to bury himself in the bouclé and stay there, Olivia's face shifted from disbelief, to amusement, to full-on laughter.

"Oh my God," she said between laughs, clutching her stomach. "You did. You came. You are adorable."

"I thought I was a stud," he muttered, pulling the tie on his pants now, suddenly feeling the need to throw them somewhere far, far away. "Give me a minute. Or…five?"

Olivia sat up and mimicked his pose on the couch, fingertips on his jaw as she lazily kissed him, brushing at the wetness on his lips with her thumb.

"You can be both," she told him. "You didn't think you were going to come, did you?"

"Your voice, it…it turned me on. A lot," he explained, pressing his forehead against hers. "You do things to me, evidently."

"Sana everyone."

Mon chuckled, but didn't feel very much like correcting her. Olivia moved off the couch, robe still open and billowing behind her as she made her way to the bedroom. Presumably she was off to take a shower, this was as far as they were going to get tonight.

But Olivia looked over her shoulder instead.

"Job's not done, Moning," she told him. "Grab a drink of water, get hydrated and come to bed."

Thank God for American tap water being potable, because Mon was sure getting water from a dispenser was never going to be fast enough.

"I got you water," he announced a minute later, walking into her room—an almost exact, Pinterest-worthy duplicate of his, except she had actually unpacked, and didn't just have a half-empty maleta open in the middle of the room. Mon tripped on it every night, but did he ever move it? No. Also, not the point.

"You didn't have to—thank you." She reached for the water and took a sip.

The lights were off, but there was more than enough illumination coming in from the streetlights for him to see clearly. Olivia Angeles waited for him on the bed, pulling a condom from a nightstand after she placed the glass of water on the table.

"Come here." She opened her arms to him, and he came over, catching her lips in a kiss. Mon wasn't a fan of lying on top of bedsheets—something about his outdoor germs in the bedroom—but he lay on this back next to her anyway, looking up innocently at Olivia. She was haloed in the warm yellow light, her finger tracing shapes on his chest, making a loop around his left nipple and down the center of his torso. He felt languid and warm, maybe because he came really, really hard on that couch.

"I would like to be in a rom-com," Olivia told him, resting her arm on his chest and her head on her arm. She made it sound like a wishful, fanciful thing that could never happen, but between the two of them, it was more likely to happen for her than it was for him. "I want to be in one where

I don't have to put on an accent, and it's not weird that I like sisig and lechong paksiw, and I don't have to explain it."

"Sisig and paksiw, huh?"

"Yeah, with mountains of rice? Yum." Oliva made a funny face that made Mon laugh. "They don't make it the same here. Not enough onion, too much mayo, and they cook the egg, which makes no sense."

"Okay, but rom-com?"

"Right. I want to just be able to play it right. Being FilAm, without assuming anything of Pinoys either. I don't want to be the best friend, or the bitch that tries to steal the man. Sometimes I don't even want to be the outer space queen who has to keep everything together all the time." She sighed deeply. "There's a scene in *Big Fish* where the leading lady opens a window, and Obi-Wan Kenobi is standing in a field of a thousand yellow daffodils."

"Obi-Wan Kenobi?"

"And he's wearing a navy suit, and he has the biggest smile on his face for her." Olivia looked like she had been there. And Mon had seen the movie, but he had never seen her so happy. "I want to be a part of big moments like those."

"In real life, or in movies?"

"Both," she decided. "I could be in both."

"I'll be sure to send you a thousand santan flowers." Mon grinned.

"Don't try to cheat me, Mon. They should be orchids at least." Olivia wrinkled her nose, but he could easily imagine that for her. A woman in love was a beautiful thing to behold, and he was a firm believer that love was for everyone. For him, yes, but for her, definitely. A thousand or-chids' worth, for sure.

"Anyway. That's my big revelation," Olivia pronounced. "Being a best friend is great, but I want a story, you know? A really good story."

"You deserve it," he agreed, placing a hand behind his head. "You've thought about it a lot, huh?"

"I always think about it," Olivia admitted, looking away. "I just don't say it out loud because...you know. It might seem disingenuous. And there's the power of words. Mani-festing and all that. I don't want it to backfire on me."

"You know that sounds like the kind of thing you should be able to work on if you wanted to," Mon mused. "Like make those things happen for yourself and for people like me, if that's what you wanted."

"Like, now showing, an Olivia Angeles original?"

"Something like that." Mon chuckled, even if he could so clearly picture that happening for her. Expanding her career the way she wanted, taking her to places where she would thrive. He wondered how he would fit into those plans, idly, in the back of his mind. She shone so brilliantly in front of him it was hard not to look away, and the more he basked in that light, the more Mon wanted to be a part of it. "You like making decisions."

"I do."

The room went still, and quiet, and Mon knew he was pushing Olivia more than she was ready for. But she could always opt out, and he wouldn't be upset. He didn't need her to tell him everything.

"Were you disappointed?" she asked suddenly. Mon looked at her in confusion when she turned her head to him. "When you realized I was Olivia Angeles. Some people are. They wish I was actually a coldhearted ice queen. They wish I was in love with Colin."

He didn't pretend that the thought didn't sting. But Olivia hadn't said it to make him jealous. In fact, he had nothing to be jealous of.

"When I met you, you were wearing a dress—"

"A fucking Heleyna Campos dress." She smiled. "There's a difference."

"My apologies. A fucking Heleyna Campos dress." Mon chuckled, rubbing her back with his free hand. "You were putting yourself on display. The parts you were comfortable sharing. Then you wanted my pancit canton. I could never be disappointed by that."

"Heyyy. Stranger danger is real, okay," Olivia pointed out. "I'm lucky it hasn't happened yet but it *does* happen. Seriously though, Mon. I can't be the celebrity you imagined."

"Of course not." He snorted, and she was frowning at him. "Because what I imagine is a face and a few details you're comfortable sharing with the world. That's not a person," he explained. "You like vanilla and other boring flavors—"

"Okay, no cheesecake for you next time, noted."

"—you like feeding people, and you love what you do so much you throw yourself into every role," Mon continued, pretending not to hear. "And you can't stand for it to not go the way you want. Which is a compliment."

He reached up to thread a hand through her hair, brushing

his thumb against her cheek. It was an intimate touch, but it was necessary. He wanted her to know how much it meant to him, that she opened herself up to him like this. Because these were the parts of herself she chose to show him, the parts that made Olivia the woman he was in love with.

"You hide the softest heart," he told her. "I don't take it lightly that you've shown it to me."

He smiled and brushed his thumb against her bottom lip, like he was leaving a kiss. He encouraged her to open her mouth, but Olivia frowned and lightly bit the top of his thumb instead, making him jerk back in surprise.

"What!" he exclaimed. "You bit my finger!"

"That was barely a bite." She laughed. "Also, you're not in charge anymore."

"What?"

"Nope." She shook her head before she placed her leg over his thighs so she straddled him, her smile wide and happy. Her hair tumbled over her shoulders, the lights giving her a warm halo. "You had your chance, but you blew it. Pun intended."

He wanted to touch her, and he reached out to do so, because he needed to kiss her, and tell her how beautiful she was—but Olivia smacked his hand away again. Playfully, but still. Again.

"I wasn't kidding." Olivia kissed him, her tongue dipping inside his mouth and Mon moaned. She did not seem to notice. "I'm in charge now."

Mon tried to touch her thighs again, but she caught the movement and took his wrist. Then she joined it with his

other wrist and placed both over his head. To be fair, Mon
wasn't exactly unwilling.

And now that he had demonstrated his willingness to
comply, Olivia reached down between his legs to grasp his
half-hard cock.

"Getting hard already, Mon?" she purred into his ear, and
his insides melted, more so when she started to stroke him
with her hand. "You like this?"

"Mmm," Mon gasped, and he knew it wouldn't take
much for him to be ready again. She kept stroking him,
and he responded so easily, putty in her hands. Mon's hands
squeezed around the top of the headboard. It killed him that
he couldn't touch her, but Olivia seemed determined to
make him wait until the very last moment before she gave
him permission.

He was fully hard now, moisture dripping from the tip
of his cock. She spread it around to make the motion even
smoother. Mon moaned when Olivia twisted at the tip,
arching his back.

"Oh my God, Olivia. Olivia, fuck, you have to stop, I'm
going to—"

"You know you're blushing," Olivia noted, but she
stopped, slowly releasing him. She ducked out to grab the
condom, and Mon put it on himself. Olivia straddled him
again, and when he was ready, she sank onto him, her head
tilted back. She gasped. "Ohhhh."

"Now?" Mon asked, pushing his hips up to meet hers.
"Can I touch you now?"

"No." She shook her head, but the smile on her face

was all satisfaction. She bent down to kiss him, stealing the breath from his lungs. He craned his neck, just to get more of her, but she sat up again and resumed the pace she wanted, her hands on his torso to keep herself steady. She was right. This was torture.

"You fill me up so well, baby," she told him, closing her eyes, sinking her hips into him, harder. This wouldn't do. Mon wanted to touch her, wanted to make her smile that much himself. He just needed to change the angle, do *something*.

He took advantage of Olivia's pace to raise his knees, feet on the bed, and used that as leverage to haul himself up so Olivia straddled his lap. She blinked in surprise, but didn't break her rhythm, holding on to Mon's shoulders instead. He was pushing up and into her now, and it took his pleasure much higher, even as he didn't touch her.

"Oh you clever boy." She rubbed her nose against his, kissing him back. The change in the angle was exactly what they were both looking for. "I'm almost not annoyed. You're so good at this."

"Yes," he said. "Yes, I am."

They continued their pace, her noises that filled the room encouraging him to go faster, deeper. Because he wasn't allowed to hold her, Olivia kept slipping. But she was nothing if not tenacious, muscles clenching to keep her place.

"Now?"

"No."

Mon could feel his orgasm building for the second time that evening, his stomach tightening, his toes and hands curling. Their bodies were slick and wet, and Mon ached to touch her. Ached to keep her steady in his arms.

"Now?" he asked. Her inner muscles squeezed around him. "Olivia—"

"Now," Olivia gasped. "Mon, touch me now, I'm almost—"

He didn't need to be told twice. He smoothed his hands over her thighs, then her back. He gave her breasts a squeeze, sucking the tip of one, then the other. But now that he could touch her, there was one thing he wanted to do.

"Mon!" Olivia gasped when he pressed his hands to her bottom, slamming her into him. Her inner muscles clenched around him and she was coming, gasping into his ears as her fingernails dug into his skin. Mon thrust up against her, once, twice, three times. The emotion exploded in him, and the next thing he knew he was coming with a shout, holding her tight because he didn't want to let her go. His body stiffened as he came into the condom, and every jerk and movement that came after felt out of control.

He collapsed backward on the headboard, Olivia on his chest as they both came down from the high.

"That was—" He began. Nope. He didn't have words anymore. Filipino, English? Nothing.

"That was," Olivia agreed, and there was a short moment of silence before she giggled. "God, you came hard, huh?"

"Yes, yes, I did. With you, I do." He wrapped his arms around her, taking a deep inhale. "Humph. Amoy araw."

"I never knew what that meant," Olivia said, but she seemed to understand it well enough to poke his dimple again as if in punishment. "You 'smell like the sun' sounds wonderful."

"You know the sun is an oppressor on my side of the world." Mon chuckled. "The bane of moms and Lolas alike."

"It brings light and warmth! And there are some days it just hits perfectly." Olivia's argument brought to mind the first day they'd actually spent time together, walking around New York with music. The sunlight had been perfect that day, and made his heart flutter at the thought.

He made a noise in assent, but Mon slowly realized he was tired. Exhausted, in the way he was exhausted on a good day. He was relaxed and languid, and maybe after orgasming twice he deserved some kind of rest.

Olivia must have sensed he was going out like a light, because she chuckled and patted his chest.

"You're still inside me, babe. Clean up muna. Drink water."

He grudgingly agreed, only half-awake as he disposed of the condom and washed off. When he came back, Olivia was under the sheets, on the left side of the bed, clutching a pillow and smiling at him. The light was hitting her, perfectly contained in a rectangle of it.

"You make me happy, Mon," she told him. "Really happy."

"Me too," he said, and even with the noise of the city outside, the sun coming up on the horizon faster than they thought, the words still felt louder, more loaded and more significant. They filled the room and made it feel even warmer. "Exhausted. But really happy."

And it was when he came back to bed, holding Olivia in his arms, that Mon wondered if he would have more nights like this with her. He hummed a new melody, waiting for sleep to take him as Olivia snuggled his chest, her hands folded under her head. Mon wrote music on her skin when she slept, writing lyrics and weaving harmonies in the dark.

He wanted to get used to this, he really did.

But in the back of his mind, he had the feeling he wouldn't be allowed to keep her.

It was that part of the movie where everything went absolutely right, absolutely, perfectly normal—until something happened to irrevocably change it all.

He held Olivia close and chased the feeling away, keeping the music to himself before he finally fell asleep.

Nine

@OliviaAngeles story: [a photo of an unidentified Chipotle store in New York, posted 3h ago] The American diner experience was not groundbreaking enough for him.

@KimVia For WHO?

@Tala_Star91 [sent story to @LadyTalaQueen] Soft launch ba itey???!!!!

@MaxAngeles HEYYY how come we didn't go to Chipotle last time I was there???

"There are *so* many restaurants in New York." Olivia collapsed dramatically on the hard, plastic seat across from Mon. As ever, the man looked calm, observant and very, very handsome. His new glasses made him look like he studied ancient tomes in a library, and he wore a T-shirt maybe a size too big, but he just made it look effortless and cool.

"So many," Mon agreed, crossing his arms over his chest and peering at her above his glasses. His dimples popped out for extra effect, and Olivia wanted to sit on his lap.

"We could have had onion, poppy seed, or even everything bagels with a whole mess of fillings."

"*I* could eat all those bagels with a whole mess of fillings. *You* would order—"

"Yes?"

"A bagel with plain cream cheese. Whole wheat if you were feeling adventurous."

Damn it. And he must have known he was right, because Mon looked immensely proud of himself, until he started to giggle, his cheekbones prominent as he gave her his full eye-crescent smile. But Olivia was not to be deterred, and elected to ignore him.

"We could have had a classic American diner experience at Denny's."

"There's a Denny's in Manila. There are actually multiple Denny's in Manila. IHOP closed down. Personally though, Pancake House parin." He shrugged. "Their spaghetti is awesome."

"Shake Shack!"

"Also already in Manila," Mon pointed out, grabbing another corn chip from the free bag. He seemed to be enjoying the corn chips a lot. "They have an exclusive ube shake flavor, but I prefer Manam's. Shakes should not be that custardy."

"Olive Garden?"

"Opening soon, I think. But Mama Lou's is pretty tough to beat in the overpriced pasta market."

"To think that when I met you, I thought you were this quiet, unassuming sweetheart," Olivia mused, resting her chin on her palm as she grabbed a corn chip, too.

"Surprise. I'm a highly opinionated monster." He grinned and gave her a wink, which was pretty endearing until he tried to open the bag of corn chips more and it kind of exploded in his hands. And *that* made the whole morning trip to Chipotle worth it for Olivia.

It was her morning off—there were no shoots today, no interviews, auditions, meetings or callbacks, just a party tonight that they were both invited to. So they had time for this, for her to feel herself around him.

After lunch, Mon declared his newfound love for Chipotle. ("I can totally make it at home."—"Please don't. I don't want you cutting off your thumb for an avocado.") The two of them walked back toward the apartment building, holding hands and enjoying the lovely afternoon sunshine.

It was almost too perfect, the two of them walking to the park with an old subway station and sitting on the benches while sipping their little coffees and gigantic cookies from Levain that they'd made a detour for. It was a perfectly touristy afternoon, and Olivia had missed having afternoons like this. It was just a nice, normal day out, and she soaked it in like a sponge. But there was something familiar about this place. Like she'd seen it before.

"Oh my God," she said, when she recognized it. "This

is the park from *You've Got Mail*." Olivia seemed absolutely thrilled as she looked around. "'I hope your mango's ripe'?"

Mon watched her, confused. "What?"

"That scene in the movie, where they go to a farmer's market? And Tom Hanks is eating a pretzel and has a single, sad mango?" Olivia lived and breathed her romantic comedies. She'd grown up with them, and her ideas about love were formed by lines like, "I hate the way I don't hate you. Not even close, not even a little bit, not even at all," and "I'm so stupid to make the biggest mistake of falling in love with my best friend!" In those worlds, things could still be wrong, could still be unfair and have their hurts, but you were carried through by the promise of hope and happiness at the end. Who wouldn't love those?

Rhetorical question, thanks.

"What does a sad mango look like? And I've never seen—"

"What! Okay, we're watching *You've Got Mail* later." She shook her head, excited. "I mean I know it doesn't really hold up, but it was 1999, and it's just so delightful. Enchanting, even."

And they just…kept talking. They wove in and out of every single thing that popped into their heads, because there was nothing else they had to do. They stayed in the park because there was nowhere else they would rather be. Olivia had missed this, missed talking like this to people who weren't Max. Their conversation started deep, and then went so light and frothy she was describing her favorite cartoon koala, "his ears fall off when he gets surprised, and he has an endorsement deal with a ramen company in Korea!"

Mon talked about the hundred-year-old narra tree at his sister's private school, how he used to be afraid of going near it when he picked his Ate up from school, because his yaya told him there was a nuno that lived there.

"And I totally believed her, until one day our driver laughed and was like, 'nunos don't live in narra trees. Kapres do.'" His voice was deep like he was recounting a gruesome horror story, and she was totally buying it. "I never left the car when we were picking up Ate. Whenever I misbehaved, all she had to do was remind me of the narra tree and I would immediately get my shit together."

"Poor baby Moning," Olivia cooed, imagining a little Mon with chubby cheeks and small eyes, terrified of a tree. Olivia could only understand about half the things he was saying, but she was riveted. Mon was a funny storyteller, his hands waving around, but he focused on remembering details, pulling his audience in. She supposed it was leftover from him being a performer, but she wanted to keep listening to him.

She was about to ask him how he got over his fears when her phone started to ring. She pulled it out, wondering who would be calling her on her supposed day off (humph).

"Sorry. It's my agent," she said. Mon nodded and took a sip of his coffee. "Mercedes, I don't want to—"

"Oh my God. Are you sitting down?"

Olivia froze. She knew that quiver of excitement in Mercedes' voice. Her agent usually tried to compose herself when delivering good news, usually preceded by a little victory dance before calling. Mercedes had done it in the girls' bathroom after her crush asked her to prom, and Olivia liked that her friend still had not outgrown the habit.

"That depends," Olivia said, speaking slowly to get a rise out of Mercedes. "You sound excited."

"They want you." Her words came out in a breath, making up for the seconds Olivia had dragged out. "*Luna's Landing* officially wants you to play Inez Duhatan."

All the breath left her lungs. She'd expected Mercedes to tell her about *Conquerors*, but this...this was completely unexpected. She smacked her hand on Mon's thigh, making him jump before looking at her like a wounded bird.

Oh my God. She mouthed the words at him, but only got the face equivalent of a *?* in return.

"They want you in Indonesia in three months, then Barcelona right after," Mercedes was saying. "It's going to be grueling, I'm not gonna lie. Especially if *Conquerors* starts filming too."

"But I thought—"

"The author is apparently a big fan of yours," Mercedes continued. "I saw she liked that photo of you at the MoMA. And the one at the Edward Hopper exhibit. And the Basquiat. So I tracked her down and said *you* were a fan. The author later tweeted about you being a fan and said you would make a perfect Inez. One of the studio exec's kids is a fan of the author, and watches *Conquerors* religiously. She tweeted at her mother asking why they hadn't cast you yet. So the mom went to the production team and they pulled out your audition tape, and here we are."

Olivia couldn't believe it. The chain of events, the conversations that must have happened in between. She'd been too afraid to ask for the role, but Mercedes had been one step ahead of her. The author had advocated for her, and this *rarely* happened for people like her.

"Fandoms save the world, wow."

She noticed that Mon had his palm up on his thigh next to her hand, patiently waiting for her to hold it. She reached for him, squeezing to release some of the tension. She was *not* about to cry in the middle of the park in *You've Got Mail*.

"That's amazing," she managed to say. "They want me as Inez for *Luna's Landing*."

Mon's jaw dropped, and the happiness on his face was brighter than the sunshine. Olivia felt overwhelmed with joy.

She'd thought that when she landed Lady Tala, it would be her last big role. But *Overexposed* blew it out of the water (outer space and contemporary New York were different things, but still). She legitimately thought that after this, she would have to go back to speaking fake accents and passing for not-Pinoy characters.

But here she was, with another role of a lifetime. And they said that while two was a coincidence, three was a pattern. This was a pattern she was more than happy to be stuck in.

Mercedes gave her more details, talked about contracts that needed negotiations, schedules that needed to be worked around (just in case), but the role was hers. In three months, Olivia would fly to Indonesia for a month of shoots and training, then to Barcelona where she would presumably pretend to steal a Juan Luna painting. She was thrilled, to say the least.

"Congratulations." Mon's voice was warm after Olivia hung up. "You'll be an amazing Inez."

The name out of his lips stole the breath from Olivia. Right. Mon. What would happen with Mon? Could they still have this, post-*Overexposed*? Loneliness was waiting, but Olivia refused to acknowledge it. Not yet. And if she could have this? There was no reason for her not to have everything else she wanted.

"I know I will." Olivia smiled, reaching out to lightly scratch at the nape of Mon's neck. It was oddly soothing, and she slowly recalled it was something her Dad would do when they were sitting at Mass, and he was bored. Before she could think too much about it, Olivia pulled Mon in for a kiss. He tasted sweet, like coffee and chocolate chip walnut cookies.

"Hey Olivia," he said when they split apart for a breath. "Let's have sex."

Olivia was not a very sentimental person. But she felt it anyway as she and Mon kissed on his couch. A kind of fondness that didn't need to be said out loud. It hit her how a month ago, she didn't even know that Morningview could kiss like this, or that he would make her feel this happy.

Now she knew Morningview had a sweet tooth, but liked his coffee black. That he liked afternoon walks but didn't have places to do it, that the insightful things he rapped about in his music paled in comparison to the things he said in real life.

But she knew all of that now, and as she took off his T-shirt and smoothed her hands over his warm, brown skin, she wanted to know more. The feel of his erection between her legs was hot, wet, and Olivia moved her hips over him quick, seeking her release.

"Slow down." Mon chuckled, filling her with his cock and setting a slower, more languid pace. Sex was supposed to be fast, and hard. She liked it that way. But he kissed her, and she knew he was trying to distract her somehow. "Let me be in charge again."

"Okay, fine," she said. But Olivia had to admit, there was something luxurious about this, about Mon being able to go deeper inside her, spend the time to shower kisses on her breasts, to squeeze her hips and tell her how beautiful she was. "You want it to last longer."

"Ah, can you blame me?" he asked, and that grin of his was going to undo her. Then he did something with his hips that made Olivia's eyes roll to the back of her head in pleasure, and maybe she was a fan of the slow sex. Her entire body tightened with every press of his hips, making her twist and writhe so much that Mon had to press a hand to steady her.

"Be good," he said, the words firm but amused before he kissed her so she couldn't say anything back. Olivia could get used to this, to Mon being calm and so perfectly in charge.

"I'm always good," she said anyway, but it was getting harder and harder to speak, or even think when they were moving like this. Her orgasm burst through her body without her knowing it was about to happen. It whipped her, and she clutched Mon, squeezed her thighs as she milked his cock.

"Oh my God," she gasped, collapsing backward on the couch, her arms over her head in total surrender to the feeling. *"Mon."*

Her voice came out in a sigh of ecstasy, and it gave her endless pleasure that Mon moaned in return. He slid out of her, his cock still hard and stiff as it curved against his stomach. Olivia was too lazy to get up, so she slid down the couch and slid the condom off of his erect penis. She pumped him, squeezing hard and lightly raking her nails against his balls. It took little for him to come, bent over and spilling against her stomach and torso. Olivia felt a lovely satisfaction wash over her, like a cat stretching under a patch of sunlight.

"Yup," she said, palming the slick spread across her body. "I definitely like it when you're in charge. We should do it again next time."

A funny look crossed his face when she said that, but it was gone before Olivia could start to peel back the layers of what he was feeling. It was the strangest thing, watching Mon grappling with his own thoughts without saying a word, as they cleaned up, and she showered. She decided to give him his space, because she certainly wasn't ready to handle these discussions yet either.

"You've Got Mail!" Olivia exclaimed excitedly, seeing what he'd pulled up on his laptop screen while he sat with a bag of Trader Joe's dill popcorn. Olivia was a butter popcorn kind of girl, but he'd been fascinated, and who was she to deny him? "You remembered."

"Of course," Mon said, like it was an obvious thing, letting her take the popcorn bag and drape her thighs over his.

Mon had the best thighs, strong and dependable, and very, very fun to bite. "Okay, explain the premise—"

"It's 1999, email is exciting, and everyone was still comfortable talking to strangers," Olivia said dramatically, as the opening credits started to roll. Mon chuckled as he put on his glasses and munched on popcorn. "Ordering Starbucks was still funny, and in Upper West Side New York where we lay our scene—"

Her dramatic exposition was cut short by a buzz from her phone. She glanced at it and saw it was a video sent from Max on Telegram.

"Why is my brother eating birthday cake on the street?" she asked out loud, squinting at the video. It showed Max standing in a crowd so thick he was almost shoulder to shoulder with the people around him, Martha behind the camera asking him to describe what he was seeing.

"Someone brought birthday cake, and it was Estrel's, so I had to ask," Max explained, *holding up his plate that had a large slice of caramel cake, complete with a deep pink buttercream rose. Max's lips were already slightly stained pink, too. She knew they were in the middle of the street because there was a stoplight hovering above his head, but there was little room to move around in the massive crowd.*

"And what did the tita say when she gave you the corner piece?"

"She said I was too pretty not to get it." He made a frowny face, *but ate the cake anyway.* "Sarap naman."

"Happy birthday, VP!" Martha giggled. Max winked and came close to the phone to give her a kiss. "Shot puno!"

"He's at the Pasay rally," Mon explained as Olivia held the phone up to him. She couldn't describe the look on his face. Like he was...jealous? Proud? "Wow, that's a *lot* of people. They were counting four hundred thousand earlier."

"Four hundred tho— Why are they rallying?"

The shocked silence she was met with was heavy, like Mon just realized an elephant stood in the corner of the room behind her. Olivia didn't exactly keep up with current events in Manila, but clearly it was a thing for Mon, and her brother.

"Look at the video again," Mon said gently, pushing her phone back to her. "Tell me if you see it."

So she did, watching again. Then she understood what she was seeing. While she didn't know why Ariana Grande's "Break Free" was playing, she knew what "Never Again," and "Never Forget" meant. She didn't know why kulay rosas ang bukas, but she knew why people were angry, why this rally was a declaration and a celebration.

Mon seemed at a loss for where to begin. But Olivia's political knowledge only made it to 1986, when her parents left Manila after the EDSA revolution, and Mon filled in the rest. "I felt so bad coming into this presidential election season," Mon explained. "I was being given a buffet of terrible choices in the middle of a poorly managed pandemic. Just...terrible candidate after terrible candidate, all with selfish reasons for running."

"Marcos Jr.?"

"The worst of a bad bunch." He shuddered. "Anyway. On the last day to file candidacy, the vice president announced she was running. The one person with some competence said she was willing to fight, and it gave me hope. Hope like I couldn't imagine feeling. I might have cried a little."

She squeezed his hand. "Aw, Mon."

"That's why your brother is out on the street eating cake," he said. "Why Teddy is there, managing the concert. They're all there because they believe in hope, and want to do something to fight for it."

And while Olivia didn't have the shared experience they had, she understood fighting for hope. She understood making a stand, and making decisions about who to support.

"It didn't occur to me to ask," Olivia said, frowning as the video played again. "I knew there was an election, but I never asked who you were voting for."

In her circles, there were few people you could count on, much less people you could count on to agree on basic human rights, even fewer people who fought for them. "I'm like, apolitical," was a sentence she'd heard too often.

Even Olivia to some extent projected that. She made her donations, supported people who did the fighting, but never out loud. Never asked either. Never walked out to the middle of a busy street during a pandemic to eat birthday cake and support a presidential candidate's platform.

"Marcos is not a hero. And his son has no business running for this position." Mon snorted. "But I would vote for Leni for president any day. It physically hurts thinking about what she could bring to the job. The hope she represents."

The words hung strangely in the air between them, like they were in the same place, but Mon's head was completely elsewhere. Somewhere Olivia hadn't been in a long time.

"I'm really looking forward to voting when I get home."

The emotion in his voice was palpable. Strong. It meant a lot to him, and she didn't question it. But it felt strange, being alienated from something that mattered so much to him. He understood the nuances and every single moment of Max's video, while Olivia could only grasp the broad strokes. She knew Marcos was bad, that the EDSA revolution had happened, that her parents moved to the US because *their* parents feared for them. But details were never talked about, never shared.

And while nothing had changed between Olivia and Mon, something had...shifted, kind of. She could feel it in the air. A reminder that they weren't the same, that what he knew to be true wasn't hers.

They were about to rewind the movie back to that scene at the Starbucks (one of many) when Olivia's phone started to ring again. She flipped the side button to move to silent and saw the name flashing across her screen—War. Her stylist. She sent him a quick message that she couldn't answer right now.

Are you not at home? War texted instead. **Your manager said you needed to be ready by six.**

It was three. But Olivia knew better than to argue with their schedule. War was likely dressing more than one client tonight, and she didn't want to put the team behind.

"I have to go," she announced, sighing.

"Oh." Mon looked as disappointed as she felt, hitting Pause on the movie. "You want me to pause it here? We can watch later."

She smiled and kissed him, because he was so sweet, and she liked him so much. "I think my brain's too scattered to watch anyway. I'll see you tonight."

"Okay," Mon said, tugging at the hem of her shirt before Olivia kissed him again. And if she held on to him a little too tight, and let the kiss linger a little too long, then that was for her to know. "Wait. What's happening tonight?"

Now Playing: "Is This How You Feel?"—The Preatures / "I Belong in Your Arms"—Chairlift / "Rainsong"—Imago

"I love Regine Velasquez," Mon said, shaking his head in awe of the actress and her impassioned speech at the Pasay rally.

"She's a fucking superstar." Teddy's voice was choppy but he still heard it over the roar of the four-hundred-thousand-strong crowd. "I never knew!"

Teddy had initiated the call just after Olivia had gone, but the call itself didn't last because the signal was so terrible. But that was fine. Mon's head was already in a completely different place, where all the things he kept on loop restarted. Olivia had gotten the role of her dreams, and Mon wanted to go home. Thoughts that didn't fit with each other, no matter how he tried to rearrange them in his head. And with Olivia getting ready for tonight's event, he didn't have a way to release or process it, so they stayed with him, all the way to the evening. As he put the snacks away, as he got dressed, as he got in a car to go to Brooklyn. Or to Dumbo, the distinction wasn't made completely clear to him. Basta all he knew he was going to some event, or some party, and Leo was picking him up.

"Look at you looking sharp!" Leo said as Mon loaded into the provided SUV. "What a difference slightly skinnier pants look on those thighs, hmm."

"Er…thanks?"

"I've also been asked to ask if you forgot anything. Phone, keys, wallet, condom?"

"Why do I need a condom?"

"Aww, aren't you cute." Leo patted his thigh as Mon closed the door.

When Mon signed the contract to write music for the movie, he forgot the part where he might be invited to like, events and stuff. In fact, the thought never occurred to him, after living with the pandemic and online meetings for the last two years.

So when he learned he was expected to show up to this party tonight, he'd scrambled for a last-minute outfit fifteen minutes before Leo texted he was picking him up—slacks his Mom made him bring "just in case," his trusty turtleneck, and a black blazer with delicate white piping he'd picked up at a thrift store. Thrifting in a first world country was pretty amazing.

"We're gonna be stuck in traffic," Nelson, the producer for Colin's song "Hopelessly Hopeful," said from the front passenger seat. "Who thought it was a good idea to have a party in Brooklyn on a Friday night?"

Said party being held in honor of Colin. Apparently when you land the cover of *Vogue Korea*, you get a huge party at a warehouse theater in Brooklyn to celebrate that fact. Mon had never seen anyone as stressed as Colin's assistant was on the days leading up to this, but she seemed as thrilled as her boss that it was happening.

So there they were, on a lovely, starry night, after an hour of traffic, sipping champagne from flutes, eating tiny bland food with names he couldn't pronounce and observing a blown up half-nude shot of Colin with a lion. Mon was legitimately wondering why this was, what it was, and if he could pull off loose pants like that.

"He looks like Zoolander," Leo said behind him, sipping on his champagne flute while Mon choked on his. "In all the good ways, of course. Cheekbones and such."

"And such," Mon muttered to himself, as Leo found someone else he wanted to talk to. It was still kind of early in the evening. Nelson had been so concerned about the traffic that they somehow made it to Brooklyn in record speed. In fact, they were so early the guest of honor wasn't there yet. Mon didn't know anyone else at the party, and didn't feel like getting to know anyone else at the moment either.

"Morningview!" a familiar voice exclaimed, and Mon looked up to see JobJams walking up to him with the effortless ka-wapakels-an that came naturally to people in the music industry. "Hey man! Fancy seeing you at an event like this."

"I could say the same to you." Mon chuckled. "Did Leo invite you?"

"No, I'm dating one of the editors for the magazine. Small world!" he said, giving Mon a casual bro hug. He felt very cool. "Anyway, I actually wanted to call you. KST *loved* the track you sent. They really want to work with you on a lot more stuff."

"Oh, wow," Mon said, genuinely flattered. He made pop music a lot of the time, but to be recognized by the biggest boy band in the world right now was incredible. "Thank you, that's—"

"They're *really* interested in working with Triptych," Job-Jams continued. "I showed the guys that performance you and Teddy put on at that university fair a few years ago."

Yeah, he knew the one. It was UP Fair, and they did a cover of Parokya ni Edgar's "Yes Yes Show" and turned it into a whole rap battle. The crowd loved it.

"Turns out Beom-ie studied in Manila for a semester and saw it like, live. He got really excited and looked into you and Teddy. Thank God you told me about Triptych. I don't think they would have been as interested if you were tied to Swan Song, no offense."

"None taken." Mon shrugged, but it was true. He had built something in Manila, and it was certainly a hell of a lot more than what he had here now. Their studio was indie as indie could get, but it was something he'd spent the last seven years of his life working for.

"They'd love to fly you guys to Seoul to discuss work-ing together," Sungjoon said, handing Mon a business card for KST's agency, and his official title as "producer" under the same agency. "Shoot me a call or an email when you get back to Manila, yeah? I'll be back in Seoul then and we can arrange a trip. Tiger Balm's got a show at Rolling Hall in Hongdae. You'd love it."

"Cool," Mon said, slipping the card into his front breast pocket. Teddy was going to shit himself. Mostly because Mon was doing exactly that right now. JobJams gave him a wave and walked off to talk to someone else, and Mon was alone again.

He didn't really feel like mingling, didn't see much point after KST (holy shit). So he decided to walk out to the little garden, fenced in by brick arches that framed gorgeous views of the Brooklyn Bridge, the...other bridge he didn't know the name of and the carousel. It was like an anteroom of portals where you could walk through an arch and end up in a different world entirely. The river nearby made the evening chilly, but he had to admit, the view was beautiful.

His phone vibrated in his pocket.

There are two pizza places near the party. Juliana's or Grimaldi's. Choose one.

Is this a personality test? A choose your own adventure?

It's pizza! You can't go to New York without having pizza.

What is your idea of an original flavored pizza? Margherita? Pepperoni?

Yes.

Also, it's a date.

Ay, wait. I should probably ask you properly.

Do you want to go out on a date?

> I think it's Margherita. Which is fine,
> because I love Margherita.
> And yes. I would love to.

I'm giving myself one hour in that party,

then we're going to Juliana's.

For Margherita pizza.

Excited. ☺

> Can't wait. ☺

"Look at you, grinning with dimples and all," a familiar voice commented, and Mon looked up to see Colin Sheffield adjusting the watch on his wrist and smiling brilliantly. "Care to share?"

It took all of Mon's energy not to laugh, because Leo had put Derek Zoolander in his head and now he couldn't unsee it. He hadn't even noticed Colin come in, which was surprising given the fuss he'd generated.

Colin was the picture of a perfect movie star—perfectly styled blond hair, sharp, but conservatively dressed in a deep green suit that matched his eyes. People moved around him, fussed around him, and yet none of that seemed to faze him.

This was a man who knew he was tonight's star, and wasn't giving that up to anyone, for anything.

"Hey Colin," Mon noted, slipping his phone into his pocket. He half expected Colin to have extremely great hearing. The man radiated superhero vibes. "Great party. I love the lion shots."

"Well, my big three are all Leos, and I guess the Koreans wanted to celebrate that."

They shook hands, as men who didn't really know each other do, although why they did it, Mon wasn't sure. Until Colin pulled him in by the hand and drew Mon into his very tall, very handsome orbit. Colin was suddenly so close Mon could see the tic on his clenched jaw, his hand squeezing Mon's to a degree that was both unmistakably aggressive, but still socially acceptable. A very fine line.

"I'm really looking forward to when you have to leave." Mon was taken aback by the viciousness in this man he'd barely spoken a hundred words to. "I need her back to normal."

"Belligerent doesn't suit you," Mon remarked, smiling politely and putting distance between them.

Colin smiled back at him, but even his great acting couldn't hide the lines of tension forming in his face. Mon had no idea what Colin's deal was, and why he felt the need to say what he had.

"I knew her first. Back off." Colin stepped closer, his six-foot-whatever figure towering over him.

"Do you really want to do this here?" Mon asked, glancing around at the people who were starting to notice something was up. All the buzzing and fussing around Colin was going quiet, eyes wary and phones at the ready. Colin seemed to notice the same, and his jaw relaxed. "I didn't think so."

Mon knew when to fight and he knew when to back away. And this wasn't the time to fight. Clearly Colin had issues surrounding Olivia, and Mon wasn't a part of that. It was just…odd to see someone so confident (Colin) display his insecurity to a stranger (him). Was Colin really that fragile? Mon didn't care to know or find out.

Without waiting for Colin to have the last word, Mon walked off, suddenly sick of this party. He tucked his hands in his pockets and walked through the arch that led to the carousel. It was as good a place as any to get away. He had a feeling he knew what Colin's problem was, but the fact was that it was not *his* problem. There wasn't anything to do about it.

He sat on a nearby bench and sighed, watching the carousel that had a separate roof and doors. The bridge that was not the Brooklyn Bridge spanned next to the carousel, and the water from the river caught the lights shimmering from Manhattan on the other side. It was beautiful and surreal, to watch all this now.

All Mon wanted was to go home. There was work to do at home. *A lot* of work. And it was work he was willing to do, and commit to, no matter how hard it got, no matter how muddy the waters could become. He'd seen Olivia do the same, and he knew in his heart of hearts that he could do it too.

He pulled a pen and notebook from his breast pocket, JobJams's card safely tucked inside. And with the view in front of him, and the light that was just enough for him to see, he started to write. About loneliness and isolation, being there but not feeling like you belong at all.

He got a text. Leo.

Mamoncito, where are you? I want a photo
of you me and Olivia so I can caption it,
'as always, i am right.'

She's there?

Just arrived. Quickly please.

Now who was Mon to deny Leo anything at this point? He chuckled to himself and slipped his notebook and pen into his pocket, taking a quick photo of the scene in front of him to share to the group chat later. A small crowd had gathered at the garden. Clearly everyone agreed that the night was too nice to linger inside. And as Mon approached, it was hard to miss why.

Olivia was in the middle of the group. She looked absolutely dazzling in a red dress with big sleeves. Her lips were painted a deep shade of red. Her smile lit up the entire garden as people approached, asked for a photo, kissed her cheek, made her laugh. All Mon could think was that her sleeves weren't pizza compatible.

"How do you feel about what Colin said in the interview, that your relationship was special?"

"Olivia, here please! Thank you, darling."

"It's so great you showed up to support him, really sweet."

She looked up, and through the crowd, the rush of people around them both, their eyes met. Time seemed slow around him, like the dark, gray world was regaining color because of her.

"Congrats on landing *Luna's Landing!*"

"You'll make an amazing Inez."

She smiled. Then she did that thing where she nodded, but in a way that meant "come here nga," then pursed her lips in his direction. It made him laugh as he started to push through the crowd to her.

He was almost there. Just a row of people left before he made it to Olivia's side, where he could also see Leo standing nearby, speaking to someone Mon had never met. Sol was taking a picture with Olivia, and she was just about to say something to him when the crowd parted behind him, and a hush fell over the room.

Which could only mean Colin was right behind him.

And he was, striding through the space in the crowd like this was a scene from fucking *Conquerors*. There was a steely determination in his gaze that was hard to look away from, and even Mon stepped aside to let him through.

"We did it, Livvy!" he exclaimed. Mon had never heard anyone *ever* refer to Olivia as Livvy. He couldn't even recall a moment when anyone tried. "I just got the call. They're renewing *Conquerors* for two seasons, and Lady Tala is alive!"

"What!" Olivia exclaimed, the shock in her voice genuine as everyone around them cheered. It was so surreal to watch this moment—Olivia and Colin, him holding her by the waist and spinning her around, Lady Tala and Lord Aries celebrating a win. Lights and camera flashes surrounded them, and everything was glittery and beautiful.

"They want us in California tonight to celebrate," Colin said, finally putting Olivia down. "Are you game?"

Mon felt his heart sink a little. Olivia would say she didn't owe him anything, not even a pizza date at Juliana's, but still. Even he wouldn't blame her if she chose to go to California. He felt himself pull back, fully prepared to disappear from the crowd.

Their eyes met. He smiled, to let her know it was fine.

"Oh. Sorry, Colin," Olivia said. "I have to take a rain check on that."

She pulled Mon in. Through the people, through the cameras and phones, and deep into the inner circle. Until he could smell her perfume, could feel the warmth of her body beside his. "I've got a date."

"Olivia, you—" Mon started, but she squeezed his hand, giving him a wink because she had everything under control.

"Hungry? Fuck yes," she said, slipping her arm around Mon's and leading him out of the party.

They turned another corner, and the entire world fell silent, as they were finally alone. She stopped and grinned. Olivia looked up at him, the lights from the buildings in her eyes as she pressed him against a brick wall and kissed him.

Nothing could touch them in that moment. He placed her hands on his waist, letting her lead the kiss, letting himself melt into her.

Mon could hear music, a song that petered out into an echoey vocal like a whisper in the night. Two figures walking together on a darkened street corner, happy and quiet.

And as they kissed, he imagined a gritty rock ending, two guitars coming in to fill the space, and another playing a solo before the drums and bass joined them. It was a hot kiss, one that was happy and promising.

Then the entire band played together in a euphoric finish, filling the air with music and romance that made you feel *alive*, before it all went away.

He pulled away from Olivia, the outlines of her face perfectly clear in the night.

"Pizza?" she asked.

"Pizza."

Ten

@StarzNews: Spotted @OliviaAngeles and her mystery Tik-Tok dreamboat sharing a pizza in Brooklyn! The two were also spotted being "sweet" at @ItsMeColin 's Vogue Korea launch. Long live the kween! #ConquerorsTV

@LordAriesConquer new roles, new man? my girl is thriving

@PinkLavarn Infair, cute din sila. Chemistry daw!

@ConquerorsStansForLeni #LadyTalaLives my god im too happy about CQ S3 to react properly to this

@Hobibi dafuq that's @MorningviewMusic?????????????????
    @StarzNews Hey @hobibi we sent you a DM, babe!

"Aw, baby's first paparazzi pics," Olivia cooed later, lying on Mon's lap on her couch. Mon looked bemused as Olivia showed him a picture of them through the window of Juliana's. Mon's back was to the camera while Olivia laughed at something he said. He'd taken off his blazer and his elbows were on the table, leaning toward her.

"I've never seen the back of my head like that," he mused.

"We look cute. I'm using this as my profile picture," Olivia announced, doing exactly that on her phone.

Then she swiped at her screen and the photos changed to ones of them leaving the restaurant.

She was still wearing her dress, even if her shoes were off and her hair was down. Even Charlotte Tilbury's revolutionary matte lipstick didn't survive against a Margherita pizza, but it was at that point in the evening where she was too full and too happy to care.

The date had been really good—they'd ended up taking a walk around the park after dinner to help it all digest. They talked about their first times on planes, and funny travel stories. Mon told her about being taken to a foam party in Siquijor, and Olivia recounted her love affair with Orangina on her first trip to Paris.

Low key, low stakes. They were walking among other couples on dates, joggers getting some time in before the end of the day. It was all wonderfully idyllic. They even split ice cream from a place Max insisted they try nearby. Olive oil was definitely not Olivia's first flavor choice, but she was asking for it by going to a place called OddFellows.

There was no mention of what happened at the party, at the news Olivia had gotten tonight. There was plenty of time to celebrate her wins. Tonight, she just wanted to hang out with Mon.

Colin is calling.

Olivia swiped the notification away. Colin had been calling every time his car was at a stoplight on his way to Teterboro, texting to ask if she was sure she didn't want to fly, if she was sure she wanted to stay.

Fucking Colin. She didn't know if he genuinely cared about her or just found it convenient that he needed her so much. She had no plans of going to California, at least not tonight.

Not until she asked someone a very important question.

"So they're together, and she just…forgives him after he puts her out of business," Mon said finally, after that first, only and final kiss of the movie. As Harry Nilsson sang "Somewhere Over the Rainbow" and the camera pulled up, up, up and out, on a typical day in New York. "A business she inherited from her mother, that she loved, and was *everything* to her."

"Pretty much." Olivia smiled fondly at the screen, her hands tucked under Mon's thigh like a pillow. The *don't cry, Shopgirl, don't cry* line always got to her. "Don't you think New York can be just as much a cliché as Paris?" It was certainly gate-kept about the same.

"Seems a little too neatly wrapped," Mon continued. "Ganun lang? Well, not 'lang,' like I'm diminishing the entire journey we went through, it was fun. But I think I just want to see that resolution, or how they would navigate their new relationship."

"You wanted it to last forever." Olivia smiled, still watching the credits roll. "That's how you know it was a good one."

There was silence. Mon was obviously thinking about what she was saying.

"But—"

"Let's fanfic this," Olivia said, rolling over so she was looking up at him. The poor boy's brows were knitted, almost as if he was concerned for the fate of a former bookshop owner and the guy who loved her.

"Fanfic…?"

"Yes. I'm still an active member of a couple of fandoms, trust me I know my stuff. Do you know Hanahaki Disease? ABO?"

"What?"

"Never mind. So they're together, and yes, the bookstore is still an issue. A big one," Olivia continues, quickly coming up with a story. "So he quits his job with the corporation and helps her open a quaint little bookshop in Brooklyn, because the Upper West Side gets too expensive. Or she gets a book deal, and has a book launch at his store, and now they have to fight her publisher for movie rights. Life will move on, and they will be fine because they're white and they live on the Upper West Side. The important thing is that they're together, that they loved each other through letters—"

"Emails."

"And trusted each other. The end."

He seemed unsatisfied. So Olivia stretched it out, just a little more.

"The arguments will come, but as long as they stay com-

mitted, and they're happy? It's worth it to have those conversations, don't you think?"

Mon said nothing, and Olivia could practically see the
wheels turning in his head. She sat up instead, tucking her
toes underneath her thighs, getting Mon's full attention
when she squeezed his thigh.

"Am I selfish because I want more?" he asked her suddenly. Olivia shook her head and kissed him. She let the kiss
go slow and deep, rushing neither of them. And when their
lips parted, and she looked into those light eyes, the ones
that saw everything and nothing at all, she knew it was her
cue. If there was ever any moment to ask him about this,
it was now.

"Mon," she said gently. "Do you want to come to California with me?"

Her question was met with sudden, pregnant silence. The
air was thick with words he wasn't telling her, things he was
processing in very real time. But Olivia had been giving this
a lot of thought, had allowed herself the fantasy.

"Why?" he finally asked. She'd expected that question.

"Because you didn't like New York, and I can't stay anyway. I want to bring you to all my favorite places. You would
love the Getty Museum. They had a photography exhibit
once that I loved. I think it's still there. I've never been to
the LACMA, but I'm sure we could—"

"Olivia, I—"

"And Santa Monica! There's a place by the pier that has
amazing fish tacos. Max introduced it to me and he's held it
over my head ever since. And funnel cake, of course. And

Porto's Bakery? I think you would love it. We could even go to a big Target."

"But—"

"And when *Conquerors* wraps, we can go to Indonesia for *Luna's Landing*," she continued. She had this strange feeling that all she had to do was say the right words, find the right reason, and Mon would stay. She didn't even entertain the idea that he wouldn't want to. Why wouldn't he want to?

Of course she knew why. Deep down, she knew this was a futile effort. That she just didn't want to admit there was a problem looming on their horizon, and neither of them were talking about it. "I've never been, but Mercedes was telling me that we were flying in to Kuala Lumpur then Bali. And Bali sounds amazing, I mean based on what you've told me from your trip."

"It is, but—"

Her heart seized in her chest, like a hand had reached in and gripped it tight. He was going to say no. Oh God. Olivia scrambled for what to say next.

"No." The word was sudden, and firm, and it slipped out of her lips before Mon could say anything, because she could see it. Could tell he was about to give her all the reasons why he couldn't. She didn't want to hear why he couldn't. "I mean, don't give me an answer yet. Not tonight."

She placed her hands on his chest, trying to breathe slowly so the panic would recede. Was this panic? She should know, she'd played panic plenty of times. But it was always hard to compare something she summoned from inside to the experience of actually feeling it—her toes and fingers cold at the idea of rejection.

"Please think about it," she told him, and if it sounded like a plea, she was fine with it. Mon's fingers caught hers, his warmth spreading. He wrapped his arms around her, letting her bury her face in his chest. She didn't think he could hear her when she whispered, "I don't think I can bear the idea of letting you go."

The silence filled the room again, heavy and thick. It threatened to tear them apart before either of them could give an answer. Olivia couldn't help but feel like this was a perfect time for someone to yell "cut."

Now Playing:...

Well, well, well. Mon could almost hear Scott say, *How the turn tables.*

Why was it that life insisted on tearing people in different directions? And yes, by people he meant himself and Olivia. He supposed the tides of coincidences and destiny that brought two people together could also pull them apart, because randomness needed its opposite forces.

The chance of a lifetime or the girl of his dreams. It was almost cruel.

"It was cruel of her to ask you to stay," Ava announced over video call, unimpressed. "You know in some cultures, saying something like that can be considered emotionally manipulative."

"Ava." Mon groaned at his screen as Ava frowned at him from the other side. She'd been his first call after he left

Olivia's apartment. He couldn't even fully remember what excuses she made to end the night at that point, but he knew Olivia wanted to give him his space to think about what to say. It was just that he needed to talk to someone else about it. And Ava did say when he was ready to process...

And if he was truly honest with himself, if Olivia had asked him on any other night, on any night before this one, he would have said yes. He would have fully given himself to the idea of moving to the US. Would have committed to being the boyfriend of a celebrity, and whatever that meant. It might even have given him time to work on whatever Morningview was supposed to work on next. (But he was doing that already.)

But she'd asked tonight. On the night he was shown the things he had to go home for. Things he could still go home for. The Colin thing had concerned him, but it paled in comparison to KST, to staying Teddy's business partner.

Mon told himself he would finish the master for "Over-exposed," but here he was instead, calling Ava at five in the morning from his bedroom. Five a.m. his time, not Ava's, obviously.

"She was telling me how she felt. That matters."

"I know. But using your emotions to convince another person to do what you want is the definition of manipulation."

"It's not. You're the one who taught me these differences matter, Miss Attorney Juris Doctor."

"Please, Mon. Attorney is my father."

It made Mon laugh, and it was nice to share a laugh with

his friend, even if everything around him felt dire. There was a weight on his chest that only seemed to get heavier the longer he stayed away, the closer he got to leaving.

"But, okay. As your completely logical friend, I can tell you she's basically asking you to give up everything here and move to the US. Which is *not* easy."

"I know." He felt chastised, shifting on the bed where he was sitting.

"But you love her, so logically, you want to be with her."

"Logically." Mon sighed. Love wasn't logical, but it was strong. And he still felt it, even as he contemplated its end. Fuck. Was that why he called Ava? To mourn a relationship? There was still a voice in the back of his mind saying there was an answer, one he would find if he just kept thinking. "So given all the factors and the processing, your answer is…?"

"That I can't give you an answer." Ava shrugged, like she was almost sorry for him, and Mon could feel her Mama Hen vibes from halfway across the world. "Number one, I'm not a computer that can just make a big life choice for you. Even in this AI-generated universe."

"You certainly try."

"I tell you to put on sunblock, not follow your heart and move to the States," Ava scoffed. "Number two, I *don't* have an answer, because I'm not the one in love with Olivia Angeles."

It was strange. The way Ava said Olivia's name was different, like there was a weight to it wholly unfamiliar to her. But it wasn't to him.

Ava was right, and of course he'd known that when he started the call. But as much as he'd been thinking about this, for as long as he had, things certainly changed when he was being asked about it point-blank. Like noticing golden hour streaming through a window, only to blink and realize it was nighttime already and you'd spent an hour daydreaming.

"I don't know if I can make this choice, Ava," he said, feeling the weight on his chest bear down on him. "All the reasons are split, too good, not good enough. It's fucking awful."

"Then you have to tell her that. Or at least discuss it with her. Sometimes you have to have the hard conversations, Moning. It can't always be a thought exercise."

There was the sound of a door opening off camera, and Ava smiled at whoever walked in, then Scott's face came on-screen to give Ava a kiss. The moment was quick and sweet, even funny as he wriggled himself to fit on the chair next to Ava, or somewhat on top of her ("Babe, I'm a payatot, we can do this!").

And really, that was all Mon wanted for himself. He wanted to come home to Olivia, to kiss her hello and tell her she looked beautiful. He wanted for them both to be happy—for her to thrive in a career she could be proud of, for him to be able to keep making music. Where they could do that, or how, he didn't know.

"Go to sleep," Ava told him, and there was that Mama Hen voice again. "It'll be better when you wake up, I promise."

He wanted to tell her all the reasons why that wasn't going

to be necessarily true. So he said goodbye instead, giving in to Scott's request of giving them both flying kisses (fuck, he *was* the baby of the group) before he closed his laptop and finally fell asleep.

Eleven

Now Playing: "Langyang Pag-Ibig"—Ben&Ben / "Crying Over You"—Honne / "Landslide"—Fleetwood Mac

Mon felt a renewed sense of purpose the next day. Ava was right. Everything felt a lot less like it was crashing down around him when he woke up.

Was he exhausted because he hadn't slept, and thirty-year-olds really shouldn't be pulling all-nighters anymore? Yes.

But he felt better, like the fog had cleared up in his head, and he had the physical energy to deal with the thought process of what to do about Olivia.

Physical energy yes, mental energy, not so much.

Thank God he still had work. He finished the master of "Overexposed" in the apartment and sent it off to Leo before breakfast. Then he'd gone on a run around Central Park without hiding in a hoodie. A hot dog vendor had made a passing comment about the coming summer being "a scorcher," and

Mon just smiled and nodded. That was cute, considering he lived in a tropical country.

After a shower and lunch from a deli, he went to the studio and dived into the master for "Surrendering." Olivia's song. He got into a groove sometimes when he worked, like everything around him fell into place, and he knew exactly how to take the song from great to perfect, how to make the listener feel like they were standing in the crowd at Times Square with her. He was being a bit of a perfectionist about it, but hey, he was a Virgo, whatever that meant.

Your file "Surrendering (mastered)-Final.mp3" has been sent!

And that was that. Job done. Mon always felt a sense of finality when he sent off a song into whatever ether where it needed to go. Like the emotion had been fully unpacked, processed and released. His breath came out in a shudder, like he was trying not to cry.

But that was that. There was nothing left for him to do here, except pack and grab last-minute pasalubong for absolutely everyone in his life. There were a couple of pasabuys too, but that was a problem for tomorrow, or the day after. Right now, he just wanted to savor being done.

He closed his eyes and played the song one more time, feeling how tight his muscles were, how tense his body had been. He got a few messages from Leo.

Hey. Got the songs. Can't wait to give them a listen.
Also thank you.
Also they're doing the last reshoots at the High Line.
The observation deck.
Just saying.

He decided not to reply. There was nothing to say yet.

Mon stretched his arms over his head, rolling his neck. He had no idea what time it was; he usually never did when he was working. He looked around the studio, taking one last look at the furniture, at the way he'd rearranged things, made the place his own. He assumed someone was lined up to take over after him, but that didn't make the place any less his.

Then again, there was a much smaller office in Marikina waiting for him to leave his mark on it. Mon could build himself back up to this. And it wasn't going to be the last time he would work at a place like this, with people like Leo and Sol, even Colin.

It was a comforting thought.

The observation deck, as it turned out, was a short walk away (look at him finally understanding Google Maps, like a grown-up!). Security blocked the entrances, but Mon found a way through with an easy wave at security and his name.

He'd seen the High Line from the Whitney, and had meant to visit before he left. Mon had always liked the idea of repurposing outdated public utilities to become public spaces (the Huashan Creative Park sprung from an old brewery in Taiwan was his favorite). Here was something reborn into something else, just because someone had made the time and effort (sana all!). It wasn't the most beautiful park in the world, but it was a lovely walk. Mon had always enjoyed his lovely walks.

He could see the river on the left, the city on the right, and the streets below. He passed old train tracks with overgrown plants. The wind whipped at him and he stuffed his hands in his pockets and his hoodie over his head. Whether he was going to miss this weather was still up in the ether (ba dump tss), but it made for a nice walk. It really made you feel like things were better than before you started walking up here.

The shoot had taken over this entire stretch of the High Line, a member of the security team commenting it was to make sure nude bathers didn't show up (but why build sun chairs facing the river if you couldn't bathe nude in them?). The actual shoot was taking place at the observation deck a couple blocks from where Mon had entered. He could see a glass panel wall overlooking the busy street below, framed by the row of buildings that stretched into the horizon and sets of stairs where people could sit. It was a significantly smaller crew today, security aside, so it took very little to make his way closer.

The sky was spectacular. The sun was setting from behind, making the glass on the buildings look like they were made of amber, the rest of the sky painted in soft shades of pink, purples and cool blues.

And watching them were Olivia and Colin. Or, sorry. Jessamyn and her husband's name, whatever it was. Mon couldn't hear what they were saying, but they were looking intensely into each other's eyes, saying lines. Olivia bowed her head, shoulders dropping, before Colin traced a very delicate finger along her jawline, lifted it up and kissed her. Then the camera pulled away as they parted, farther and farther back, as much as they could.

And they lived happily ever after.

"And, CUT! That is a wrap on *Overexposed*, people!" Sol exclaimed, and everyone cheered, celebrating. Colin and Olivia hugged again, and Mon wanted to walk away, feeling crumpled. He forgot why he was here, wondered *why* he was here. He was being petty, but his heart was a fragile little thing, unfortunately.

He took a step back, ready to leave. He should have just waited for her at the apartment. He didn't have to come.

Just in time for Olivia to look up and call his name.

"Wait for me?" she asked him, her eyes still glassy and wet from the scene, her cheeks still flushed from feigned happiness. "Please."

Dread pooled in Mon's stomach. But he nodded.

"I'm sorry I made you wait," she said, after she managed to untangle herself from Colin, after she thanked Sol and hugged Leo, after she said goodbye to the wardrobe and makeup people, after she changed out of her costume and took off the mic they'd slipped into her clothes. She came to Mon after she managed to get her stuff back together, after she gave her assistant her keys so she could start packing up the apartment for her.

"It's no problem."

The network wanted Olivia and Colin to go on a bit of a mini press tour to promote the new season of *Conquerors* before they started shooting, so they had to prep for that. The new script was due soon, and they were officially in preproduction for *Luna's Landing*, after some last-minute negotiations. Olivia had signed on to be a producer, and she was thrilled, ecstatic. Over the moon. There were a million things to do, a million places to be.

And yet there was nowhere else she wanted to be than here.

"How did you know to find me here?"

"Leo told me," Mon explained as they walked back on the High Line together, their shoulders touching while their hands were too nervous to actually do anything. "He's...done a lot."

"That's saying something," Olivia agreed, and they reached a break in the walk where they had a clear view of the city, past the river and all the way to Hoboken. The sun was setting slowly, like it had all the time in the world. "So."

"Hmm."

"Have you thought about my question?"

Olivia was still a little raw from that last scene, from the entire process of shooting this movie. Normally she took this time to sit with herself and her feelings, to de-Jessamyn, if that made sense. But there was little time for either. She was due back in LA in a couple of days, and she wanted to go home, get her life back together to get ready to be Lady Tala again.

But all of that paled in comparison to how much she wanted Mon there. She couldn't put into words what he meant to her, what she wanted this to become. But she didn't want to risk him not being there.

"I have to go home," Mon announced. "I have to vote."

No.

"Your visa is valid until the end of the year, right?" Excuses, she was making excuses. But, God. *No.* "You can come back after the elections. Summer in LA isn't too bad. We can drive to San Francisco or San Diego. Or Disneyland! I bet we can get a guided tour. We can even watch a nerdy documentary on ride histories before."

She suddenly couldn't imagine LA without him there. There was no appeal in going thrifting at the Rose Bowl if he wasn't there to comment on the art. She'd pictured all of it, how she wanted their next three months together to be, coming home to him writing new songs and her with new scripts. Then Bali, then Barcelona. She would have loved to visit the Sagrada Familia with him.

Olivia had refused to accept the possibility that a life with Mon wasn't going to be her reality. It made her stomach turn.

"What happens when my visa runs out? I don't even know if I'd qualify for a tourist visa if it does. And you have work, which is great. But I have work, too. It was fine here, because I could walk and do things—"

"There are parks in LA."

"I can't drive," Mon explained.

Something inside Olivia was slowly shattering, and she could feel it, pieces rattling in her chest with every breath she took. She held on to the railing, trying to keep steady.

"Are you jealous of Colin, is that it?" she asked, because it couldn't just be visas and elections that kept him away from her. Yes, they were big things, but they were things that could be overcome, surely.

"I'm jealous he gets to spend all this time with you," Mon

said, touching her elbow before pulling his hand away, like he couldn't stand to touch her anymore. "And I don't have much of it left."

"Maybe I just don't mean that much to you."

"That's a fucking lie," Mon disagreed, wrapping an arm around her shoulders, pressing her against his chest as he kissed the top of her head. Olivia wanted to bury herself there and never let him go. She wrapped her arms around him, committing the moment to memory, telling herself it would be fine. It had to be fine. "You've come to mean everything to me, Olivia."

"But not enough to let go of your life in Manila."

"You're offering me museums and beaches, this whole LA experience. You want me to give up everything I've built in Manila, in exchange for an experience," Mon pointed out, and she felt laughter rumble in his chest as she held on to him.

"I wanted to be the one to lift you up."

"I was already as high as I wanted to be," Mon told her, and God, *ouch*. He didn't need her. He didn't need her at all, and yet she meant everything to him? But he wasn't going to stay?

"But is that the only reason why you want me around?"

"No!"

"So why, Olivia? Why do you want me to stay with you?"

"Because!" she exclaimed, and God, she didn't know what came after that. She felt it in her chest, an emotion trying to burst out of her, but she didn't have the right words for it. "Mon, please don't test me. This isn't fair."

"Asking me to leave everything behind was unfair," Mon

reminded her, and he was right. Totally right, of course. She'd made assumptions about his life and made a decision that hers was infinitely more preferable, without asking him what he wanted.

God. She'd done things wrong. Horribly wrong, and Mon was being so generous with her. She didn't deserve any of it, or him, for that matter.

"So that's it?" she asked, looking up at him even if it was going to hurt her, even if it was the memory she would carry with her forever—of her and Mon breaking each other's hearts before they properly bloomed, letting go of a good thing before either of them were ready. "All this, and you're just going to go?"

"So are you."

"I know, but—"

Now it was Mon's turn to silence her with a kiss, sweeping her breath away. Olivia held on to him like the train tracks around them were about to crumble into the river. Tears brimmed in her eyes, but she didn't let them fall. The kiss didn't distract her from her thoughts, not at all. But it did bring him close, as close as she was ever going to get again.

In the back of her mind, she still knew there was a way to write them out, a magic wand someone could wave to fix all this. But at the moment, her entire chest felt like it was full of blooming flowers, all threatening to choke her.

Mon brushed a hand through her hair, his eyes sad and his mouth pressed like he was piecing together the perfect words to end this. And Olivia could see he was about to walk away, the time they had so recklessly spent together was about to run out.

"Being with you was a dream, Olivia."

She didn't know what to say after that. Even if she wanted to, she was sure the words weren't going to come out, all stuck in her chest between the tears, the flowers, the roots and petals in vines that had grown around her heart.

"Don't say goodbye." She was angry. She was hurt, and she didn't want him to leave. "Don't you dare say goodbye."

"I'll see you again," he said instead.

They took one last look at each other. It was too trite to take pictures, to mark the occasion with anything else but a last look, cementing each other in their memories. Him, standing on that edge with her, with the sky alight in gold, pink and purple streaking behind it.

Then with a small smile, Mon lifted his mask back up over his nose, stuffed his hands in his pockets and walked away. The farther he went, the tighter Olivia's chest felt, and the words were all trying to tumble out of her.

But it was too late for any of that now.

She wished the car service driver good-night when they came back to the apartment. Olivia smiled at the concierge when she got the Postmates she'd asked her assistant to order. Things were fine.

But when the elevator doors opened on her floor, she had a sudden vision of the first time she ever met Mon, the pathetic looking guy sitting on the floor with all his belongings. She tried not to listen for sounds of him moving around his apartment, or his music, as she'd gotten used to doing in the last month.

Olivia entered her own apartment and closed the door behind her. Everything felt too empty, too quiet, even as nothing had changed. This wasn't even her place; she had no attachment to any of the belongings here. But still it was there, that feeling of everything being too still and too stale. *Hello, old friend*.

Olivia toed off her shoes and switched to a pair of house slippers. She padded to the kitchen and started to unpack her order—mild Laksa, catfish mango salad, fried crab cakes— it felt like too much food, like her PA had expected she wasn't alone.

Olivia pulled out her phone and started to navigate to her brother's number for a FaceTime call, stopped before she hit the button. She knew he would answer and hum about how Banana Leaf in Manila had excellent pad thai until she finally got around to telling him what was wrong. He would tell her she was not the asshole, and assure her she would be okay. That she hadn't done anything wrong.

But Max was proposing to Martha today. And she knew that because he updated her, sent her messages, made her feel like she was a part of it even if she was thousands of miles away.

She was supposed to start reading *Luna's Landing* too, but she felt too raw and at the end of her emotional rope for anything other than food and a sad girl viewing of *The Lake House*. Keanu in that glass house just encapsulated everything she was feeling, and Sandra's shaggy cut was cool now, so.

She was halfway through the movie when Colin proposed splitting a matcha cheesecake with him via text. She barely looked at her phone when she replied. **Pass. And you should know better.** Sol invited her to celebratory drinks downtown, but she didn't feel like bringing down the mood. Olivia had just sent her reply about needing to pack when her phone chimed with a notification from Leo. The subject made her entire body feel cold.

Surrendering—Final Version

There was no note, just an attachment. And because she was dramatic AF, Olivia slowly laid her phone on the coffee table, pushing the device's volume up to max before she hit Play.

The song started with two notes, repeated over and over. Then she heard her own voice, perfected and smooth, singing about wanting love, about wanting not to feel alone anymore. Mon had made the music perfect, and everything she wanted it to be.

The effect of her being recorded live was that it created a lot of audible space in the song, evoking images of her being alone in a room, with a single light spotlighting nobody but her. Making it more vulnerable and open. The recording picked up every quiver of her voice, every time she slightly strayed from Mon's demo. But still he made it sound like that was how it was always meant to sound.

Morningview had always been good at what he did. So good he'd built an entire career in Manila, so good he'd reached her, and made it here.

He didn't need LA or the LACMA or any of that. He had

a fan base in Manila, a job, a life. And Olivia hadn't offered what he really wanted, which was her. Her love, her distaste for anything she considered "too flavored," her taste in movies.

I would have wanted to stay just for you.

The song reached its climax. It was perfect and it made her want to get up and dance, spin around the room and open herself to absolutely every emotion that came.

But instead, Olivia wrapped her arms around her legs, pulling in close, and started to cry. Not because she was sad or unhappy. But really feeling everything was overwhelming, and allowing it all to come to her in one go meant tears had to come out.

For Olivia, who always had perfect control of how she felt, this was overwhelming and beautiful as much as it was difficult. And Mon had been the one to pull it out of her without him having to be there.

She played the song again, and it felt like physically releasing every emotion lodged inside her. Change was never easy, and she let herself feel it all. And in feeling, she found the words she wanted to tell him. Could find the real question she wanted to ask.

God, she *was* the asshole. But there was time to fix this. There had to be.

Twelve

Now Playing: "Ladyfingers"—Herb Alpert & The Tijuana Brass / "I Miss You"—Mamamoo / "No One"—Cold

"Well, this is a mood."

Teddy appeared at the door of Mon's shiny new office, leaning against the wooden jamb with his arms crossed over his chest. It was late in the afternoon, maybe. Mon didn't know what time was these last three days. Between coming home, the elections, the result...there was very little reason to keep track of time.

"Is that what the kids are saying these days?" Mon muttered from where his head was resting on his desk. It was his favorite feature of his new desk; it was the perfect height to rest his head on without totally fucking up his back. Good to know when his entire world felt off-kilter, or when he was so bone-tired he couldn't keep his head up, he could lie on his desk like this and feel relatively comfortable.

"Girl Crush hit five hundred thousand subs on Tik-Tok." That was excellent news, it really was. But the way Teddy said it made it sound like he was commenting on the weather. "We got a couple of brands approaching us for sponsorship, and the Wish Bus people want a couple sets with them."

"That's great." Mon was ecstatic, even if it wasn't obvious by his voice. The girls totally deserved that. "Can we vet the sponsorships to make sure none of them are apologists or something?"

"The reps found out about Girl Crush because of the Pasay and Makati rallies, it's fine." Teddy waved a hand around. It was scary how well Teddy had run Triptych while Mon was gone, enough that Mon felt guilty he wasn't fully adjusted yet. But Teddy was patient, and kept Mon looped in. He was a more generous friend than Mon deserved right now.

"Thank you, Teddy." Mon sighed. "I know I haven't been the best business partner—"

"Eh. You would have done the same for me." Which was true. "But you know you've been home for three days. By New York time, it's ten. You love ten. You're usually fully functional at ten."

"Things got screwy around the international date line. Or maybe it was the Greenwich meridian. Or maybe it was spending nine hours in line at the fucking precinct on election day."

"You're lucky. I heard a couple horror stories of people who weren't able to vote at all."

He knew that. It didn't make it any less unfair anyway.

"You've barely left the office. Even for me, it's a record."

Teddy walked in and sat on the couch at the opposite end of the room—a leather, bright orange thing Mon salvaged from his parents' hoarder stash. He could only perch on the end there because half the couch was doing an excellent job of holding the books that hadn't managed to fit on Mon's bookshelves, including the *Collected Works of Marc Chagall* and *MoMA Now: Highlights from the Museum of Modern Art*. They were new.

"I'm getting used to the new space."

"You're not a cat."

Teddy also started folding up a bunch of jackets, also on the couch. Mon had a terrible habit of leaving jackets everywhere—he simultaneously got too hot and too cold when he was working, and this was a side effect. It was also how he realized he'd left his "the future is female" hoodie in New York. He'd gotten it three months ago with the intention of wearing it to his polling precinct, only to be unable to find it anywhere.

"The quiet makes it easier to work," he explained, refusing to look at Teddy and his "I'm only judging you because I love you" face. Mon could see that face in his sleep. Saw it last week when Teddy asked if he was serious about maybe moving to the US.

"You could spend the quiet time trying to sleep."

"Sleep is for the weak." And for the devastated. The ones who were a little sad, a lot scared. He couldn't even say it out loud. He left New York, Olivia was in LA and the new president was a Marcos. Suffice to say, it was easier to be at the office, where he could arrange and rearrange his furniture and still feel in control. Where he could sit and work on the tracks he'd left behind.

Not songwriting, though. He knew it would be a while before he could articulate this feeling. And he wasn't trying to force anything out, not anymore. What Mon needed was a good meal, and sleep. Then maybe he could figure out what tomorrow was going to look like.

"You seem like you're in mourning," Teddy noted, tugging a loose thread on his T-shirt.

"Can you blame me?" Mon asked, looking up now to grin bitterly at his friend.

"Not at all." Teddy sighed. "We lost."

They did. They lost in a way that left everyone in disbelief, some angry, some accepting. Mon felt like throwing something at the wall in sheer frustration at his own fucking country. *Ang hirap mo mahalin, Pilipinas.*

"The whole world feels off-kilter today," Teddy acknowledged. "Not just for you. And we can only hope."

"Fuck hope." Mon leaned back against his chair, yawning as he tilted his head back. "I'm done with that. Tired of it. It's not worth it. Better to accept that things are going to turn to shit and adjust accordingly."

"And here I thought I was the pessimist."

"Well, I'm jet-lagged," Mon pointed out. His voice was angry and bitter, so much that he could almost taste it. "I had already adjusted my life around the idea I would get what I was hoping for. I pinned my hopes on a long shot.

That everything would work out the way I wanted. I don't know how to go back to the way my life was before all this."

"Because you'd hoped for better." Teddy nodded, and Mon was whining. He knew he was, because there were people a lot more devastated than he was. "You go to New York once..."

"What a fucking cliché, right?"

"Stop." Teddy shook his head. He looked almost worried, which worried Mon. "You're the positive one, Mon. The one that's too happy for his own good, you know? And that stuff you said about hope, long shots, disappointments. I think it only means you have to hold *tighter* to hope, not let it go. Because you saw a way things could be different, or better. It's a reason to keep fighting. Or else what was the fucking point?"

Mon said nothing in response, because he didn't want to respond. That weird, elusive thing called hope was hard to hold on to, and yet he'd needed it so much to get through the last month. And he was holding on to it still, even as the proverbial doors were closing, as his visa slowly expired. He knew Teddy was watching, and he didn't know what his friend could see, but Mon dropped his hands.

"You really loved her, huh."

"Yeah." He still did. When he thought about Olivia Angeles, it was starting to feel like a memory, to get blurry around the edges and change into what felt better, felt perfect. And that sucked.

His phone lit up the darkened room. His blackout curtains were drawn. Mon glanced at his screen and saw it was a message from Ava.

Is that you in the MV teaser for Olivia's song?????

Mon had no idea what she was talking about, so he opened the link that Ava had helpfully provided.

It was a short clip, less than a minute long, and featured vague, close-up shots of Olivia's magenta jumpsuit, of her fingers wrapped around the shiny pink microphone they got especially for the shoot. Everything was slow motion, and the color grading made it seem darker and moodier than he remembered. "Surrendering" played, a pared-down studio version without Olivia's vocals. It seemed pale in comparison to how the final song had turned out, but Mon was biased, and this was a teaser.

The song was ramping up to the chorus, and they heard Olivia's echoey, soft exhalation of "surrender to you," before the last scene showed her running into his arms at Times Square, cut so you couldn't see Mon's face, except he was wearing the denim vest his friends endlessly roasted him for. You could see him squeeze her tight on-screen, and everything faded to black, until white text appeared on the screen.

"Surrendering." *Olivia Angeles. Directed by Sol Stanley. Soon.*

The video had seven hundred thousand views already. The comments below were appearing as he scrolled, ranging from exclamations like "oh holy shit, I'm not ready???" to "oh my god another actress turned singer. how original."

But the song had been properly teased, and an audience intrigued. They must have rushed the cut of that teaser to get it out so fast.

"What the fuck. I've seen that vest before," Teddy said behind him, and Mon jumped, totally forgetting his friend was in the room, and now he stood right behind Mon. And he had no idea what facial expression he had on, but it was hard to hide from Teddy, whose eyes widened. "What the fuck, is that you?"

So Mon had no idea. *No* idea that Sol had still been rolling the cameras when that hug had happened. All he knew was Olivia needed to feel safe in his arms, he had to hold her as tight as he could because she needed him. He certainly hadn't been thinking about the way it looked on-screen, because it looked...it looked amazing.

Olivia was right. The camera really did something to soften the edges of a moment, make it feel less than real. But he knew what it had really been like, to be in that moment with her. Sol had seen the glitter and the romance, but in that fleeting moment, she'd seen that comfort too. That feeling of bringing comfort to someone you loved, when they needed it.

He didn't know they were going to release "Surrendering" first.

"Um."

"That's all you have to say? 'Um'!" Teddy exclaimed, and Mon genuinely couldn't tell if he was about to burst into laughter or kill him, which was a fine line for Teddy.

"I don't know what else to say...?"

"Okay, but that's you, right?" he asked, jabbing his finger on Mon's screen, which lit up again to show his arms wrapped around Olivia's. "I've seen Colin Sheffield's arms. They do not look like that. He doesn't have a chest like that."

"Uh—"

"Andi follows him on Instagram, his thirst traps are effective."

"Ah."

"Now is not the time to be monosyllabic, dude," Teddy reminded him, placing his hands on his hips and pouting. Mon really didn't have an answer for him. But the pouting didn't last long. Teddy's face softened as he dropped his shoulders. Mon realized his friend was genuinely worried for him, or at least unhappy that he didn't know what was going on. "I know I didn't really ask, but…"

"But?"

"I'm going to need you to tell me everything that happened between you and Olivia in New York."

So Mon told him. It was shockingly easy to lay out the way he felt, to choose his highlights when he was doing it for Teddy, because Teddy understood when Mon was going off on a tangent, when he didn't want to elaborate beyond a certain event. And the funny thing about talking about how he felt was that it seemed like he was letting go, bit by bit—the parts he'd kept to himself, the parts Olivia had willingly given away.

It helped that he trusted Teddy with his life, as Teddy trusted Mon with his. But by the time he talked about the

High Line, his eyes were wet and his entire soul was exhausted.

And through it all, Teddy had only crossed his arms, nodded and asked very few follow-up questions. He was absorbing it all, and Mon appreciated it.

"I asked because there might be legal implications to them filming you without knowing, but…are you okay with it?" Teddy asked. "That people might guess it was you, might connect the dots between you and Olivia?"

"I was ready for it," Mon admitted. His imaginings of staying in the US had been surface level—they had been long, rambling thoughts where he mentally played out scenarios of people finding out they were together, navigating the press, releasing a statement. Real Korean drama things like that.

In hindsight, it had been bold of him to assume all of that, but he could only be himself.

"What happened?"

"She…felt differently," he said, his brow furrowing. Was that what happened? He'd been ready and willing to stay, except he'd looked at all the things he was giving up, and decided there was only one argument he could hear for moving. And it wasn't the same argument Olivia made.

She kept offering him museums and parks, restaurants and things he could find here. Well, could *mostly* find here. She wanted him to have the American Experience, but that wasn't what Mon would be staying for. Sure, it would be nice to be near all the capitalism, but…she would have been enough.

"Or maybe I just didn't want to hear how differently she felt about me."

"People *are* different. She's not a mind reader, and you're not as transparent as you think."

Mon knew that Teddy knew that Mon already knew that. But it was always hard to remember in the moment. Just because you wanted to think one way, didn't mean the other person would think the same way.

It was a hard lesson he was still learning. It was why meeting someone you got along with felt so miraculous. If among the randomness of the universe, the difference in space, in age, in birth order and freaking astrological sign (if you believed in that), you met someone who liked you, and understood you, and who you understood back.

And it devastated you every time when they had to leave.

"I'm sorry it didn't end the way you wanted," Teddy told him.

"Me too." Deep sigh. The kind that ended all his sighs about Olivia Angeles. "But right now, all I want is to crash."

Mon put his phone down. The next video had autoplayed, one of Olivia and Colin crushing a couple's game for some magazine that they were both going to be on the cover of. That had been all over Mon's social media, and he figured he'd had enough of the internet for now. "Preferably on my couch."

"Your couch is too full of shit."

"The shit can go on the floor," Mon mumbled, feeling himself sway as he wandered over to the spot Teddy had left. He picked up the Chagall book and dropped it to the floor. Then handful by handful, until his couch was nothing but a layer of jackets and hoodies, and the perfect nest for him to burrow into.

He looked up to find Teddy staring at him, his friend's brow furrowed like he was deep in thought. "Yes?"

"You love her," Teddy said. "You still do."

"Of course," Mon agreed. Because through all the hurt and the disappointment, the frustration and weariness, he still loved her. If only they could talk, if only they could figure this out together, he would be willing. But right now? "Good night. I have no idea what time I'm supposed to wake up tomorrow."

"Well, it's about 10:00 a.m right now, so—"

"A.M.?"

"Yeah, dude." Teddy walked over to the window and opened one of the curtains. Mon winced at the sunlight, and sure enough, it was full fucking daylight outside. He should have known. He swore he heard a taho vendor yelling. Good morning, Marikina. "We usually have an update meeting in the mornings, which was why I came in."

"Fuck." Mon dropped his head forward. He was fucking exhausted and running on a very, very small amount of sleep. "I need coffee."

"And breakfast," Teddy agreed, patting Mon on the back. "Get out of here. I want to nap on your couch. Your aircon is already cold and your couch is softer."

"How is that fair?" Mon groaned, standing up as Teddy shoved him aside to flop on the neon orange leather. It was a surprisingly comfortable couch, but only when the air-con was on.

"Ask me after my nap. Now go," Teddy said as he closed his eyes. Mon was a good boy so he headed out of his own office, starting to get dizzy but determined to start the day (continue his day?) with a good meal.

What happened after a downpour? The sun came out again. Somehow, it always did, especially in the Philippines. He was going to be fine.

"Anyone want coffee?" Mon yelled into the hallway, knowing he was within hearing distance of all the staff who were in today. Depending on their schedule, there had to be two or three people here, the rest encouraged to work from home. As far as he knew, the studio was empty today, so if everyone wanted coffee, all he had to do was juggle… what, five cups? Easy.

Mon jogged out to the garden, savoring the warm summer sun. The old preschool's guardhouse was currently empty. He and Teddy had been meaning to open it and set up a small take-out coffee stand. They had plans to turn the garden into a relaxed seating area, then make the backyard a walking garden for Mon. It would bring a bit more income if they managed to figure it out. And hey, they could host events or open mic nights or something.

Big plans. All he could start on tomorrow.

His phone rang in his pocket, cutting off his future café thoughts. *One business at a time, Mon.*

"Morning, Moning!" Scott's voice was cheery, and Mon smiled even if his friend couldn't see it. It was always nice to hear from Scott, even if Ava had described them as "two brain cells rubbed against each other," when left to their own devices. "Did you get that? Morning, Moning?"

"Vaguely," Mon said back, too sleepy to give Scott a proper response. He loved Scott with all his heart, but he was too grumpypants at the moment to be much of an audience.

"Are you still feeling blue?"

"Well, pink is apparently overrated, so." Ha ha election joke. Too soon. "What can I do for you? Is this about your studio time?"

Scott ran a very successful YouTube channel called *EatCute*, and when he felt like mingling with society, graced Triptych with his presence to record his voice-overs. His only requirement, when he invested in Mon and Teddy, was that he be allowed that. Well, that, one-third of the shares and a channel jingle Mon came up with in the shower.

"You sound like you could use some breakfast there, bud." Scott's voice was perky. A little *too* perky maybe.

Somewhere in the back of Mon's mind, he knew Scott was trying to pull *something*, possibly orchestrated by Teddy, but that remained in the back of his mind, because he was currently using all his brainpower to stay awake.

"Grab a Grab and meet me at this magical food park you won't shut up about. I'll buy you anything, because I want to buy everything."

"NomCom?" Mon's head cleared enough to remember mentioning the Nomnom Commons Food Park in Pasig to Scott once, how nice it had been that it was right across from where Triptych was first born. Mon had moved before Scott had a chance to visit, and apparently today (of all days) was going to be the day they would go. "But, work—"

"I'll call Teddy and tell him I've stolen you away. You know he loves me."

"Who doesn't?"

"Exactly! So come meet me na." Scott's tone brooked no argument, and why the hell not, right? It was probably early enough that a rideshare to Pasig wouldn't be so catastrophic. It would be good. He could also get Teddy a milk tea when he came back.

One long Grab ride to Pasig later, he spotted Scott at the entrance of the food park, posing for selfies with subscribers with his mask still on. Nomnom Commons was bright and cheery as ever, the repurposed container vans seemed to welcome him home. The old narra tree at the center of the dining area seemed to have opened its arms for Mon especially, old childhood fears aside.

"Monching!" Scott exclaimed, enveloping Mon in a hug. And it was so nice and comforting that Mon squeezed his friend a little tighter. Scott was a man who believed in the power of a good hug, and patted his friend's back warmly. "It's been a long month for you, huh."

"Exactly." He sighed, and the two friends stared at each other, exchanging smiles. Mon had known Scott most of his life, and it was because he had known Scott for most of his life that he could see his friend looked…nervous? Excitable? Granted, excitable was Scott on a normal day, but there was something that went well beyond his food park anticipation. "Did you really drag me all the way to Pasig just to eat?"

"Which one of us is the seafood allergic guy who drove all the way to BF for sushi?"

"It was a date! And they had good...gyudon?"

"Talaga lang ah." Scott looked amused as he and Mon walked into the food park together. "Do you see that Negrense dessert stand?"

Scott pointed to Azucarrera de Papi across the way. Mon's stomach grumbled at the possibility of piaya with a sweet muscovado center.

"I will be there if you need me," Scott continued, and he was using his "dad tone," the one that was slightly condescending but overall protective. "Chef SJ is coming on *EatCute* and I want to know my barquillos from my merengue."

"Oh." Mon was confused. "Do I not get to know my barquillos from my merengue?"

"Hmmmmmmmm." It was almost embarrassing how long Scott pretended like he was thinking about it. "No."

"Boo."

"Now be a good boy and wait for me by the narra tree, okay?"

Then Scott literally skipped off toward Azucarrera. And, look, Mon was not fully dense, he knew something was maybe possibly up, but he was much too tired and sad to figure it out.

He approached the narra tree anyway, kapre-free as it was, and sat on his favorite spot by the trunk. He'd written a lot of songs in this particular spot in the early days of Morningview. When he was still figuring out what he wanted to say, worried there would be nobody to hear it. He would come here and write, and when he needed a drink, the first clue to the little treasure hunt to find Dr. Do's Gin Parlor was right above his head. This place was amazing.

Mon felt himself drifting off to a nap. And he was in that strange, in-between state when he thought he could smell Olivia's perfume. He was terrible at identifying smells, but it was familiar. He'd buried his nose in that scent enough to think of her. It pulled him out of sleep, blinking awake. He looked up.

"That's my hoodie."

"Well, it's mine now," Olivia said, very much in front of him, eyes sparkling with delight, the rest of her face hidden behind a mask. "Hi."

"Hi." He made no move to get up. "You're here."

"I'm here," she repeated.

"For me?"

"Well. Max got engaged, and I wanted to officially meet his fiancée. Martha happens to be friends with your friend Ava, and Scott is very good at getting you to do whatever he wants without question."

"It's his special talent." Mon was definitely fully awake now.

"But yes. I'm here. I asked him to bring you here because I wanted to see you." She crouched in front of him, hugging her knees like she was examining a leaf on the side of the road. "May I sit?"

Mon nodded, unsure of what to say. Unsure of words in general, if they would fail him. If he thought it was surreal meeting Olivia in New York, it was even more surreal to have her in Nomnom Commons, under the tree where he wrote Morningview's first songs. The ones she loved so much.

Her thigh pressed against his as they sat together. Her hair was cut short, her face drawn and tired. But it was her, and Mon's heart twisted in his chest. She felt unreachable, even as she sat there with him, even as her fist opened and closed like she was waiting for him to hold it.

"I realized I owed you an apology," she began, and it was a good start. "I wasn't listening to you, and I made assumptions about your life and mine. But LA can be terrible too, right? Finding a real connection with someone is so rare and precious, even if it's what we all want. And I thought I was offering you all these things—"

"Don't," Mon said firmly. He didn't want to hear them again, the reasons why he should feel a certain way about somewhere else. It wasn't going to be better.

"Right." Olivia seemed taken aback. Surprised, maybe, but why? He hadn't been shy about telling her why he didn't want to hear all those reasons. What did surprise him was the bright, glossy shine of her eyes. Tears? "I wasn't trying to…I mean, I…and you're just *so*…"

"So?"

Olivia made a sound that was almost a growl, and pulled down her mask in frustration. She definitely had tears in her eyes, stubborn little things that seemed to want to hold on forever. But then she exhaled, and they fell. They fell among reddened eyes and cheeks, a sniffly nose.

Mon learned that when Olivia Angeles cried, it was ugly. Ugly and loud and made her sound like she was out of breath. He handed her a pack of tissues from his pocket, and the sound her nose made would have made him laugh if he wasn't trying not to hug her and tell her it was okay.

"I'm sorry," she said, blowing even more into the poor piece of tissue. "This is a new thing. I cry. It's ugly."

"It's beautiful," Mon insisted. "It's you."

That made her cry even harder, which he didn't think was possible. "How can you say that, after what I did?" she asked, shaking her head. "I was the asshole, and I misread everything, or I wanted to, but…"

He said nothing, and waited.

"I think I'm falling in love with you, Mon. And I'm scared. Love shouldn't be scary, but I want it with you, or whatever version of it you want to have with me."

He said nothing. Mostly because his brain had short-circuited, and for once he had no words, but also because he had a feeling there were more things she needed to say. Those movie star eyes of hers were so filled with longing and worry, but also love. So much love, more than Mon ever thought she would feel for him.

"I think I will mess us up, but I want to do us until I can make a mess of it."

The words hung in the air, the possibility of the *us* sparking between them. And Mon had been wrong about New York and possibilities, because it was here. It was her.

And he didn't want to let it go. He wanted to hold on to hope.

"You are not very good at this emotional speech thing," he finally said. It was hard to hide how warm and fuzzy he felt, because his cheeks were hurting from how much he was smiling. He held her hand, and warm, happy relief flooded him.

"I usually have a script for scenes like this," she grumbled, briefly pressing her head on his thigh. And when she lifted her head, her hair haloed in the late morning sun, and in the shadow of the narra tree, Mon smiled. It looked like a scene from a young love hot dog commercial. But it was her. It was them, and the us they were slowly building together.

"Olivia."

"Mon?"

"I love you too."

"Was that all I needed to say?" She laughed, tears springing to her eyes, but she wouldn't let them fall. Happy tears were harder to come by, after all. "You make it sound so easy."

"It takes a lot of practice." He tilted his head forward to press it against hers, and everything was right in the world. It felt like the ending of *You've Got Mail*, their moment at the park, meeting each other again, except Mon didn't have a dog, and "Somewhere Over the Rainbow" wasn't playing. "Rosas" was. "We'll figure it out."

"With flowers, next time?"

"A thousand orchids. I didn't forget."

He kissed her, and she tasted like sunshine and happiness, like eroding edges making way to better things, and herself. Olivia Angeles, the love of Mon's life.

Epilogue

One Year Later

If relationships aged like fine wine, Olivia liked to think her relationship with Mon was much closer to a fine, smelly, soft cheese. Just because they were so cheesy.

"Like…Jesus. The two of you. Stop," Teddy complained, wrinkling his nose as Mon buried his face in Olivia's neck. If he was sniffling a little, Olivia was not going to be the one to mention it. "Andi and I weren't like that when we left Manila, right?"

"Well, no, but it's generally accepted that you become a sourpuss when she's gone," Olivia commented, giggling at Teddy over Mon's shoulder, who gave her a flat, unimpressed look.

They were making a spectacle of themselves in the middle of JFK, Olivia Angeles hugging her man for dear life while her assistant, styling team and a bodyguard all waited. But that was where they were, and what they'd been dealing with for the last year.

What they failed to tell you when you started a long-distance relationship were the logistics involved—Olivia would be in Bali, could Mon see her? Could Olivia sneak a trip to Seoul to see the autumn leaves while he was working there? Was there time to still pass by Manila and see Max and her parents? Mon's travel agent had joked that his travel plans and visa applications alone had helped their agency recover their pandemic losses. Because of course Olivia didn't need visas most of the time.

It was *a lot*.

But then there were moments like this, like last night, where they both attended the premiere of *Overexposed*, and officially "debuted" as a couple. The entire thing had been calculated by Olivia's publicist, and Mon really had looked so dashing in his suit, his hair back to being longish and styled off his forehead.

If they made out in the projection room, nobody had to know.

"And you have everything?" Teddy asked, because, as Olivia found out, while her boyfriend was a badass rapper and the named president of a record company, he was basically a baby to all his friends. And because Mon was a baby, Olivia was automatically Also Baby. And it was fine, because Mon was always going to be Daddy, too. Heh. "Snack, mask, hand sanitizer?"

She actually liked it? The friendly, warm affection of fellow Filipinos who cared about what she had for breakfast, lunch, merienda or dinner?

"Nicola's got it." Olivia nodded to her assistant, who nodded back. Between shooting *Conquerors*, *Luna's Landing* and figuring out how to get incorporated (because apparently you needed that when you wanted to produce things, where was the adulting class?) she'd needed an on-the-ground assistant. "I'll see you in Manila, Teddy?"

That was his cue, and he took a step back. "I'll go check on our gate."

Mon lifted his head, his eyes a little wet, trying his hardest to smile. Olivia smiled back, but it still broke her heart every time they did it. The two of them were achieving dreams left and right—Mon and Teddy still had a couple of meetings in New York with KST's American distributor to discuss the possibility of more work—but the more they did, the more it seemed they were doomed to keep meeting in these stolen bits of time.

She didn't tell him that Nicola knew not to speak to her on the first hour of plane rides, knew that every day they were apart was another day she wanted to give all of this up to see him.

"I can't believe you're flying to Paris to shoot a sexy perfume ad with Colin," Mon muttered, which she knew was very *not* what he was mad about.

"Colin is a traitor. I fully intend to use my powers and make them shoot a scene where I duct tape him to a chair and not in a sexy way." Olivia shrugged, because she was an adult and could be petty. Because Colin, the traitor, had left *Conquerors* midseason because he was cast in a Marvel movie. The service didn't think Olivia could carry the show on her own, so she made them write an ending where Lady Tala wins the entire Time War after losing Lord Aries.

But hey, the perfume people were willing to pay millions to make them play nice. She wasn't going to complain. Decent homes in Manila went for quite a lot. And she'd been checking.

"I hate that this isn't getting any easier," Mon mumbled, pressing his forehead to hers and kissing her deeply. "I hate watching you leave."

It was harder for Olivia to say these things out loud, but she tried. She held him closer, kissed him back. She'd even sent one of those bands that played at a barrio fiesta to serenade him with "Officially Missing You," and Mon retaliated by releasing a song called "Lucky Me Original."

Like she said. Cheesy.

"Hey, I always come back," she assured him. "I'll be home soon. Wherever that is. Wherever you are."

"I just..." There were novels full of feelings in those two words, and Olivia knew them all. But instead of saying them, Mon pulled something from his backpack instead.

"You think I should read a book?" Olivia asked, holding up the shockingly chonky little book. "Thank you?"

Her boyfriend managed to give her a sarcastic look with tears in his eyes. Olivia looked at the cover.

"A sketchbook of a Philippine garden...oh my God."

"There are only about a hundred and twenty orchids in this one," Mon explained quickly, sniffing. "But it's a start.

I know we're not ready to talk about anything more permanent yet—"

They weren't, but this was exactly what she thought he was going to say. That there was a need to be tied to each other a little more. That terabytes of messages, photos and videos in between trips were less and less satisfying.

"—but it's a start. And I want us to start."

"Mon, are you asking me to marry you?" Olivia thumbed through the pages, her eyes a little wet. This was what she wanted, the smart and shockingly simple gesture. Mon's version of standing in a flower field.

"Not yet." He pressed a kiss to her forehead. "Just that I will miss you. And I will see you in Cannes in two weeks."

See? Cheesy really was their thing. Thank God Olivia liked cheese.

She threw her arms around his neck and leapt into his arms for a kiss. Lucky Mon was always ready to catch her. He held her close, the boy who made her favorite songs and opened up her heart. The boy who didn't know she was coming to Manila to stay. Production companies needed a base *somewhere*.

A fan had snapped a photo of the moment, and by the time Olivia landed in Paris, her publicist sent her reels and TikToks, asking if the caption was a good thing or no?

Shet, haba talaga ng hair ni Ate Olivia! Sana all!

★ ★ ★ ★ ★